Echo

Book 1

A novel by

Richard Glenn

Echo

Book 1

A novel by Richard Glenn

Dedicated to my family.

Acknowledgements

As any other author would agree, no book gets written by one person alone. This book would never have made it this far without the following people who, without their help, *Echo* would never have been ready to start its journey into the public realm.

To start, I would like to thank my family for their belief in me and their support while I've been on this ride. Also, a thank you for tolerating my "zone out" moments when I would suddenly begin to think about plot points, usually without warning and often at inconvenient times.

I would like to thank my good friend Mark, from Splash Design Birmingham LTD, for all his hard work in not only designing my book cover and webpage but for also convincing me to keep going every time I felt like throwing in the towel.

I'd like to thank my editor Jacqui Corn-Uys, for all her hard work, help and patience with a new author who often had no idea what he was doing, and in asking questions of the story I did not realise needed to be answered, making a huge difference to the story.

Thanks also to my beta readers: Les, Lara, Matthew, Holly, Laura, Steven and Yvonne for taking time out of their lives to read my story and provide much-needed feedback.

Finally, I would like to thank you, the reader, for choosing my book and giving my story a chance. I hope you enjoy meeting the characters and joining them on their journey as much as I enjoyed bringing them to you.

Richard Glenn.

What is history?

An echo of the past on the future;

A reflex from the future on the past.

Victor Hugo

Chapter One

Jackson woke suddenly from a deep slumber. Stretching, he winced as he felt the ache settle into his back from spending another night in his chair. Looking around and still groggy from sleep, he realised the computer had been left on. It sat quietly humming to itself, and the screensaver of him in his army uniform glowed from the screen. Papers were in several untidy piles and a half-empty bottle of whiskey sat next to a coffee mug; the source of the dull pain currently making its presence known behind his eyes. Drinking at work. If he wasn't his own boss, he would probably fire himself.

The office was a simple one. A single room, slightly bigger than the average living room. His desk sat opposite the only door in or out, with another chair on the opposite side of the desk for when he met with clients. A second desk sat in the corner and was currently unoccupied. This held a larger, more expensive computer system on it. Though this one was silently waiting to be switched on. Filing cabinets stood in rows along a wall and a single window let the morning sun filter into the office. Finally, a pot plant on the windowsill which had long since given up on life stared forlornly at him.

It was a small, unimpressive place, but it was his. A sign beside the door read: *J. & A. Private Investigators. When the police cannot help, try us.* Jackson looked at the whiskey again.

God, he was such a cliché. A P.I. who drinks too much and sleeps in his office. All he needed was a trench coat and a fedora hat to complete the look. He sighed and picked up the case file in front of him with reluctance. Reading through it he realised he was still no closer to solving it. When he had started the agency, it was to help those who needed it, instead, he seemed to spend his time involved in marital disputes and proving business fraud. Hearing the door open, he looked up to see his business partner enter.

Allister was thirty, the same as Jackson. He was average height but slightly overweight, not that he would ever admit to it. His short blond hair was thinning, so as always, he wore one of the many beanie hats he owned, regardless of the weather outside. He was carrying two paper cups of coffee in a cardboard tray in one hand and a bag containing what smelled like bacon sandwiches in the other. He took in the dishevelled form of Jackson sitting at his desk, sighed, then smiled sympathetically.

"Pull another all-nighter then, mate?" Allister asked, placing a coffee and a sandwich in front of Jackson.

Jackson nodded his thanks, took a sip of coffee and grunted in affirmation. He held up the paperwork before him. "I just can't seem to get anywhere with the Winstable case."

Allister sat down at his own desk and began pushing buttons and flipping switches to boot up his very elaborate and, to Jackson, complicated computer layout.

"I keep saying if you let me hack into her husband's email accounts, I can find all the evidence we need. If he's cheating and with whom, and where he's been moving all of his money to."

"You know how I feel about that sort of thing, Al," Jackson

said. "Once we start breaking the law, we're no better than they are."

"Who are?"

"I don't know. Them."

"Who's them?"

"The bad guys, I guess."

"We don't know for certain that they're bad," Allister said taking a bite from his sandwich.

"Granted. So, we need to find out."

"So, you need to let me hack Mr Winstable's accounts!"

Jackson sat back in his chair and looked at his friend. "No, Al. We don't do stuff like that. Mrs Winstable is certain her husband has been cheating and hiding money from her. I'm confident we'll find something on him the old-fashioned way."

"Have you found anything out the old-fashioned way yet?"

By way of an answer, Jackson took a large bite from his sandwich. "It's cold," he grumbled. "Also, what time do you call this, anyway?"

"Tastes better that way, and you know me, I do my best work after 11am."

"You work? I hadn't noticed. Look, I understand what you're trying to say, really I do. I just believe that we are too reliant on gadgets and gizmos these days. The world's problems won't be solved by a computer. You can't save lives with a mobile phone. My dad didn't rely on any of this stuff," Jackson gestured toward Allister's computer. Nodding at the window he continued, "He solved crime out there. On the beat. In the real world."

"I think you underestimate the power of technology,

Jackson." Allister looked somewhere between amused and baffled. "Everything is done online now. Everybody and everything are all connected. As for your dad, I'm sorry, mate. But it's not the 1980s anymore."

The room descended into temporary silence as they ate. Allister eventually decided to try a different tactic. "So, have we made headway at all on any of our workload?"

"One or two cases," Jackson answered looking through a different untidy pile of papers. "We have a couple of leads to follow up on I think."

"How about I get some digital copies and we work on them at lunch? By which I mean the liquid kind, and by which, I mean the pub."

"I guess we could go for a drink..."

Allister looked him up and down, distaste clear in his eyes. "But for the love of God, freshen up first, would you? Sorry, but you look like crap."

"I'm sure I don't look that bad," Jackson replied. He stood and walked to a full-length mirror hung on the wall. The person who greeted him was more than a sorry sight. His dark brown hair was untidy, eyes ringed with the shadow of tiredness and his clothes were crumpled. Stubble showed he had not shaved in who knew how many days. He looked closer to forty years old than his thirty. He wasn't sure, but he suspected the stale smell in the air came from him too.

"See?"

"You may have a point," Jackson conceded.

"Ok, so we are agreed. Get yourself home and make yourself look a little less dead, and I'll get together some files. Then we'll go to the *Wheat and Barley* for some refreshments. I checked our bank account this morning and it looks less alive than you do, so we need to get some more money coming in, and fast."

"I'll see you there in an hour."

***

The afternoon in Leeds city centre was a busy time of day. The lunchtime rush drew crowds to the many bars, cafes and restaurants that were scattered along the streets. Music came from many such places, competing to be heard in the hopes of enticing new patrons. People weaved in and out the masses of bodies, trying to avoid the charity collectors or joining a queue at one of the street vendors for a bite to eat.

Allister negotiated the streets, past all of these as well as the many people who were more interested in what was on their phones than directly in front of them. He would be the first to admit that he loved technology, though sometimes wondered if it stripped away part of a person's humanity. Everywhere you looked were people posing for selfies, or posting updates about every aspect of their lives as if searching for some kind of validation from someone, somewhere. He could certainly understand Jackson's reluctance to embrace it. Even if it frustrated him at times.

He knew from experience that it would take Jackson longer than an hour to get ready, so Allister decided to take a walk around the local shopping centre to pass some time. He had worked at cultivating friendships in many of the stores to be able to get the inside scoop on sales for merchandise he was interested in. Though nothing had come through so far.

As he wandered among the shops, his attention seemed to be drawn to his left, almost as if some outside force was acting upon him. So, he took a look, even though he had no idea why.

Allister was not sure what had made her stand out. A teenage girl sitting alone on a bench. She had long blonde hair tied in a ponytail and was dressed in a school uniform. However, as it was lunchtime, that did not particularly make her out of place. It was just something about her appeared lost. Nobody else seemed to notice, though. Then again, she would need to be on fire to attract most people's attention here. Something made him decide to check and see if she was ok. If he was told to go away, then at least he could leave knowing he had tried to do something.

He crossed to the other side of the shopping centre and stopped a short distance away, hoping that she wouldn't feel threatened by his presence.

"Aren't you supposed to be in school?" he asked, in the most jovial tone he could muster.

She looked up at him. Blue eyes seemed to bore into his person, making it clear that his presence was not welcome. But behind the obvious annoyance, it was also clear that something was wrong. Something she was trying to push away. She was studying him closely, most likely trying to decide if he was any kind of threat.

Obviously deciding he was probably safe, she replied, "Shouldn't you be at work?" Her voice was tinged with evident sarcasm as well as a slight accent he couldn't immediately place. Her face remained impassive as she waited for him to reply.

Allister was already beginning to regret his decision to approach her, but he pressed on. "To be honest, I kind of am," he replied with a shrug.

She started to scrutinise him again suspiciously; those blue eyes analysing his face. He took a moment to examine her too and guessed her age to be around fifteen or sixteen. There was an obvious intelligence in her face, but then he saw that look of being lost again. Almost a kind of loneliness, but far from helpless.

After what felt like a very long pause, she finally asked, "Then what? Are you the police?"

"No. Definitely not the police," Allister answered.

"In that case, can you leave me alone? I'm having a bad day and I'm not in the mood to be hit on by some guy..." she paused as she looked at him again before continuing, "who must be at least twice my age." She then looked away, took out her phone, and began tapping on its screen. It was clear that for her, the conversation was over.

"I'm not being funny, but you're not actually my type."

Her answer was deadpan, which seemed to bring out her accent even more. "Really? You don't like blonde-haired girls?"

"I like blonde hair fine," Allister clarified. "I just don't like girls."

She looked up at him again with a confused expression. "Oh?" Followed by realisation spreading across her features. "Oooooooohhhh. I see!"

"Is that ok with you?"

"Sure, being gay doesn't make you a sexual deviant."

"Great. Can you tell that to my dad, please?"

With a soft laugh, she held out her hand, "We may have gotten off on the wrong foot. I'm Chloe."

"Allister," he replied. "But you can call me Al."

Chloe smirked. "Pun intended?" she asked.

"What pun?"

"You're kidding me, right?"

He smiled, "You'll never know."

"I'm not really a fan of abbreviating names; it feels lazy. So, Allister, what do you do for a living? Or is hanging around shopping centres talking to teenage girl's kind of your thing?" A twinkle in her eyes made it clear she was not serious.

"I'm a private investigator. I have an office just outside of the city with my partner."

"You work with your partner? That's kind of cute."

It was Allister's turn to be confused. "It is?"

Chloe stood and picked up her school bag. "I do need to get back to the hellhole they call school now, Allister. It was nice meeting you. Take care of yourself." She began to back away, before giving a small wave and turning to walk off.

"Ok, you too," he replied. It was only as she left the shopping centre without a backwards glance, that he realised he never asked her if she was indeed ok.

***

Chloe left the shopping centre feeling frustrated. She was not sure why that guy Allister had approached her. But the way things had been recently, it had initially worried her. He had seemed genuine enough and her gut said he was not somebody to be concerned about. But why approach her? Had he seen something in her? Was it that obvious that she was losing her mind? If she was. She had to hold on to the possibility that she was still having trouble adjusting to the move here. Though she knew that the 'if' was starting to look more like wishful thinking every day.

As she headed toward the bus stop, intent on returning to school, she stopped. What was the point? There was no chance she would be back in time for afternoon classes now. She figured if she was going to get into trouble, it may as well be for not turning up rather than going in late, so decided instead to find something else to do.

As she walked with no fixed destination in mind, she thought about how much she missed Australia. She had always been happy there, with friends and extended family. Somewhere she felt she really belonged. Then her dad got this stupid job in England. He wasted no time moving her mother and herself literally halfway around the world. To Leeds of all places. London or Manchester she could probably have coped with. But she had never even heard of Leeds. Nobody she knew had.

That was two years ago. To begin with, everything seemed to go fine. She settled into school and was making friends. Everybody wanted to get to know the new Australian girl. It was actually starting to feel like home again. There had even been invites to a couple of insane parties; the sort you never got in Australia. They were not really her kind of thing, but she wanted to be part of what went on, maybe be one of the popular kids again. She still felt ill just thinking about how much she had had to drink. It was fun and she was fitting in.

Then *it* started. Chloe could not even be sure what it was or even when it began taking place. But gradually over time things she could not explain were happening more and more often. The feeling of being watched. Of being followed. She could never be certain by who as they always remained a shadow in her peripheral vision. Gone as soon as she tried to focus upon them. She could not even be sure if it was male or female. Or more importantly, why it had chosen to torment her.

Eventually, the whispering started. At first just at night, but soon during the day too. Only ever when she was alone. It was fast and barely audible. Occasionally she picked up on a word or two, but never a whole sentence. She tried to record it on her phone one night, but all she got was white noise. The only thing she could be certain of was that whoever was doing the whispering was not looking out for her best interests. They meant her harm.

She was so lost in her thoughts; she didn't realise she had strayed onto a canal path. She hated these things, especially when she was alone. A second later, however, she realised that she was not the only one there.

"Hey there, sweetheart," said a voice that cut straight through to her fear.

She turned and found herself face to face with a man who, at first glance, looked surprisingly ordinary. He was only a little taller than Chloe, but he was stocky and obviously very strong. He had ordinary brown hair, ordinary clothes and an ordinary face. Not attractive, nor particularly ugly. In fact, if it was not for the way he looked at her she would not have found him threatening at all. His eyes betrayed him and his intent. He looked at her like she was prey; with grey eyes that seemed cold, almost devoid of emotion.

"What do you want?" Chloe asked, her voice shaking more than she would have liked. She slowly took a small step backwards, increasing the distance between them.

He, in turn, took a step closer and smiled. If his eyes freaked her out, it was nothing compared to his smile. "I saw you all alone," he replied. "I thought maybe you needed company." Even his voice was ordinary, despite the menace it carried.

"No. I'm fine, thank you." She took another step back, not daring to take her eyes off him.

Moving so fast it took her by surprise, he lunged forward and grabbed hold of her wrist. His face had turned into a hateful mask that was anything but ordinary. "I wasn't actually asking!" he snarled.

Without thinking Chloe swung her free hand toward his head, her nails clawing at the attacker's face. She felt them make contact, and she dug deep into his exposed skin. He let out a gasp, releasing her wrist as he reached for his cheek. She twisted away, dropping her school bag, and wasted no time in taking off running. She was fast, always had been, but the shoes she was forced to wear for school were slowing her down. Already she could hear the pounding of his feet as he gave chase, could sense that he was gaining on her. She did not dare look over her shoulder, but she knew that he was not far behind.

Turning right she was forced to come to a stop. A gate blocked her path, and she knew there was no way she could climb it. The rusty chain and padlock showed it had not been opened in some time. She had no choice but to turn and face Mr Ordinary. He was walking around the corner casually, knowing full well she was trapped. In one hand he was carrying her bag, which he threw to the ground beside him. She looked at his face and was pleased to see she had done some damage. A large gash that dripped blood was ripped in his cheek. It looked deep and would definitely need stitches. His hunter's eyes blazed with hatred and she knew her victory would be short-lived.

Reaching into her coat pocket she searched for something to fight back with. Chloe felt the sharp point of a pencil poke against the skin of her hand. She quickly wrapped her fingers around it and prepared to pull it out as a weapon when he was close enough. She was trembling, knowing deep down she stood little chance against this man, but her instincts refused to give in without a fight.

"You'll regret that, you little bitch!" he hissed.

He took a step forward then stopped. First, he looked confused, and then terror spread across his face. He was suddenly pulled from his feet, landing face first on the concrete path. He reached out to Chloe almost pleadingly before being dragged back around the corner, his fingers desperately trying to find something to stop him. His hands were only briefly able to grab hold of the metal base belonging to a signpost which momentarily slowed his momentum. But there was a powerful yank, and she heard a loud crack as his wrist broke. A second later he disappeared from view.

Chloe was back on the canal path and running before he had even begun to scream. The sounds of a struggle were behind her as she ran so she could not see what was happening, and as the screams grew louder, she refused to look back over her shoulder. Almost as loud were the sounds of ripping skin and muscle and the breaking of bones. Tears were already sliding down her cheeks, but she wouldn't let the feelings in, for fear of collapsing to the ground and being unable to get back up again. She didn't even stop when the screams abruptly ended and the silence was loud in her ears.

"Not again," she whispered to herself. "Not again!"

Chapter Two

Jackson turned off the shower and stepped out, grabbing a towel to dry himself. He walked to his wardrobe and began selecting some fresh clothes. As he was dressing, he noticed a light flashing on his phone, indicating he had received a new message. He finished dressing and crossed the bedroom to his bedside table.

Picking up the device, he swiped the screen and tapped in his pin number. The phone lit up, showing that he had received a multimedia message. He clicked on the file to open it and was met with what looked like a news report from the Leeds Daily News website. The bold headline was in capitals followed by a brief article:

LOCAL MAN FOUND MUTILATED ON QUIET CANAL PATH!

By Jane McArther

West Yorkshire Police were left confused yesterday by the discovery of a body belonging to local Leeds man, Michael Johnson. He was found just after 3pm by a member of the public who wishes to remain anonymous. Mr Johnson had been subjected to such a violent and sustained attack, only the driving licence in his wallet could be used to indicate his identity.

Mr Johnson was well known to the police for a string of petty offences and was jailed in 2008 for seven years for the attempted kidnap of a 14-year-old girl in Sheffield.

So far, the police have no suspects to this vicious assault. However, CCTV shows a young girl walking on the same path around the suspected time of the attack, shortly before Michael was also recorded alive for the last time by the same camera around 2.30pm. But as yet nobody has been able to identify her. Police would like her to come forward in order to eliminate her from their enquiries.

The report continued to list the various crimes of the deceased and a plea from his family for witnesses. Jackson was unsure as to why he had received this. He checked the number and it was unknown. In fact, it did not even look like any kind of phone number he had seen before. He looked to see when it had been delivered. Ten minutes ago.

He clicked on a link at the bottom of the article that took him to the home page of the Leeds Daily News, but he could find no mention of the story at all. Not even in their breaking news section. He clicked back and returned to the original article he had been sent and read it again. Shaking his head, he went to the desk he kept in his bedroom for when he worked from home and picked up the landline's receiver, dialling Allister's number.

Allister answered on the first ring. *"This call had better be to tell me that you are on your way,"* he said, his tone only half-serious.

Jackson got straight to business. "I need your help. I've

received something strange on my mobile."

"Really? What is it? If it says it's from your bank, ignore it. It's called phishing."

"It's nothing like that. I've been sent a news report about a man being murdered in Leeds yesterday."

"That's a bit messed up, but why is it strange enough to call me instead of telling me when you get here?"

"When I checked the Leeds Daily News homepage, there's no mention of it. And I mean nothing. I checked new and recent stories."

"I guess that could qualify as strange," Allister said, sounding intrigued now. Jackson heard the sound of keys being tapped and guessed that Allister must have his laptop with him. A moment later he said, *"I can't find anything about a murder in Leeds. Not on the local or national news. Are you sure you read it right?"*

"Positive. I've just this moment read it. Twice!"

"Let me see..." more tapping, *"and you're sure it's from today?"*

"I think so." He looked at his mobile again, read the date at the top of the headline and froze. He sat on the corner of his bed and stared at the phone trying to make sense of what he was seeing. He was brought back to reality by the tinny sound of Allister calling his name. "Al, you won't believe it. This makes no sense!"

"What are you talking about? What doesn't?"

"The article. It has tomorrow's date," Jackson said, still in disbelief.

This time Allister was silent for a moment, then he began

to laugh, *"Good one, mate. You almost had me there for a second."*

"I'm serious!"

"Of course you are. Sorry, Jackson, I'm not biting."

"When do I ever joke, Al?" Jackson snapped, sounding annoyed.

Allister was quiet again. *"That's a very good point. What exactly does it say?"*

"Mutilated body found on a canal path yesterday, or rather today, just after 3pm."

"Well clearly it can't be genuine," Allister said, his rational side coming through.

"Probably not." Jackson thought for a moment, "What time is it now?"

"Two thirty-five. Wait! You're not thinking what I think you are, are you?"

"I'll call you back."

"Jackson, hang on a—"

Jackson slammed down the receiver, grabbed his car keys and headed for the door.

***

He drove his second-hand 1980s Ford Escort as fast as he dared through the streets of Leeds. His car was his pride and joy. It was battered and didn't start on cold mornings, but it had belonged to his dad so he was reluctant to let it go. He drove down a street close to the canal and pulled into a free parking space. He climbed out into the warm afternoon air, locked the door and ran toward the canal. He checked his watch: 2:53pm.

He slowed his pace when he reached the canal and began looking for anything suspicious as he moved down the path. He looked into bushes and checked patches of long grass, trying not to miss anything. His mind told him he was being stupid, that none of this could possibly be real. But somewhere in his gut, he wondered. Wondered if the rumours from his childhood were true. If maybe what had happened before could be happening again.

In the end, what he was looking for was not hidden. There appeared to be no attempt at all to conceal the body. If it could even still be described as a 'body'. In the middle of the path was what looked like the bloody remains of a person. He could only be sure that it had been human when he saw the remnants of a hand and a patch of brown, blood-stained hair. Finally, the smell hit him. Putrid yet sickly sweet. It reminded him of the smell of something that had been dead for a long time, a smell he had encountered more times than he cared to remember. A sensation began in the pit of his stomach and before he knew it, he was bent over the edge of the canal emptying the contents of his stomach into the water, finding himself reunited with the bacon sandwich Allister had brought him. Once he was sure he had finished, he stood and checked his watch again: 3:01pm.

He took his mobile from his pocket and dialled emergency services. A voice answered almost immediately. *"Which service do you require?"*

"Police, please."

***

The police arrived around ten minutes later with the sound of wailing sirens. They quickly cordoned off the area while one began taking a statement from Jackson. He was asked a lot of questions, most of which he could not or was reluctant to answer. After capturing his details and telling him they may need to contact him for further questioning, the police let him leave. He checked his watch and realised he had been there for over three hours. He was looking forward to getting away from the scene, and hopefully the memory.

Sadly, he realised that neither was going to happen immediately as he found himself face to face with several members of the media. Dictaphones were pushed toward him as each reporter attempted to shout questions at him. He was still dazed and confused from the afternoon's events and found it difficult to deal with the noise. Eventually, he chose to remain silent as they all tried to encourage him to give them answers or a quote.

He was unsure of what to say or do when he saw Allister pushing his way through the throng to reach him. He stepped in front of Jackson and turned to face the media.

"Now then, vultures," he began, looking at each of them in turn. "I know there has been a tragic event you would love to earn a few bob from, but my client has nothing to say on the matter to any of you. So, take your little recorders and go back under your rocks, or I'll inform these lovely uniformed people about your harassment and request that they remove you!" He raised his eyebrows to emphasise his point.

Reluctantly the journalists started to break away and began writing notes or making phone calls. Jackson noticed a woman in her early 50s with red hair and green eyes watching him with interest. She looked as though she recognised him somehow. A Leeds Daily News ID card hung on a lanyard around her neck, but he could not make out the name. He considered talking to her, but she turned and walked away quickly before he could approach.

"Thanks, Al," Jackson said, his voice still a little shaky and all thoughts of the woman flew straight out of his head.

"I hate those cockroaches. I love an opportunity to put them in their place."

"So, I'm your client?"

"They tend to listen more if they think you're a lawyer."

"How did you know where to look for me?"

"I hacked the emergency services mainframe. Found out where the police had been called to."

Jackson looked mortified. "Oh, my good Lord... You hacked what?" he spluttered.

"Shhhh. Bloody hell, Jackson. Keep your voice down, mate. Don't worry. They'll never know."

"That's hardly the point, Al. I must say, I am very disappointed by this."

"What's done is done. Best just to move on," Allister said with a shrug and a grin. He glanced over at the police, "Are they done with you now?"

"They took a statement, asked how I found him."

"What did you tell them?"

"Not the truth obviously. I told them that I was out for a walk and there he was."

"Good. Best to avoid saying that you read it in tomorrow's news."

"I still don't know what to make of that," Jackson said.

"It does sound a bit crazy. I'm still struggling to believe it if

I'm honest."

"But that's not even the part that is the craziest."

Allister looked at him as if he was not sure he wanted to know. Finally, he sighed, "I'm listening."

"I overheard a police officer talking to the paramedics. Apparently, Michael Johnson looked as though he had been dead for weeks. Not less than the hour they suspect he may have been here instead, as the blood around him still appeared to be relatively fresh. How can that be possible?"

"I think you need that drink now," Allister said, setting off down the canal path.

***

They found a quiet pub a short walk away, and Allister went to the bar while Jackson chose a table. He opened his phone again and began to reread the article as Allister returned with two pints of lager and two shots of whiskey. He placed them on the table then sat opposite Jackson. He slid one of the whiskies to him.

"Here," he said. "I figured you might need to start with something stronger to calm your nerves."

Jackson took the shot glass and drank it down in one. He pulled a face as the taste hit him, then sighed, almost in relief. "Thanks. I definitely needed that."

Allister sipped his lager and thought for a moment. Finally, he spoke, "So, are we going to discuss what happened here?"

"It seems pretty simple. Somebody, somehow, sent me a message about the future."

"I don't think that should be the conclusion that we jump straight to."

"What other possible conclusions could we jump to?" Jackson asked incredulously. "I received a newspaper report about the violent death of Michael Johnson. It said he would be found just after three pm today. Then I find said Mr Johnson dead, clearly from a very violent attack, at one minute past three. What other options can we possibly consider?"

"You said the police think he may have been dead for weeks. Maybe he was murdered, hidden, then dumped on the canal with a fake news article designed to look like it was from the future?"

"I have considered that possibility. However, even I could see that the blood was still fresh and there appeared to be no signs of animals making a meal of him, which trust me, you would expect from a body that had been left out in the open for such a long time. Also, if what you said was true about all this being a setup, then why send it to me? I'm just an unknown private investigator who follows cheating husbands around and looks for missing people. Before you ask, we have not been asked to look for a Michael Johnson."

"I know. Photographic memory, remember?"

Jackson drank some more of his pint before continuing, "However unlikely it is, I think we need to accept that this is a possibility."

"I don't get it," Allister said with a shrug.

"Get what?"

"This. Ever since we were kids, you have been the world's biggest sceptic. Yet you seem to accept this with remarkable ease."

"I'm not sceptical."

"Oh please, that time I showed you evidence about aliens

living on the moon, you said it was utter nonsense!"

"It is utter nonsense. This, however, is different."

"Aliens are a no-no, but messages from the future are entirely believable?"

"I just have a feeling about this," Jackson said, clearly becoming irritable. "Don't ask me why. It's personal."

Allister raised his hands in surrender, "Hey, no problem. I'm just glad you have an open mind for a change."

"I do not have a closed mind!"

"You kind of do, mate."

"Could we please just drop this and change the subject?" Jackson asked, looking annoyed.

"Of course. In which case; new subject. It's your round."

***

Chloe sat on the bed in her room. Her knees were drawn up to her chest, and she rested her chin on them. She ran her fingers through her hair repeatedly, a nervous habit she had developed when she was stressed or anxious. She still could not believe what had happened today, even though she had seen 'accidents' before. Nicola Ritchie at school, who had bullied her for months, suddenly falling down the stairs for no apparent reason. Also, the time her crush, Brandon Davies, seemed to stumble into the road and the path of an oncoming car as he walked her home. There was no explanation why, though. He said afterwards, when he still acknowledged her existence, that it felt like he had been pulled. He was lucky he had only broken his leg, but it was more than enough to ensure that he called her less and less until her phone just stopped displaying his number.

She had never seen anybody attacked like that man before, though. His screams still rang in her ears. She had tried blotting it out with television and music, but nothing worked. She had even considered doing coursework until she remembered she had lost her bag on the canal path when she turned and ran. It had her name and the name of her school written inside, which meant it could be traced back to her. *I guess I should be expecting a visit from the police soon.*

Everything was so messed up. The accidents people kept having around her made sure that she eventually had no friends at all. Even though she was never directly accused of anything, the fact that she was always nearby when something happened was all the evidence most people needed, and they tended to give her a wide berth. Now when she did go to school, she sat alone in class and ate by herself. Eventually, she was away from school more than she was there. So much for the popular girl she had been in Australia.

"Chloe, sweetheart?" her mum said through the door. "You didn't eat any of your dinner. Do you want me to make you a snack?"

"No thanks, Mum," Chloe replied.

"Are you sure? It's no trouble."

"I'm fine."

"You have to eat something..."

"I said I'm fine!" she snapped, more harshly than she intended. She heard her mum hesitate a moment on the other side of the door before sighing and going downstairs.

When had she started being such a bitch to her mum? They used to be so close. More like best friends than mother and daughter. Yet another thing that seemed to be destroyed by this goddamn move to this god-awful place. If she wasn't ignoring her parents, then she was just being flat out mean or rude to them. They probably thought she was being a typical teenager. But she knew it was more than that.

She felt, more than saw, the shadow pass by her window. But she knew immediately what it meant. It was here. A little later than usual perhaps, but here all the same. She was familiar with the torment now. It was almost as much a part of her existence as breathing was. Though maybe she didn't just have to accept it anymore. Maybe she needed to start doing something proactive. At least try to fight back. Maybe today she had been given a way to do just that. She got off the bed and crossed the room to her desk, powering up her desktop.

"Chloe!" The whispering always began with her name. She guessed it was to get her attention, though that was certainly unnecessary. It was not as though she could ignore its presence.

She sat down and began typing. Her fingers flew across the keyboard in a blur. "Not tonight, aye?" she said, feeling emboldened by her idea.

The whispering grew more insistent, ignoring her request. As always, it was mostly unrecognisable gibberish with the occasional word she could understand *"... hate..."*

"Seriously, is there nobody else you can pester?" She searched the internet for what she was looking for, the voice seemingly growing louder, as if it was trying to envelop her. Since she was distracted by the computer, it seemed determined to get her attention back. What she was looking for was harder to find than she had anticipated, requiring some creative thinking on her part, but she eventually found who she was searching for.

"... stop..."

Chloe had stopped wondering why it had chosen her such a long time ago. It was not to do with the house being haunted, her first thought when it had begun, as it followed her seemingly at will. The only place she seemed to get any respite was when she visited her dad's cousin in Manchester. Almost like it was confined to Leeds. Except for her safe place. It never went in there.

"... can't..."

She would need to go to her safe place soon. It was clearly getting angry, and that never went well for her. At best it would be a sleepless night. At worst, well, it was best not to think about the worst. She took the info she found, copied it to her phone and began to head for her bedroom door. She froze suddenly when the whispering became a scream.

"YOU... WILL... DIE!"

***

As the evening progressed, the small pub they found themselves in had gradually grown busier. Music played in the background, loud enough to hear but not so loud as to drown out conversation. Jackson and Allister were slowly becoming very drunk. Several empty pint glasses sat on the table as Jackson returned with two fresh drinks. He passed one to Allister.

"Thank you, my good man," Allister said taking a sip. "Though to be honest we probably should make these our last ones."

"Let's not be hasty, Al," Jackson replied with a smile. "It's not even ten o'clock yet."

"I know. But it's been a stressful day and let's not forget that last night you slept in a chair."

"Perhaps you do have a point. However, it is not a point I find favourable!"

A bar worker approached the table and began taking the empty glasses. "Hey guys," she said. "Are you having a good night?"

"Yes, we are, thank you," Jackson replied, his face instantly lighting up at the sight of her. "And how are you?"

"I'm good. Except that I'm at work obviously." She laughed, then winked. "But don't tell my boss I said that."

"Your secret is safe with me," Jackson said in a conspiring tone and ignored Allister who was rolling his eyes. "So, is this a full-time job?"

"God, no. Just a part-time thing. I actually study law at Leeds Uni."

"Really? That sounds as though it could be interesting." He held out his hand, "I'm Jackson, by the way."

"Lucy," she answered taking his hand. Jackson held her hand a moment longer than necessary as they shook. She had long auburn hair, which she wore in a ponytail and green eyes. She was in her mid-20s and had a stunning smile that lit up her face. He let go of her hand as she continued, "So do you both work in the city?"

"I have a small office just outside in Armley." He nodded toward Allister, "He works for me."

"I what?" Allister asked looking offended.

"I'm actually a private investigator."

"Wow. That is impressive," Lucy said. She literally looked

genuinely impressed instead of the usual bored look he received from girls when he told them what he did. "Did you have to study to do that?"

"Not really. I used to be in the British Army. I did two tours. So, I kinda just learnt skills on the job."

"That's amazing. My brother is in the Parachute Regiment. He's actually overseas now."

"Oh, I was more involved with behind the lines work," Jackson said hesitantly.

"You mean like special forces?"

"Well..."

Allister interrupted before he could continue, "He means behind our lines. He was a chef. He's single-handedly responsible for putting more of our troops in the hospital than the enemy. He has a certificate and everything."

"Al!" Jackson said, clearly mortified.

"Don't worry, Jackson," Allister said giving Lucy a playful smile. "I'm just winding up my *boss.*"

Lucy smiled in return and placed a hand on Jackson's shoulder, "Hey, you know what they say, an army marches on its stomach. So, you're still a hero in my opinion." She smiled again, finished collecting the rest of the glasses and walked back to the bar.

"Believe it or not, mate," Allister began, "I think she likes you."

"You honestly think so?" Jackson asked, uncertainty in his voice.

"Almost definitely. She must like that old man charm thing you do when you talk to girls. Though what was that part about me working for you?"

"People always seem to get the wrong impression when I tell them you're my partner."

"What are you talking about?"

Jackson looked uncomfortable, "They assume we are in a relationship."

"Don't be ridiculous. I tell people all the time that we are partners and nobody ever thinks that."

"I'm telling you, Al. It sounds weird."

"You are really overthinking—" but before Allister could continue his phone buzzed with a text message. As he picked it up and read it, his brow furrowed slightly. "I have to go," he said suddenly. He took another sip from his drink and stood.

"Is everything alright?" Jackson asked with concern.

"Yeah, I think so. Are you going to be ok here?"

"I'll just have a couple more and head home."

"Do you promise? Seriously, you need some sleep."

"Scout's honour," Jackson said with a small salute.

"You were never in the scouts!" Allister pointed out.

Jackson just shrugged and continued to sip his drink.

***

After calling a taxi, Allister travelled to the outskirts of Leeds and an upmarket area known as Colton. The houses were expensive and far out of his league. They made him feel a little ashamed of his one-bedroom apartment. He paid the driver and got out of the car. Taking out his phone he opened up a map and followed the coordinates that took him down a path until he reached a park. It was the kind with a slide and a roundabout he used to play in when he was young. There was a steel gate with a simple catch lock at the entrance to the play area.

It was nearly completely dark with just a little light from the nearby street lamps to see by. The park was almost entirely in shadow, and the various play items were more or less unrecognisable. The only sound came from the squeak of the chains on the swings. He entered through the gate wondering why anybody would want to meet in a place like this at this time of night. He briefly considered returning to the pub where it was at least warmer, but quickly decided against it. He jumped slightly as the gate swung loudly closed again.

Heart now pounding he ventured farther into the park. If he were more like Jackson, he would be convinced by now that this was some kind of trap and that he should be ready for anything. He did not expect any real danger here, but neither did he feel like he should let his guard down at all.

"Hey, Allister," a voice said from the darkness, startling him a little once more.

Turning to face the direction the voice came from, he could just make out Chloe sitting on a swing a short distance away. He almost did not recognise her as she now wore her hair down and was dressed casually in jeans and a jacket. She swayed slowly back and forth, the squeaking following her steady movement.

He walked toward the swing set and sat on the empty seat beside her, "Hey back."

"Thanks for coming," she said in that accent he was annoyed to find he still could not quite place.

"How could I resist? I'm more than a little intrigued as to

how you found my personal number. I've gone to a lot of effort to keep it private."

"There are not many private investigators called Allister. Only one in Leeds. So, I just went from there. I have what you may call... a knack with computers," she replied with a shrug.

"So, you're a hacker I see?" Allister asked, feeling more than a little impressed.

"Allegedly." Chloe shrugged again but said no more, signalling that the subject was closed. He could respect that. Hacking was far from legal, and you had to be careful who you told.

"Are you ok? Your text said that you needed help."

"Yeah, I do." She looked sideways at him, "How much is it to hire you and your boyfriend?"

"Boyfriend? I don't have a boyfriend."

"I'm sorry? You said you worked with your partner. Did you guys break up?"

Allister understood then and groaned. "No! No, no and finally no. I meant business partner. Eww. I've known Jackson since we were kids. He's like a brother to me. Also, he's straight."

She covered her face, mortified, "Oh my god! Me and my big mouth. I'm really sorry. You said you were gay and that you worked with your partner. I just put the two together and assumed."

"It's fine. I should probably have clarified." He laughed out loud. "It also shows that Jackson was right about something. Not that I'll tell him." He looked back at Chloe, "Why do you want to hire us?"

She looked uncertain for a moment, and Allister wasn't sure if she would reply. Then she seemed to nod to herself as if deciding to continue, "I'm being followed."

"Followed? You mean..."

"Stalked, I guess."

"I know this may sound like a silly question, but do you know by whom?"

Chloe laughed sadly, "It'll all sound crazy to you."

"I love crazy," shrugged Allister. "So, who is it?"

"That's the thing. I don't know. I don't know who it is. I don't even know what it is!"

"What it is?"

"I've never actually seen it."

"I have to ask, Chloe, but how do you know you are being followed if you've never actually seen anybody following you?"

Chloe looked directly at him now. Even in this light, he could see that she was close to tears. Her voice had a hard edge as she continued, "I need you to believe me, Allister!"

"I believe you," he replied sincerely. "But you have to understand that this doesn't make a lot of sense."

"Really? Do you think that I don't know that?" she snapped in annoyance.

"Just tell me what you know," he said gently.

"It's been going on for a while now. It's strange. More a sense of a person than actually seeing a physical one. Like somebody is watching me. As if there's a shadow moving in the corner of my eye, but when I try to look there's nothing there."

Allister let out a breath, "It's certainly a lot to take in. Have you tried talking to the police?"

"Yes. They treated me like some kind of messed-up teenager. Not that I can exactly blame them." She laughed humourlessly. "I certainly feel messed up."

"You say it started a while ago. Do you know exactly how long ago that was?"

"About eighteen months ago. Not long after I moved here from Australia."

Allister clicked his fingers. Finally, he knew the accent. "Of course. You're Australian. I knew I recognised the accent!"

"I'm not filled with confidence in your ability as an investigator if you didn't realise I was from Australia," Chloe said with the first smile he had seen from her tonight. "It's literally the first thing everybody in this country notices about me."

"I have difficulty placing accents. It's... a flaw I guess."

Chloe bit her lip, clearly a nervous habit. "So, can you help me?"

"I think we can. I will need to run a few things by Jackson. He'll probably want to meet you to discuss your case."

"How much will it cost?"

"Don't worry about that. We'll waive the fee," Allister replied, dreading telling Jackson that piece of news. Things were already tight financially. But he knew his friend and was sure he would understand. Hoped he would understand, at least.

Chloe let out a huge sigh of relief. "Oh my God. Thank you. You've no idea—" She was suddenly cut short as a loud bang shattered the relative silence, making them both jump. "What the fuck was that?" she whispered, clearly terrified.

"I don't know," Allister whispered in reply, feeling more than a little unnerved himself. "But it sounded like it came from the entrance."

He stood and began to walk slowly in the direction the sound came from. It was almost silent again, but for the slight ringing in his ears from the sudden noise. He heard Chloe start to follow him and considered telling her to stay where she was. But how could he be sure that this wasn't a trick to draw him away and leave her vulnerable? It was not a risk he was prepared to take.

"Stay behind me," he whispered, "but be ready to run if I tell you to."

"This isn't right!" she whispered in reply. "I'm supposed to be safe here!"

"What do you mean?"

"It never comes into the park. I don't think it can." She was clearly growing anxious now. "It's my safe place. I'm supposed to be safe here!"

Unsure of what she meant, he continued to creep forward. He kept looking and listening for anything that could potentially be a threat. Soon the gate that led into the park came into view. It still stood closed and looked to be intact. He scanned the area and could not see or hear anybody else around. He took his phone from his pocket, turned the torch on and swung the beam of light around for a better look. But all it showed him were trees and empty spaces.

"Whoever or whatever it was, I think they've gone now," he said, trying to sound more confident than he actually felt.

"No. Fucking. Way," Chloe said from beside him.

He glanced at her and saw she was looking at the gate. Her face had drained of all colour so she looked ghostly pale, but above all, terrified. Allister followed her gaze and saw something dangling from the gate he had not noticed before. Walking closer for a better look, he aimed the torch directly at it and gasped. There, from one the metal posts, hung a school bag, and as the light illuminated it, they could see that the bag was covered in wet blood.

Chapter Three

Jackson began to stir slowly in his bed. Even with his eyes still shut he could tell that it was daytime, the sunlight visible as a soft red glow through his eyelids. Ever since his army days, he had been able to keep track of time easily, almost as if it was an extra sense. It was a handy trait to have learnt and also saved him from needing to set an alarm. His brain, however, was still groggy from a night of drinking and he had difficulty trying to piece together the previous evening's events. He struggled to recall his memories as once again, pain fired through his head randomly when he tried to think too hard.

He knew he had remained in the bar until it had closed at midnight. Without a doubt, Allister would not be happy about that, but what was done was done and couldn't be changed. He had spoken to Lucy again briefly, but as the bar became busier, so had she. Instead, he had ended up passing the remainder of the evening with two elderly men who had been police officers during the 1980s. Since his dad had also served around that time he had asked if they remembered him, but neither did. Once he was sure Allister was not returning, he had ordered a taxi and headed for home.

Rolling onto his back he groaned. In part because of his pounding head, but also at the sudden realisation that he had left his car parked somewhere near the canal. Did they have restrictive parking there? He could not remember. But if they did, he would almost certainly have a ticket by now. With the way finances were at the moment that was all he needed. He already had three under his belt from following leads or being too drunk to drive home.

Maybe Allister can erase it from the police computers for me he thought but immediately regretted it. He was annoyed he would even consider something like that, after all the times he had complained to Allister about the morals of hacking.

He lay there for a moment longer, allowing the consequences of the hangover to punish him a little more. It was cut short, however, when his phone let out a sharp beep that just seemed so impossibly loud and announced the arrival of a message. Seconds later it beeped again, a second message for his attention, forcing him to acknowledge that it was time to face the world.

Throwing the bed covers off, Jackson stood slowly. Once he was steady on his feet, he crossed to his bedroom desk and picked up the phone. Squinting slightly, he punched in his pin number and found two messages waiting to be read. The first was from Allister informing him of a new client the firm had taken on. He did not give many details, just that her name was Chloe, she was in desperate need of help and she would be in touch. He guessed that this Chloe must have been who Allister had left so abruptly last night to meet with. The second message was another multimedia file. He was immediately filled with dread, and he was ashamed to admit, also slight excitement as to what it contained. He tapped the screen to open the message and caught his breath. It was another article from the Leeds Daily News. Again, it was dated for the following day:

STUDENT MURDERED ON UNIVERSITY GROUNDS!

By Jane McArther

The city of Leeds was once again in a state of shock this morning after the body of a female student was found in the grounds of Leeds University, near the drama department, just before midnight. The police and paramedics were called, but she was pronounced dead at the scene.

Lucy Silverman, 25, was studying law while working part-time as a barmaid in the city centre. She is believed to have been on her way home from a night out with friends, before being attacked as she made her way alone through the campus. The reason for the attack is currently unknown, although evidence points to there being a sexual motivation.

The police have arrested a male suspect found a short distance away who they believe to be responsible for the attack, but have currently released no further details. They are, however, still appealing for any witnesses to come forward.

Jackson found himself feeling very sober all of a sudden. He read it again and froze as his mind began to make connections. Lucy. Studying to be a lawyer. Works as a barmaid. It couldn't be the same person, could it? He quickly dialled Allister's phone number.

"Hi, Jackson," Allister said upon answering. He sounded annoyingly not drunk. *"Is this about Chloe?"*

"Not now, Al," Jackson replied quickly, more abruptly than he intended to. He decided he could apologise later. "The bar worker from last night. Can you find out her name?"

"I probably can. I'm not sure if I should, though. To be honest, mate, it's a bit creepy."

"That's not the reason I'm asking. It's important!"

"I understand, Jackson. I'm not blind to attractive women. But there are laws against online stalking. You can get into a lot of trouble."

"Listen to me, Allister," Jackson said firmly. "I've received another newspaper report sent to me with tomorrow's date. I think she dies. Tonight!"

***

After ending the phone call, with Allister finally agreeing to do what he could to find out Lucy's surname, Jackson was on his way to collect his car before it was towed away. A local taxi company dropped him off on the same street, he paid and stepped out into the unreasonably cold day.

He walked a short distance and saw his car still beside the kerb where he had left it. Fearing the bright yellow penalty fare notice glued to his windscreen, Jackson was surprised to find there was none. He opened the door and sat down in the driver's seat. As he was searching for his keys, his phone began to ring. He retrieved it from his pocket and saw Allister's name on the display.

"Did you find anything, Al?" he asked immediately after pressing accept.

"I did," Allister replied. *"It would seem that the woman from the bar last night, is indeed named Lucy Silverman."*

"Which means, if the latest news report I've been sent is correct, she is murdered tonight," Jackson said sadly.

"We don't know that for certain."

"Come on, Al. I think we need to accept that these news reports may well be real."

"Or they could be part of some sick and twisted joke," Allister pointed out.

"They could. But are you really prepared to ignore them if there's even a small chance that they could real?"

Allister was quiet for a moment. Finally, he conceded the point. *"Ok fine. Let's say they are real. What are we supposed to do with this information?"*

"Yesterday there was nothing I could do. I got the report too late to make a difference. But this time, we have a few hours until it happens. We have time to stop it. We have to do something!"

"Like what?" Allister asked warily.

Jackson thought for a moment, "Can you find her phone number?"

"Why? So, you can ring her and tell her that she is going to die? How do you think she will react to that, Jackson? Guy from the bar she works in whose table she clears, somehow gets her number and calls her to say she's going to die. Do you think she will thank you? Or even believe you? You only exchanged a few sentences. She will most likely call the police on you."

"You're right," he let out a frustrated growl. "Then what am I supposed to do? I can't just let this happen."

This time it was Allister's turn to be silent. As he waited for a reply, Jackson had a feeling he would not like what was coming. He was right.

"I think you have to consider the possibility that if she does die tonight, and I'm not entirely convinced that she does, then maybe it's because she's supposed to."

"Are you kidding me, Al? You cannot seriously believe that? How can you say she deserves to die?"

"I didn't say that she deserved to die," Allister clarified. *"I was saying that we all have a destiny. Who are we to interfere with that? We are not God."*

"You're right. We're not God. Nobody is. Because there isn't one," Jackson said through gritted teeth, then hung up.

***

Allister lowered the phone then placed it onto his office desk. He had known that Jackson would not like what he had said, but he had to be honest. If messages predicting the future really were being sent, then that future must have already happened, somewhere. How could they possibly believe they could alter what was coming? Who knew what the domino result of that would be? But then why had the message been sent if they were not supposed to intervene? Allister was not a particularly religious man anymore, but he did believe everything happened for a reason.

His computer sat idly waiting for the next command; a quiet humming emanating from it. In the near silence of the office, it was the only sound. On the screen was a picture of Lucy Silverman. It was from some wedding she had attended recently, and she had posted it to one of the many social media accounts she maintained. So much online presence made tracking her movements simple, even for somebody without Allister's particular level of skills. It would make finding a suspect who may attempt to harm her extremely difficult.

He wondered, not for the first time, what drove people to display their entire lives on the internet. Checking into bars, photographing every place they went or everything they ate. Constant updates that seemed to be for nothing more than self-validation. He believed wholeheartedly that the internet could be a force for good. He equally believed that in the wrong hands it was just a cesspit for the garbage that people insisted upon sharing with the world.

He closed the browser window and sighed. He got where Jackson was coming from, he really did. Obviously wanting to help somebody in danger was in both of them. It made them who they were. He was doing the same for Chloe, after all. But he just could not shake the feeling that something was wrong with these news reports. Could they knowingly try to alter the future? Should they, even if they could? A person could go crazy trying to figure that one out.

He opened a file from his hard drive and began reading. All through the morning, he had been compiling a dossier on Chloe. It made for a confusing story. While in Australia she had been very active online. She seemed to be something of a queen bee among her peers, evident by photos of her at parties, trips to waterparks and even an excursion to the Outback. Wherever she went two things seemed to remain constant: she was always surrounded by friends, and she was always smiling.

Even after she first moved to England, she seemed to be just as social. Until around eighteen months ago. Since then she hardly seemed to have an online presence at all. She rarely updated Facebook anymore and her other social media accounts seemed to have been deleted or abandoned. When she did post something, it was usually mundane and lacking any real substance. The comments would still attract responses and likes, but usually from family or friends in Australia.

The most recent post he could find was on her mother's Facebook page. It was a photo that Chloe had been tagged in. It had been taken around a week ago and showed Chloe sitting cross-legged on the grass in her garden. She wasn't looking at the camera, seemingly unaware of its presence. Her mother had written a caption to the photo which simply read *My beautiful daughter, enjoying the lovely weather!*

Allister looked at the photo. He would not have said Chloe looked as though she was enjoying herself. She looked distracted. Even a little scared. She was staring into the distance, but he did not believe she was looking at anything in particular. At first, he guessed that she looked lost in thought. Thinking about a school project or something else equally unimportant. But then it dawned on him. She just looked lost.

He moved the cursor to the top right of the window with the intention of closing it when he suddenly stopped. Something else had caught his eye. He sat forward to be closer to the screen so he could try to see better. There. In the background between the trunks of the trees was... something. He zoomed in closer and what looked like a pale smudge became evident. It didn't seem to have any real discernible shape and just seemed to hover in the air, blending almost perfectly into the background.

"What the hell is that?" he whispered to himself. He downloaded the photo and opened a Photoshop application on his computer. He slowly began filtering the photo to try to get a better look at what was there. Soon, after changing the lighting and contrast, he could just make out what the smudge was. It was a face. Pale white and featureless. Except for two black, angry-looking eyes. Eyes that were clearly looking straight at Chloe.

With his hand shaking slightly, Allister closed the window on his screen. The picture disappeared, leaving only his desktop displayed on the monitor. He turned away in his chair while picking up his phone. He breathed heavily, taking several deep breaths to try to steady his nerves. His shaky fingers dialled a number, and he listened to several clicks as special software on his handset encrypted the call. Several seconds later he heard the call go through.

"Hello," a voice said, answering the call.

"Hi, it's me," Allister replied.

"Is the line secure?"

"Of course. I know the rules."

"Why are you calling?" The voice was stern, all business.

"I'm looking into a new case we've taken on. I think I may have found something of interest to you."

There was a brief silence on the other end of the line. Allister imagined a discussion taking place. *"Send us what you know,"* the voice said before disconnecting suddenly.

He slowly removed the phone from his ear. He hated making these calls, and he hated lying to Jackson even more. But he would not do it unless he believed it was absolutely necessary. He was told to keep this to himself, so he kept it to himself.

Allister turned back to his computer to compile a new file when he jumped and dropped his phone. He felt his heart pounding in his chest at what he saw. Without thinking, he instinctively did the sign of the cross over his chest, his religious upbringing guiding his response. On the monitor, instead of his desktop icons, was the picture of the pale face, except it had been enlarged so that it filled the whole screen. It was still featureless except for those angry dark eyes; which now appeared to be tinged with red. Eyes that seemed to look straight at him.

***

Jackson sat in his car feeling angry and frustrated at Allister. How could anybody possibly feel that way? How could they think that it's ok to do nothing when you knew that you could help somebody? He understood what Allister was trying to say about the possible consequences of interfering, but to hell with all this new age nonsense about fate. There was no such thing as destiny. Jackson firmly believed that by accepting a person's life was preordained and meant to follow one set path, took away the whole point of being alive.

Except that now he knew the future. He knew that Lucy was going to die tonight. From what he read, it would be a violent death. He supposed that you could call that destiny. But it didn't have to be. He knew what lay ahead and, in this instance, knowledge was power. He had the power to change things. To give her a new destiny. He was meant to stop her murder. Why else would he have received the newspaper report, if he was not supposed to act on it?

A headache began to make its presence known at the front of his skull. Not the usual alcohol-related one, though. He really needed to think this over and he also equally, needed some coffee. He was about to start the car when he noticed a fancy-looking coffee shop across the street. *I'm confused; I don't remember seeing that there before. I must still be in no condition to drive!* Jackson looked at the coffee shop again and decided that it would be as good a place as anywhere for some breakfast. He got out of his car and crossed the road.

The cafe was called George and Son's, and was a little more upmarket than he was used to. Pretentious really. It was exactly the kind of place Allister would go to, Jackson thought bitterly. The kind that would charge a week's pay for a coffee and something with kale in it. The windows were tinted with what he guessed was one-way glass, preventing him from seeing inside. He opened the door and entered; a bell sounded to alert people to his presence. He immediately realised that the bell was possibly the only ordinary thing about this place, as the inside was no less over the top than the outside. Tables that appeared to be made from recycled metal were randomly laid out in the room.

"Probably something to do with spiritual energy," he said to himself sarcastically.

He chose a table that looked as though it doubled as a modern art sculpture and sat down in a chair that was far more comfortable than it looked like it should be. He searched the table for a menu but could not see one.

"Welcome to George and Son's," a voice said suddenly from beside him. "How can I help you?"

Jackson looked up to see a Middle Eastern man standing next to him. He was dressed in black trousers, and a white shirt with a black tie, suggesting that he was the waiter.

"Oh, hello," he replied. "I was actually just looking for a menu?"

"George does not use menus. You tell George what you want, and George will make it for you."

"Are you George?"

"Of course!" George said with a beaming, slightly creepy

smile.

"I see. It's just that you are talking about yourself in the third person. It's quite confusing," Jackson explained. "Also, a little annoying."

George's entire voice and body language changed instantly. "Yeah, sorry about that, mate. It's something that I picked up from watching my dad work. The punters always seemed to enjoy it."

George looked to be a little older than Jackson. He had straight, black, shoulder length hair with a beret worn perfectly on top. His chin had a very well-groomed goatee beard, and he wore a necklace made of wooden beads and round, purple tinted glasses. Jackson guessed that the look was carefully crafted, but in all honesty, he thought George looked too much like a hipster.

"I see," Jackson nodded slowly. "Well, if you are after honest customer feedback, you should stop doing it."

George smiled again, but this time it was far more genuine. "Noted. So, what can I get for you?"

"If it's not too much trouble, I'll have a white coffee and a full English fry up, please."

"Not a problem, mate. By the way, this is a vegan establishment, so we do not serve any animal products," George said before disappearing as quickly as he had arrived.

Great. He considered leaving but figured that since he was already seated, he should be open to new experiences so decided instead to stay. Looking around the coffee shop, Jackson noticed some of the other customers. He had always enjoyed people watching. It came with the occupation. But what was odd here though, was that everybody seemed to be sitting alone. Nobody was talking, using a laptop or even a mobile phone. Every person was just eating their breakfast in silence.

A cup of coffee appeared before him. "One coffee with soy milk!" George announced. The food appeared seconds later. "Your fry up. Complete with vegetarian sausage and bacon, and scrambled tofu."

"Thank you," Jackson replied, eyeing the food suspiciously. It certainly looked like a fry up. Smelt like one too. Maybe it wouldn't be as bad as he first feared.

George studied him for a moment. "Something is bothering you, am I right?" he asked suddenly.

Jackson hesitated a moment, taken completely by surprise. Then without quite understanding why, decided to open up, "How can you tell?"

"It's a gift; I guess. Something else I seem to have picked up from my dad. Do you want to talk about it?"

"I am facing something of an ethical dilemma, to be honest."

"A dilemma is only a dilemma because you haven't found the solution yet," George replied.

"Is your dad a master of stating the bleeding obvious as well?" Jackson asked with a weary sigh.

George looked annoyed for a moment, then pressed on. "Tell me your problems. Maybe I can help."

"I'm just wondering if it's right to interfere in somebody else's life? To change their future and possibly their fate?"

"I guess it depends. Would you be changing it for the better?"

47

Jackson nodded, "Absolutely. I'd literally be saving their life."

"I suppose then, that you have a moral obligation to take whatever steps you need to. As long as you are not acting from a selfish motive, I cannot see how it can be wrong."

"That's what I thought at first too. But what about the knock-on effects?"

"Knock-on effects?"

"If I change one person's fate, what if it changes other things too? Makes them worse? Either for them or for somebody else?

"Like the butterfly effect?"

"Exactly like that."

George looked solemn "That is a valid concern. One you should consider. But ask yourself this, could you really refuse to help somebody because of the possibility of an effect? Or even the prediction?"

Jackson considered this for a moment. "I think you're right. I'm overthinking this. I can't really in good conscience sit here and do nothing." He instantly felt more relaxed. He knew what he had to do. Why he had been sent the message about the future. "Thank you, George."

"You are welcome. Now, enjoy your meal." And with that, he was gone again.

Cutting into a sausage, Jackson began feeling a lot more confident about what he needed to do. Sure, George was an odd character, but he seemed to know what he was talking about. He even made a strange kind of sense. Also, Jackson had to admit he cooked a good fry up, even if it did not contain any meat. He was so lost in thought he did not notice that he was no longer alone.

"Are you Jackson?" a female voice asked.

He looked up to see a teenage girl standing beside his table. She looked to be about fifteen and wore a school uniform. Her blonde hair was tied in a ponytail, and she had blue eyes that looked far too old for a girl of her age. She smiled and seemed pleased to see him. Almost as though she was greeting an old friend.

"Do I know you?" Jackson asked, feeling strangely off balance.

"I'm sorry, I thought you were expecting me," she replied. "I'm Chloe."

"Oh yes. Allister mentioned you." He held out his hand in greeting.

Chloe held up both of her hands in front of her, "Don't take this the wrong way, but I'm a bit of a germaphobe. It's nothing personal. I just have some serious OCD issues."

"Not at all. Please take a seat." He gestured to a chair opposite him.

"Thanks." She stepped up to the seat and began to sit. The movement somehow seemed forced, though. She sat slower than expected, then appeared to perch on the edge rather than sit. She looked at him, and she gave the impression she was kind of sad.

"Are you alright? You look distracted," he asked, concerned she might burst into tears at his table.

"Yes. It's just that, well, you kinda remind me of somebody," she said smiling again.

"I get that a lot," Jackson replied. "I think I just have one of those faces."

"Maybe."

"You're Australian, I notice."

Chloe smirked, "Well, you picked up on that a lot faster than Al did."

"He has a problem with accents, apparently. Or so he claims." Jackson moved to business, anxious to get back to his food. "How can we help?"

"I don't know if Al told you, but I think I'm being followed," she explained.

"To be honest, he was a little sketchy on the details, but I'm sure he is putting a case file together as we speak. In the meantime, however, what can you tell me?"

"I feel a little silly, really. I'm sure it's nothing."

Jackson looked at her with a serious expression, "Well, if there's a chance that you're in trouble, then you really should let us try to help."

"Truthfully, I'm not exactly sure where to start," she began. "As I said to Al, I've never even seen her."

"Her? So, it's a woman?"

A look passed briefly over her face, so fast that most people might have missed it. But Jackson did notice. It was clear Chloe had just said more than she may have intended to.

"Well, it could be. Fifty-fifty chance after all," she said quickly. "As I said, never really seen it. It could be a her, or a him."

Jackson could tell that she was definitely holding something back. But he decided it was probably best to let the slip up go for now. He made a mental note and filed it away. He knew that if she was going to trust him enough to let him help, it was not a good idea to ask too many difficult questions just yet.

"So how long have they been following you?" he asked instead, trying to keep the conversation going.

Before she could answer, George returned from the kitchen. He had a smile on his face until he noticed Chloe. His face immediately turned to one of thunder at the sight of her. He walked quickly to the table and pointed accusingly at her.

"What are you doing here?" he demanded. "You know that you are no longer welcome in this cafe!"

"Well hello, Georgie!" Chloe replied, with a bright, innocent-looking smile. "It has been a while, hasn't it? Also, what have you done to this place? It looks… hideous!"

"Not long enough," George practically growled. "And my name is George. Not Georgie!"

"Am I missing something?" Jackson asked, starting to feel awkward. "Is there a problem here?"

"No problem," Chloe answered happily. She looked back at George. "We both know that your dad is the real George. You'll always be Georgie."

"No. You don't get to talk about my father!" George said, his face red with anger.

"Hey, no fair. I've always liked your dad. A genuinely nice guy."

Jackson tried again to diffuse the situation. "Your dad is called George too?" he asked. "Does he work here as well?"

Without taking his eyes off Chloe, George replied, speaking slowly, "My father died fifteen years ago."

"Fifteen years ago? But how...?"

"I should probably go," Chloe said, standing again. "Georgie looks upset, and I don't wish to stay where I'm not welcome."

Jackson stood too. "I'll come with you. We never finished our conversation." He turned to George, "How much for the meal?"

"There is no charge here, but be careful, Jackson," George warned. "She is not to be trusted."

Chloe laughed bitterly. "Yeah. I'm the one who lets people down. Good one, Georgie." She turned and walked to the door, stopping to wait beside it.

"I'm not sure what that was all about, George," Jackson began, "but I do know that you do not speak to teenage girls that way. In fact, you shouldn't speak to anybody like that."

"Be very careful of her, Jackson. My cafe will always be here if you need it." He left and returned to his kitchen.

Jackson turned away and crossed to the exit, confused as to what kind of establishment served free food. *Probably one of those new-age hippy places that try to encourage good deeds and paying it forward. I doubt it'll last.* He opened the door and stepped outside, with Chloe following after him. They walked a short distance from the coffee shop then he turned to face her.

"So, what was all that about?" he asked.

Chloe paused for a moment before answering. "Let's just say that George and I have, well, I guess you'd call it history. Kind of. It's really a matter of perspective," she said, then quickly clarified. "Not the romantic kind, before you ask, because that would be gross. George is a lot of things, but he doesn't date teenage girls. Let's just say there was a mistake.

Things didn't go as planned."

"What happened?"

"I'd rather not go into it just now if you don't mind," she shrugged. "It's complicated."

"You said that you knew his father? But if he died fifteen years ago?" Jackson left the question open.

"I'm afraid that was me being a bit of a bitch. I kinda wanted to upset him. Not my brightest idea or my most shining moment, I admit. No. I've never met his dad. I believe he died before I was born."

Jackson decided to stop probing and let his unanswered questions go for now. Allister had not said anything about Chloe being so complicated. Still, it was in his nature to find answers, and she certainly posed a lot of questions. He was sure he would get to the bottom of it all in due time.

"Well, it was nice meeting you, Jack," Chloe said. "I really should get back to school before they notice I've gone again."

"Can I give you a lift?" he asked, indicating his car.

Chloe glanced in the direction of it and a look of amusement crossed her face. "Oh my God. Is that pile of crap still running?" she laughed again.

"What do you mean? Have you seen my car before?"

"No, of course not. It's just so old. I'm surprised it still runs."

"It belonged to my dad. So, I keep it around for sentimental reasons."

"I guess that's understandable," she said with a sincere look on her face. "But school isn't that far and I've taken up a lot of your time. I'd best be off. Say hi to Al for me."

"I will. Take care," Jackson replied. He watched her walk away, struck again by how strange the whole encounter was. "What just happened?" he said to himself.

Chapter Four

Later that evening, Jackson sat in a bar not far from Leeds University. In many ways, it resembled the coffee shop he had visited that morning. All new age decor and no atmosphere. Honestly, he would take a rough dive of a bar on the outskirts of Leeds full of football fans and cheap lager over one of these overpriced chain pubs any night of the week. But sadly, this was the sort of place that would attract somebody like Lucy, so it made sense to start there.

It was only after he had left his apartment that he realised that he did not actually have that much information to go on. All he really knew was that Lucy Silverman was out with friends somewhere in Leeds and that the attack would happen sometime before midnight near the drama department. Seeing as how he had never been to the university and had no interest in drama, he did not actually know where the department was. Since when was drama something you could even study at university? He had been left with no choice but to call Allister for help.

He sat at the bar and waited for Allister to arrive. He was dressed entirely in black, thinking that it would help him to blend in more easily and go unnoticed. All of his army training told him it was the logical thing to do. Now that he was here and looking around at all the bright clothes and colourful outfits worn by the other patrons, he realised that his choice of clothing actually made him stand out. More curious looks had come his way than he would have liked.

Taking a sip from his glass, Jackson grimaced. Mineral water. First a vegan breakfast and now water. Somewhere within the weirdness of the day, he seemed to have developed a health kick. It was probably a good thing, but at over two pounds for a glass of something that tasted like it came from a tap, he couldn't really say that he cared for it. Still, a day without alcohol would not do him any harm.

Allister arrived and sat beside him. He nodded in greeting then pointed to Jackson's drink. "Is that water?" he asked, sounding surprised.

Annoyed by the comment Jackson snapped, "Of course it is. I can hardly try to save somebody's life while I'm drunk, can I?"

"Easy, Jackson," Allister replied, raising his hands in surrender to placate his friend. "I was just joking around!"

"Sorry, Al. It's just been a really strange day."

"You're telling me," Allister replied. For a moment Jackson was sure he had caught a look in his friend's eyes he had rarely seen before; fear.

"Are you ok?" Jackson asked.

"Yeah. Just starting to wonder what we've let ourselves into."

"I've been wondering the same thing." He was just about to tell Allister about his strange encounter with Chloe but then changed his mind. He wasn't sure why, but the idea of talking about her suddenly seemed unimportant. Helping Lucy had to remain the priority now. With that in mind, he continued, "Have you been able to find out where Lucy is?"

Allister took his phone from his pocket, "I have. Right now, she is in a bar called *The Northerner*. She got there about twenty minutes ago."

"How do you know that?" Jackson asked, quietly impressed.

"It was really not that hard. She's one of those internet bores who posts her entire existence on social media. She checked into *The Northerner* on Facebook twenty-three minutes ago and has already posted seven photos of herself and her friends to Instagram. She has also let her five thousand followers on Twitter know where she is if they want to join her. You really do not need to be a hacker to follow this girl. Hang on, eight photos."

"That sounds like an awful lot of work for a night out. Whatever happened to sitting down and having a drink and a chat with friends?"

"It's not safe. If this works out you really need to have a word with her about it," Allister said, then asked, "Are you still going through with it?"

"It's the right thing to do, mate. We can't let what might happen stop us when we know what will happen. Life isn't set in stone. I can't worry about destiny when I know somebody is going to die. I couldn't live with myself if I didn't try to help her."

"I guessed you'd feel that way. I've certainly known you long enough. I'm still not completely sure if I agree with you, but I'll help in any way I can."

"Thanks, Al," Jackson replied sincerely, "that means a lot. Also, I checked the Leeds Daily News website this evening. The story I was sent yesterday is on there. And it's exactly the same, word for word. I think we have to consider this is happening."

"Yeah, I checked it too. It's exactly as you said it was," Allister admitted. "I also contacted Jane McArther, the journalist who wrote both articles to see if she could shed any light on this."

"Good idea. What did she have to say?"

"Ironically, she said 'no comment,' and hung up on me."

That was strange, Jackson thought. Though part of him was relieved, he did not want to direct the attention to himself. He decided to return to what they were here for. "Do you know how to find the drama department on the university campus?"

"Give me your phone," Allister replied holding his hand out and Jackson passed it over. He tapped and swiped the screen several times before handing it back. "All you need to do is open the maps app on your phone. It will then give you directions, no matter where you are."

Jackson looked at the app Allister had now set up and saw a little stick man on a map illustrating where he currently was in Leeds. It then showed a dotted line, which traced a route ending in a red arrow over the campus. It gave directions and also an estimated walking time. He was surprised he had never used this application before. It would make tailing someone a breeze! Modern technology still made him marvel from time to time.

"Thanks again." He checked his watch and saw that it was 9.30pm. "We've got a couple of hours before we need to be there. Do you want a drink?"

"Ok, sounds good," Allister said. He pointed to Jackson's glass, "I'll have what you're having."

"Are you sure? It's pretty disgusting."

***

Chloe was having a bad day. If you didn't count the previous day, it would quite possibly be the worst day in some time, and honestly, it had some stiff competition. It all started when she received a text from her mother. The school had been in touch with them again to let her parents know she had been absent for the first two lessons of the morning. It really had not been intentional. Sometimes there were more important things than school. But her mum had made it clear that there would be a family meeting tonight to discuss her recent behaviour as soon as she was home, and that her father was deeply disappointed in her. Needless to say, she had yet to return home.

At lunch, Nicola Ritchie and her clique had sought her out to give her a hard time again. Chloe knew why they often chose her. She was nearly always alone at school, so they clearly saw her as a soft target. She may have been alone, but she was not soft. Chloe didn't allow them to intimidate her, but she didn't provoke them either. They soon gave up when Mr Howard, the headmaster, arrived on the scene to ask what was happening. Her relief was short-lived, however, when he began to drone on about her attendance and how she could do better. He then made a comment about her running shoes not being correct school footwear. She almost told him that after being chased the previous day by a deranged rapist who was then viciously attacked, she never intended to wear school shoes again.

That had pretty much ruined the rest of her day. She coasted through the remainder of her lessons, refusing to get involved. Finally, she had been asked to leave the last period when she spent ten minutes arguing with her science teacher that Krypton was not real so it should not be on the periodic table. The discussion had raised a few sniggers from her fellow students, but she doubted it had made her any more popular. Not wanting to waste any more of her time in that place, she decided to take it as an excuse to skip the rest of the school day and left.

So now Chloe found herself watching the sky darken in the park, her safe place. It was late, and she had several missed calls and text messages from her mum demanding to know where she was. She ignored them all as she decided she was in enough trouble already and a little more wouldn't hurt. She really was not in the mood for that conversation. Probably never would be. Instead, she sat on a swing, gently swaying back and forth.

Chloe had never figured out the significance of the park and why 'it' would never come in here. She knew it was out there now, lurking among the trees, watching her. She had heard it circle the boundary fence several times already, rattling the gate to make sure she knew it was there. As if she was going to forget. As usual, by the time her head had whipped in the direction of the gate, there was nothing there. But she could hear the leaves being crunched, as if under feet, and there was the constant feeling of being observed. But for whatever reason, it never tried to enter. Either it chose not to, or it simply could not.

"I don't believe that we were finished," a familiar voice said from behind her.

Chloe rolled her eyes, stood up and turned to face her other tormentor. "What do you want, Nicola?" she asked, trying to sound bored.

Nicola Ritchie stood between two other girls from their school. She was a couple of inches taller than Chloe but slouched, making the height difference seem less obvious. She had long dark brown hair and brown eyes with a gold piercing through one of her eyebrows. She always seemed to wear a permanent scowl on what would normally be considered a pretty face and in her ears were large, fake gold hoop earrings.

The other girls Chloe was less familiar with; she knew them only as Danielle and Jade. Both were in her year and some of her classes, but they flanked Nicola like the loyal thugs they were. She despised them all, but she was not scared of these girls. She knew there were far worse things to fear now. But she was annoyed by their intrusion into her safe space. Still, three against one, she would rather not get into a fight right now if she could avoid it.

"I wanna know what your problem is," Nicola demanded.

Chloe looked at her with a blank face, "You'll have to be more specific. I have a lot of problems."

"You think you're so clever, don't you? You think you're smarter than us cause you're from Australia, innit?"

Chloe inwardly grimaced at the girl's poor use of the English language. She had heard Nicola speak before, but she never got used to it. She replied in a deadpan tone, "I don't think I am better than you because I'm from Australia."

"You better not!" Nicola said getting face to face with Chloe. "Cause if I find out that you do, I swear I'll give you a proper beating, innit."

"Are you done now?" Chloe asked calmly. She could hear what sounded like angry footsteps pacing outside of the park. They sounded impatient and anxious. If the other girls could hear them, they made no sign.

Nicola seemed to be taken aback by the question and took a while to respond. Chloe had always found that to be the case with bullies. A direct challenge often took them by surprise and put them off balance.

"For now," she said. "But I best not see you at school tomorrow, innit bitch?" she lightly slapped Chloe's cheek.

Nicola turned and began to walk away, her friends following her. Chloe's face burned with anger from the indignity of the situation. She was sick and tired of being spoken down to by people like Nicola. No, she was not popular anymore. Nor did she belong to any social circle, but she was damned if she was going to be treated like she was nothing any longer. She heard a low growl from just outside the park. It seemed as if Chloe was not the only angry one, and it emboldened her to make a stand.

"Hey, we are not done, bitches," she called after the girls. They turned to face her with looks that ranged from confusion to annoyance.

"You talking to us?" Nicola asked, sounding surprised.

"I said that I don't think I'm better than you because I'm from Australia. Which is true. You see, I am better than you because I am better than you." Chloe shrugged, then smirked at them, "Innit?"

"You're proper getting a beating for that!" Danielle replied, clearly enraged now. Chloe was surprised. She was not aware that Danielle could speak for herself.

As the three girls began to walk toward her, Chloe knew that it was a fight she was unlikely to win. Not for the first time she silently cursed her newfound temper. Suddenly there was a screech that seemed to envelop them all, then a rock landed a short distance from Nicola's group. They stopped in their tracks and looked around.

"What the fuck was that?" Nicola demanded. "Did you just throw a stone at me?"

Feeling as shocked as the other girls looked, Chloe raised her hands to show that they were empty as a second rock bounced even closer to them. Looking around, Danielle did not see the next rock that flew in from her left and struck her above the eye. It was accompanied by what sounded like a screech of triumph. Danielle screamed out in pain and her hand flew to her face to cover the injury as she collapsed to her knees. Chloe saw blood begin to trickle between the girl's fingers.

The three of them were clearly shaken now. Nicola and Jade helped Danielle to her feet, allowing the injured girl to rest against them. Danielle was shaking as blood dripped to the tarmac.

Nicola looked up with fury in her eyes until she looked over Chloe's shoulder and the colour drained from her face. She began to back away, carrying Danielle with her. Another rock landed close by.

"I don't know how you're doing this, freak," she hissed, trying to look threatening but clearly terrified, "but you will regret it. I promise you!" The three girls hurried away from the park.

After they had left, Chloe glanced over her shoulder to see what had scared Nicola so much. She drew in a sharp breath at what she saw. Several more rocks hung as if suspended in mid-air. Then slowly at first, but increasing in speed, they began to fall to the ground one by one with a thud.

"What the hell?" she whispered to herself.

From her right, she saw movement at the corner of her eye. She looked quickly in that direction, but this time something was still there. She saw the shape of a slender body shrouded in shadow, and a pale face with dark eyes that seemed to glitter with colour in the dwindling twilight. She could just make out that the face wore a satisfied smile as it slowly faded away. Soon, Chloe was entirely alone again, feeling far from safe.

Shaking, she sat back down on the swing before her knees buckled under her. What had she just witnessed? It did not seem real. And who was that? Did it mean to protect her or do her harm? She was not sure anymore. One thing she did know was that she had to stop saying 'it'. Now she knew her stalker was female. Chloe took several deep breaths to steady her nerves, then took her phone from her pocket and began to compose a message.

***

Jackson and Allister had found a table in another bar close by. They were still drinking mineral water while watching the people around them slowly getting drunk. They all seemed to be taking photos of each other or tapping away furiously on their phones. It made no sense to Jackson. Why would somebody arrange to come out with friends and then spend the evening talking to people who were not even there? He realised that almost everybody else in the bar was in their late teens or early twenties, which just made the two of them look even more out of place. When had he gotten so old?

"Bloody hell, Al," he said. "I feel like I've come to pick my kids up from a school disco."

Allister glanced around, "Student bars for you, mate. I used to hang out at places like this all the time back in the day. Had so many great nights."

"Hang on, you were never a student."

"Yeah, I know." He shrugged and left it at that.

"I've known you most of my life and there's still stuff I don't know."

"You were in the army. Besides, I only said I used to frequent student bars. It's not like I joined a cult." Allister took a sip of his drink, "So, have you figured out how you are going to do this?"

"Only thing I can think of is to head over to the drama department and keep a watch for Lucy or anybody suspicious-looking hanging about. Then if she's attacked, stop him," Jackson replied.

"Did the article say who did it?"

"No. It just said a man was arrested nearby. He wasn't named."

"That's a shame. All of this would have been far easier if he was." Allister's phone bleeped. He picked it up from the table, read the text message and looked up at Jackson apologetically.

"Let me guess; you've got to go," Jackson said.

"I'm afraid so, mate."

"The mysterious Chloe?"

Allister hesitated before answering, then nodded, "Yeah, she needs help."

Jackson sighed, "Do you need to borrow my car?"

"Yes, please, if that's ok?"

Handing over the car keys Jackson gave a mischievous smile and said, "Should I be concerned that you're spending all this time with a schoolgirl?"

Allister rolled his eyes at the jibe, "You know it's not like that, Jackson."

"I know. Still, we can add the time to her bill."

Pulling his coat on and taking a step back, Allister took a

breath before answering. "About that... I actually told her that we'd waive the fee. I knew you'd understand, see you later," he said before turning and leaving, Jackson staring after him in disbelief.

***

Nicola Ritchie was angry. In fact, angry did not cover it; she was fuming. After taking Danielle home, she had gone to her house and fetched the baseball bat that her stepdad always kept by the door in case of unwanted visitors. Now she was headed back to the park intent on finishing things with that Australian bitch once and for all.

She was not entirely sure why she hated Chloe so much. She guessed it was all the attention she received after she first arrived. How everybody crowded around her to be her friend without her even trying. Nicola had always struggled to make friends, and those she had were more hangers-on than actual friends. But Chloe just had to turn up with her blonde hair and dumb Australian accent and she was suddenly popular. Admittedly, once everybody realised that she was a freak, her popularity had nosedived and everybody moved on. Everybody except for Nicola, who had always struggled to let grudges go.

As she hurried down the street, she realised she was alone. The sun had set, and the streetlamps lit her way, but there was no sound. No sound of cars travelling along the nearby dual carriageway, or the sound of cats and dogs calling into the night. It was deathly silent. Even the leaves on the trees seemed to stop rustling as if holding their breath in anticipation. Nicola stopped walking as the strangeness of the silence began to dawn upon her. She looked around and could see nobody else there. Admittedly it was late, but normally there was still some sign of life to be seen.

She jumped as the first set of streetlights suddenly went dark right above her, one on either side of the road. This was followed by two more. Then in pairs, every light in the street went out, leaving Nicola in darkness. Even the houses that lined the street were dark. There was a brief sound of whispering that seemed to come from every direction at once, but Nicola could not make out any of the words.

Already scared, her fear turned up several notches when she heard the echo of footsteps coming toward her, loud in the otherwise total silence. Nicola raised the bat, holding its rubber grip in both hands as she saw the shape of a girl walking casually along the paving slabs. Concealed by darkness and thus unrecognisable, the girl stopped a short distance away. All that could be seen of her face were her eyes that glowed gently and seemed to change colour. Her hair hung loosely around her, dark but for a line of dimly lit purple that travelled periodically from the roots to the tips as she watched Nicola silently.

The girl looked at the bat in Nicola's hands and laughed. "Oh, you've got to be kidding me," she said in a voice that sounded musical, yet intimidating. She flicked her wrist, and the bat was ripped from Nicola's grasp then flew through the air and out of sight. "Now, maybe we can have a more civilised conversation."

"Who... who the fuck are you?" Nicola asked, trying to convey a confidence she no longer felt.

"Who I am is not the issue right now. What is, is your behaviour and what we are going to do to change it going forward."

"Yeah? What's that then?"

"We are going to talk about your treatment of Chloe. I take it you are familiar with her? You were, after all, on your way to assault her with a weapon."

"Yeah I know her," Nicola replied with a sneer. "What's she to you?"

The girl waved the question away dismissively. "That is none of your business. All you need to know, for now, is that you are going to start leaving her alone." She took a step closer, the colour of her eyes settling for a moment on red, the warning clear, "Do you understand?"

Nicola hesitated for a moment before shaking her head, "No way. That Chloe has got a beating coming. I'm gonna make sure she gets it!"

The girl's eyes grew a deeper shade of red as she raised her arm towards Nicola with her hand open. She began to close her fingers slowly, and Nicola felt her throat start to constrict, then she began to find it difficult to breathe. She fell to her knees, scratching at her neck, trying to dislodge the invisible force that held her.

"Jesus, Nicola," the girl said in a voice like acid. "I always knew you were stupid, but I had no idea you were suicidal!" Then she laughed, "Not that I'm complaining. I've wanted to torture you for such a long time."

"Let... me... go..." Nicola managed to beg through frantic gasps for air.

The girl squatted down so she was eye level with her, "I'm so sorry. I didn't quite catch that." With her other hand, she cupped her ear to mime hearing better, "What did you say?"

"Puh... please..."

"Now, listen to me closely. You will leave Chloe alone from

now on. You and your little gang. Or you will find that I can do far worse than making it difficult to breathe or pushing you down some stairs. Do you understand me?"

Nicola was by now unable to speak, but she nodded furiously. The girl opened her hand, stretching out her fingers and Nicola could breathe again. She greedily gulped down a great lungful of air and slowly began to struggle back to her feet. She stood rubbing her throat but made no effort to run, too terrified to even think about escaping.

Those strange glowing eyes began to alternate through the colours again. They regarded Nicola for a moment, settling briefly on a deep blue before changing to green. Without a word, the girl held her arm out to her left, and seconds later the baseball bat returned. It hovered in the air between them, held by the same invisible force that had choked Nicola moments earlier.

"Chloe is mine," she said, her voice becoming even more menacing. "What happens to her is up to me. Do you understand?"

Nicola nodded her head again, not trusting her voice to speak. She watched as the girl casually twirled a finger in the air, the bat started to spin on its axis, mimicking a propeller, but remaining suspended in place above the ground. In the distance streetlights began to turn back on two at a time, moving up the street toward them.

The eyes twinkled with danger, shining brighter for a moment. "I'm glad we had this little chat. Obviously, I can trust you not to tell anybody about this, right?" she asked. Nicola nodded. "Good. However, even though I am sure that you will keep your mouth shut, I don't like to leave anything to chance." She stopped twirling her finger, and the bat ceased spinning. She flicked her wrist again, and the bat swung through the air and struck Nicola's lower arm. The sound of her scream was drowned out only by the noise of the bone snapping in two. Nicola fell to the floor once more, her good arm cradling the injured one, tears falling down her cheeks. She shook as the shock began to set in.

The girl crouched down in front of her yet again. Now there was no colour in her eyes; they were just black and empty as a void. Nicola finally realised that it was the girl from the park who was throwing the rocks.

"This never happened. If you tell anybody about me or go near Chloe again, you'll find that there is nowhere in this city you can hide from me!" She looked to her right before adding, "Say hi to your mum for me."

The last comment was lost in the pain she felt in her arm, and the streetlamps just above her then lit up, bathing them both in a white glow, allowing Nicola to see the girl's smiling face looking at her for the first time. She began to scream again, though this time not from pain, but terror.

***

Allister arrived at the park shortly before eleven and decided to head straight for the swings. He hadn't heard anything more from Chloe so assumed she must still be there. Her message had worried him as she seemed to be upset even though she had assured him that she was not in danger. It had taken him fifteen minutes to drive here, so hopefully, nothing had gone wrong during that time. He reflected on why he had become so protective of Chloe. *I guess it's because she reminds me a lot of Ruby.* Out of the blue, the pain came. It had been nearly sixteen years, but the memory was still raw. He doubted it would ever get any easier.

Pushing all thoughts of his twin sister from his mind, he

entered the park through the gate where Chloe's bag had been found and headed straight toward the swings where he guessed she would be. After what happened last night, the place sent a shiver down his spine. It was creepy; the shadows seemed to close in on him and there was a feeling of being watched. How Chloe could stand to be alone in a place like this he had no idea. She called it her safe place, but the feeling was definitely not mutual.

"Hey," Chloe said from where she sat. As he suspected, she was on the same swing as the night before. "Thanks for coming."

"I would say it's a pleasure," Allister began, looking around, "but I'm not sure I'm ready to be back here yet."

"Last night was a little freaky. To be honest, it's normally pretty quiet here." She looked sad, "I hope I didn't interrupt anything important."

"Just Jackson messing with the fabric of time."

"What?" Chloe asked, looking confused.

"Never mind. It's a really long, weird story," he replied, then changed the subject. "So, what's happened?"

"I've had a really rough couple of days, and I think I should probably tell somebody about them." She paused to gather her thoughts. "Did you hear about that man who was murdered on the canal?"

"I saw something about it online," Allister replied, feeling guilty for holding back exactly how much he knew. "Why do you ask?"

She seemed to hesitate before answering as if she was trying to decide how much she should tell him. "I was there!" she blurted out.

"You were what?" Allister answered in surprise, he was sure he could not have heard her correctly.

"After I left you at the shopping centre, I knew there was no point in going back to school. Instead, I decided to go for a walk and ended up by the canal. Some guy followed me. He tried... he tried to attack me." She struggled to finish her sentence and tears appeared in the corners of her eyes.

"Chloe..." Allister began slowly, knowing he had to get what he said next absolutely right or the conversation could be over. "Are you responsible for what happened? Because if you are, we need to go to the police."

"Oh, my fucking God no, Allister!" she replied, almost insulted. "I tore a chunk of skin from his cheek, but mostly I just ran."

"So, what happened?"

"After I ran, I took a wrong turn and he managed to corner me. I thought for sure that was it, my time was up. But then he was just pulled away and dragged down the path."

"Somebody grabbed him?"

"I guess. Kinda. I'm not sure what exactly happened. I've replayed it over and over in my memory and it literally makes no sense. One moment he was walking forward, looking at me like I was food. He was so confident like he was sure he had won. The next he was pulled back as if he was on an elastic band or something. Then he started, well, screaming." The grimace on her face made it clear the memory was hard for her to talk about.

Allister smiled reassuringly at her, "It's ok."

Chloe took a breath and then continued, "I didn't see who attacked him. Mostly because I was running away from it."

"I don't blame you. I'm sure anybody would have in your situation. Myself included. I do think you should consider going to the police. I think you were caught on CCTV going onto the canal path before he was murdered."

She shook her head, "They'd never believe me. I hardly believe me. They would either think I'm guilty or I'm crazy. Neither ends well. As for the CCTV, I've already wiped them. I made it look like a random glitch. I deleted all the back-up copies too."

"You hacked the city's security cameras? I have to say that I'm impressed."

"Allegedly," she shrugged.

"So, do you have any idea who attacked him?" Allister asked, getting the conversation back on topic. "Your stalker, maybe?"

"Perhaps. I think so anyway," Chloe said. "But that's not everything. Today some girls from my school came here to give me a hard time."

"Why?"

"They don't like me. Anyway, my stalker was hanging around outside the park. When it looked as though Nicola and her friends were going to attack me, it began throwing rocks at them until they backed off. Which they did. They were looking over my shoulder and looked scared." She hesitated again, "When I turned to see what they were looking at, I saw several rocks just hanging in the air."

"Hanging in the air?"

"Yeah, like levitating..." She studied Allister a moment. "Aren't you going to tell me that I'm crazy?"

"No. I've already decided to believe everything that you

tell me," he replied simply.

"Why? Not that I'm complaining."

"It's been a strange thirty-six hours. It's changed my perception of the world, I guess. What happened then?"

"Well, the rocks just all fell to the ground one at a time. But I did see it this time! Well, kind of."

"Really? You know what it is?"

"Not exactly. Its body was mostly hidden by shadow and its face was just white, with eyes that were almost black!"

Allister looked at her. Even though he had been expecting the description, it still surprised him when she told him. He had suspected the face was connected to Chloe's stalker. But having those suspicions confirmed was still a difficult thing to accept. It all went against everything he thought he knew and understood in the world.

"Wow. This is a lot to take in," he said, rubbing the bridge of his nose.

"There's more I'm afraid, Allister," Chloe continued. "It's not an it; it's a girl."

"A girl? Are you sure?"

"Almost certain. I saw enough of her body to see she was definitely female," she paused before continuing, "and I think I know her."

Allister stopped what he was doing and looked up. "Know her? Know her how?"

"I'm not sure. It was just a feeling I got. Like I recognised her, or that we had met before. She had no face, so I didn't actually physically recognise her." She thought for a moment, nervously biting her lower lip, "That's the only way I can describe it. A feeling. Not very helpful I know."

"I do believe you, Chloe. I just wish I knew what it all meant."

"Me too," she whispered. She looked at Allister, those blue eyes full of intensity, and fear, "Allister... am I going to be ok?"

"Yes, you are. You have nothing to worry about" he said as firmly as he could, even though deep down he had asked the same question.

"I'm scared, you know? This thing has been following me for over a year. Tormenting me and I don't think it's just because she's bored. I think she wants to hurt me."

"That's not going to happen, Chloe. I won't let it. And neither will Jackson!"

She smiled a sad smile. "I want Kanga," she said suddenly.

"Kanga?" Allister was confused by the unexpected comment.

"It's a stuffed kangaroo I've had since before I can remember. Whenever I was scared when I was little, my dad would give me Kanga, and I'd stroke his fur and everything would be ok, less scary you know? I pretty much wore away his fur stroking him." Chloe laughed lightly at the thought, "Now he just sits on my desk gathering dust."

"You don't need to be scared. I will do everything in my power to keep you safe. I promise," Allister said.

"I guess it's my turn to believe you." She checked her watch. "Damn, I really need to go home. My parents will be in full freak out mode now and about to call the police. If they haven't already." She stood and picked up her new school bag.

"Do you want me to come with you?" Allister asked. "Let

them know that you were safe?"

"Thanks, Allister. But I'm pretty sure that hanging out in a park at nearly midnight with a guy twice my age, isn't the reassurance they'll be looking for."

"I see your point."

Before he realised what she was about to do, she hugged him. "Thanks again. It means a lot to know that you and Jackson are looking out for me." She released him and stepped back.

"Of course we are, Chloe," he replied.

She turned and set off for home. Allister watched after her until she was no longer in sight. Nothing made sense to him right now. Every time he thought he might be onto something, he realised how far from reality it was. He liked puzzles, but he was starting to feel as though Chloe was a puzzle he would never solve.

***

Jackson had been waiting near the university drama department for almost thirty minutes and had yet to see anything that seemed out of the ordinary. A few people had passed by him, though none of them was Lucy. He had also not seen anybody acting suspicious or hanging around unnecessarily. Except for himself, obviously. He checked his watch for what felt like the thousandth time. 11:52pm. If nothing happened in the next eight minutes, he was prepared to accept that the whole thing was probably a hoax.

"HELP!" The scream came from close by. Very close.

Jackson set off running in the direction of the voice. As he rounded a corner, he saw a man pushing somebody to the ground, a knife held to their throat. As Jackson neared, he recognised the victim as Lucy. The man was so focused on forcing her to the floor, that he did not hear Jackson running toward them. Without slowing down, Jackson aimed his shoulder at the attacker and barged into him, knocking him off Lucy and hearing a satisfying yelp of pain.

They both hit the ground, and Jackson used the momentum to roll several times before springing back to his feet. He faced the man who by now was also standing up. He was tall but skinny, and his skin and clothes were dirty. He had messy hair and a beard that were dark grey and greasy. He looked to be in his fifties, but Jackson guessed that he could be younger. What really caught Jackson's eye, though, was the deep red birthmark covering much of the left side of his face.

"Give it up, mate," Jackson said in a calm but firm voice. "Put the knife down and let's talk about this." He became aware of other people arriving at the scene, obviously drawn by the commotion. Some of them held mobile phones in their hands, and most were actually filming what was happening. *What the hell? What is wrong with these people? Are they seriously more interested in putting a tragedy on social media than trying to help?* He noticed then that at least one person did appear to be making a phone call. *Let's at least hope it's to the police.*

The man took a step forward and lunged, the blade aimed at Jackson's stomach. With perfect timing, Jackson stepped to the side and grabbed the attacker's wrist, twisting hard. The man let out a gasp of pain and the knife fell to the floor. With his free hand, Jackson punched the man twice in the face, forcing him to the ground again.

Jackson turned to kick the knife away and saw several of the new arrivals were already checking that Lucy was ok.

While he was distracted, the man got back to his feet and began running in the opposite direction.

"Hey!" Jackson called after him. "Get back here!"

He started to give chase, already beginning to gain on the other man. He may have been out of the army for some time, but Jackson had kept up with his fitness. He was fast approaching, and just as he was about to tackle him to the ground, Jackson felt his feet pulled from underneath him. *I must have tripped on something*, he figured as he hit the floor hard, the wind knocked out of him. He looked up just in time to see Lucy's attacker disappear into the darkness and slammed his hand against the concrete in frustration. Jackson began to pull himself slowly to his feet and looked for what had tripped him but could see nothing except paving slabs, which were flat and level.

Confused, he headed back to where he had left Lucy, limping slightly from a knock to the knee. He could hear police sirens getting closer. Good. Maybe they would catch the assailant. He scanned the ground, looking for where he had kicked the knife, since it could contain fingerprint evidence, but could not see it anywhere. *I hope somebody has picked it up to keep it for the police.*

By the time he got close to Lucy, she was surrounded by other students who were comforting her. He couldn't see any obvious signs of injury from where he was standing and nobody else appeared to be concerned. The police sirens were very close now, so he walked to Lucy and crouched beside her.

"Hey, Lucy," he began, "are you ok?"

She looked up at him but did not appear to recognise who he was. After a few seconds, the penny seemed to drop. Confusion then spread across her face.

"Jackson?" she asked. "What are you doing here?"

"I... was... just passing," he replied, mentally kicking himself for not thinking of a cover story. "I heard screaming and came to investigate."

She looked at him, clearly dubious. She must have decided that it did not matter as she took his hand. "You saved me?"

"I just happened to be in the right place at the right time is all."

"Oh my God, thank you," she said throwing her arms around him. "You saved my life!"

"Anybody would have done the same," Jackson replied modestly when she pulled away again.

Jackson stood up and was just about to offer to help Lucy to her feet when he was thrown roughly to the ground. His arms were pulled up behind his back followed by the cold metal of handcuffs being applied. He winced as a sharp pain shot through his injured knee.

"What the bloody hell are you doing?" he protested as he lay face down on the ground.

"You're under arrest for attempted assault," a police officer began. He continued to read Jackson his rights as he was pulled to his feet and forced toward the waiting police car.

Chapter Five

The police cell was tiny and cold. Beige walls surrounded Jackson on all sides, broken up only by a small window near the ceiling and a grey metal door opposite him. The door bore the signs of damage from previous occupants' displeasure at being incarcerated. There was a thin bed bolted to the floor along one wall, but instead, he chose to sit on the floor rather than risk coming into contact with whatever may be on the mattress.

The lights were off inside the cell, but sunlight crept in through the window, giving Jackson enough illumination to see by. He had not slept during the night. Partly due to his annoyance at being arrested, but mostly because of the banging and the shouting from the drunk in the next cell who had promised to do all manner of unsavoury things to the on-duty police officers before finally falling unconscious. Since then he had been left alone with his thoughts while waiting for the interview that was surely coming. He had been offered a lawyer but declined, since he knew that he had done nothing wrong.

Jackson replayed the events of the previous evening in his head to see if there was anything he could have done differently. It was unfortunate that Lucy's attacker had managed to escape. It was the one thing he should have made sure did not happen. Now, instead of being held in a cell, he was still on the loose and a danger to others. Jackson had told the police about him, but they had been uninterested. They were certain that they had their man already.

He considered asking Allister to try to find him online since that birthmark would not go unnoticed. Somebody, somewhere, must know who or where he was. Finding him should be a priority. If he had tried to kill Lucy once, he might try again. He kicked himself for losing him. He still could not understand what happened. One moment he was right behind him then he was down. It was strange as he was certain he had not tripped on anything. It almost felt like his legs were pulled from underneath him. That the knife had disappeared was an even bigger concern. He knew he had not kicked it far; just enough to ensure the attacker couldn't reach it.

The sound of footsteps echoing in the corridor outside interrupted his thoughts. They came to a stop in front of his cell door, and he heard the large lock sliding back. The door swung open on squeaky hinges to reveal a police officer standing on the other side.

"Jackson Clarke," the police officer said. He was not asking.

"That's me," Jackson replied, standing up. He limped a little from where he had banged his knee.

"Could you come with me, please?" The police officer stepped to one side, so the door was no longer obstructed.

Jackson crossed the room and left the cell. Outside was a corridor with several metal doors on either side and the same beige coloured the walls.

"Do I need to cuff you?"

"Not at all. This is all a big misunderstanding. I'm just anxious to get it straightened out."

"Follow me, Sir," the police officer simply replied and began walking. Without another word, Jackson followed behind him.

ECHO

***

Chloe left the house early before her mum and dad had even woken. She had no wish right now to have another confrontation after the previous night. Once was enough. They had both been furious with her by the time she arrived home. They yelled. She yelled back. They threatened to ground her. She laughed at them. They told her to hand over her phone. She refused. Then the crying started. Mostly from her mum. She wanted to know what had happened to their daughter. Chloe didn't have an answer she felt would make them feel better. So instead, she just said she hated living in England. Her dad surprised her then by suggesting that she could go live with her grandparents in Australia until she finished school. The idea appealed to her more than she admitted, and she said she would think about it.

When she went to her room, she found it strangely quiet. There had been no visitor last night, so no whispering. Chloe guessed that 'she' must have been somewhere else. Which troubled her the more she thought about it. She fell asleep more from exhaustion than anything else, and she ended up sleeping well for the first time in a while.

This morning she had woken with the alarm, showered, dressed and headed out without breakfast. She considered skipping school, so that she didn't run into Nicola, but knew that if her parents were considering letting her return to Australia, she needed to get into their good books. She felt relief at the thought that maybe she could escape what her life had become.

After grabbing a coffee from the shop near her school, she arrived almost thirty minutes early. This really was unprecedented by her usual standards. The downside was that it would mean lying low until the bell rang, as Nicola was bound to be looking for her. After some more thought, she decided that she would not hide. If she saw Nicola, then she did. Whatever happened then happened.

As she wandered the halls, she began to notice people looking at her. Normally people were either indifferent or just straight ignored her. Today though some people looked at her warily, like they thought she might suddenly attack them, while others smiled or even nodded at her. A couple of others even went so far as to say hello as she passed. It was definitely time to admit that something was wrong with the world right now.

Turning a corner, she found herself face to face with Jade. Chloe looked around to see if Nicola was also there, but she was alone and seemed as though she had been waiting for her. Jade appeared to be trying to look non-threatening, and she ran a hand through her raven black hair nervously before speaking.

"Hey," Jade said, actually sounding pleasant for once.

Chloe stared back at her in confusion, certain that this must be some kind of trap. "Hey?" she said slowly, unsure what to expect. "Can I help you?"

"Did you hear about Nicola yet?" Jade asked.

"Should I have?"

"She's in hospital!"

Chloe's hand went involuntarily to her mouth, "Oh my God! What happened? Is she ok?"

"She was beaten up last night. She has a broken arm and bruising around her neck. The doctors think she may have been strangled."

"Fuck," Chloe said, surprised that she actually felt bad for the girl who had made her school life miserable. "Do they know who did it?"

Jade looked at her with a serious expression. Her green eyes sparkled, contrasting well against her olive complexion. It was something Chloe had never noticed before. "There's a rumour going around that you did!"

"What?" Chloe said panicking. Anybody at the school would almost certainly say she had a motive if asked. Also, she did not have an alibi for the previous evening without pulling Allister into it. Her worry showed clearly on her face.

"Calm down. I know it wasn't you," Jade reassured her. "I was speaking to Nicola this morning. She wouldn't say who attacked her, but she did tell me that we have to leave you alone now."

Chloe was confused by this turn of events, "I probably shouldn't ask, but why?"

"She didn't say. She just told me to put the word around school that you're not to be touched."

Now all the looks in the hallways were starting to make sense. People thought that she was responsible for Nicola being in hospital! The reactions were a mix of wariness and support. *I suppose there are always people on both sides.*

"Is she going to be ok?" Chloe asked, feeling genuinely concerned.

"I think so," Jade replied. She thought for a moment and then continued, "I'm going to be honest with you, Chloe. I know I hang with Nicola, but it's only because it's better to be her friend than her enemy. Don't have too much sympathy for her, because after we took Danielle home, she was on her way back to you. She finally intended to have it out with you. So, whoever got to her first, they did you a huge favour."

This news, while not exactly shocking, did distress Chloe. If it hadn't had been for somebody else, it could have been her lying in a hospital bed right now. She had no doubts that Nicola would have taken it that far since she had always made her dislike for her clear, and Nicola's reputation was well known. Chloe had always prided herself on the thought of being able to look after herself, but Nicola was unhinged.

"Well, thank you for letting me know."

"No problem," Jade replied. "If you have any trouble from anybody today, let me know. I will sort it."

Knowing this may be the only chance to ask Jade a question about the previous evening, Chloe decided to keep the conversation going, "Jade, what do you remember about last night? In the park?"

Jade looked uncomfortable at the question, clearly also disturbed by the events. "I'm going to be honest with you. I don't know what I saw, but I do know I don't want to talk about it. It's best if you don't either. People already think you are crazy as it is."

Any further conversation was broken up by the school bell ringing. The two girls nodded to one another, then went their separate ways. Chloe headed toward her form class in a daze. She could only think of one person who might be responsible for the attack on Nicola, but she could not understand why. Why did *it, she,* keep protecting Chloe, while tormenting her at the same time? It made no sense. She walked into the classroom feeling, not for the first time, lost.

***

Jackson sat on an extremely uncomfortable plastic chair at the only table in the police interview room. He was alone except for the police officer who had brought him here, but who seemed unwilling to have a conversation. He just stood silently by the single exit to the room. In the middle of the table was some kind of recording device. Jackson had expected a 1980s tape recorder like they had in so many police dramas he had seen, but was disappointed to see that it was more sophisticated than that.

Just as he was starting to believe he was deliberately being kept waiting, the door opened and two men entered. Jackson found it amusing how they could not have been more different. Both were wearing suits, but whereas one whom he guessed to be ex-military was dressed immaculately, with a perfectly pressed shirt, clean shaven and not a hair out of place, the other was dishevelled and untidy. His tie was loose and his collar button undone. While his suit was clean, it was clear it had not been pressed, and he had several days of stubble on his face. Jackson smiled inwardly. Knowing he had not requested a lawyer, he figured they were probably plain-clothes police officers. It was almost like a clichéd television show after all. He wondered if he was about to be subjected to a round of good cop, bad cop.

The untidier of the two sat first and immediately pressed a button on the recording device. "This is D.I. Jacobs with D.I. Sanderson interviewing Mr Jackson Clarke," he began. "Also present in the room is Police Constable Smith. Today is the 26th of September 2018 and the time is 09:15." He regarded Jackson for a moment. "Are you aware of the reasons for your arrest?" he asked.

Jackson remained composed as he answered, "Yes, and I can assure you that it is all a big mistake."

"If I had a pound for every time I heard that one," Jacobs

replied with a chuckle.

"Except on this occasion, it happens to be the truth. I didn't do anything to deserve to be arrested."

"So, you weren't the one we received an anonymous call about regarding a suspicious male dressed in black hanging around the university campus at around 11:30pm?"

"Well, yes. That was me."

"And for the record, Mr Clarke," Jacobs began. "Why would a thirty-year-old man, who is not an employee or student, be on university grounds at such an hour?"

Jackson was just in the process of formulating an acceptable lie when Sanderson's phone started to ring. He smiled apologetically at Jacobs as he took the call.

"Hello?" he asked. "I see. Yes, that's correct. Uh, huh. Yes. Ok, send them down." He ended the call and looked at Jackson. "It would seem that your lawyer is here."

"My what?" he asked, genuinely confused. Then he rolled his eyes and groaned. Surely Allister would not be stupid enough to pretend to be a lawyer in front of the police, would he?

Moments later there was a knock at the door and Constable Smith turned to open it. Jackson felt his jaw drop as Lucy stepped into the room dressed in a suit and carrying a briefcase. A stern expression on her face challenged someone to mess with her. She looked worlds away from the friendly bar worker he had met two nights ago and appeared nothing but professional now. As she made brief eye contact with Jackson, she shook her head slightly, indicating that he remain silent.

Eyeing the two detectives, she said in a voice that invited

no argument, "I would like to speak to my client. In private."

D.I. Jacobs glanced at his colleague and shrugged, "Interview paused at 09:19." He stopped the recording, and they both stood. "You have five minutes," he said before the three police officers left the room.

Jackson stood, "Lucy? Oh my God! What are you doing here?"

"Repaying you," she replied, sounding slightly annoyed. "I called the station this morning and was surprised to find you had refused legal representation. Curious as to what kind of idiot would do that, I came down here straight away."

"It's a misunderstanding. I'm sure I can get it straightened out fast enough."

"I admire your optimism, though honestly, I can get it straightened out a lot faster," she replied simply. "But I'm going to need some answers from you."

Jackson's shoulders sagged. He had expected this, "Answers to what?"

"First of all, what were you doing on campus last night? Secondly, how did you know that I was going to be attacked? Don't you dare say you didn't. Because the only other explanation I can think of is that you were following me. If that's the reason, then I walk out the door right now and you resolve this on your own!"

He thought for a moment. Would she call him crazy if he told her the truth? Almost certainly. However, right now he had no choice but to be honest. He would have to come clean. Show her the news article and hope for the best.

"Ok, I can explain everything. But not here. Can you meet me later?"

Lucy handed him her phone, "Put your number in there. I'll call you this afternoon." Jackson took the phone, saved his number and handed it back. "Thank you. Ok, while I go have a word with Tweedle Dum and Tweedle Dummer out there, you stay here."

"What are you going to tell them?"

"The truth. That you were not the attacker. I have several eyewitnesses who will attest that you actually saved my life, and if that doesn't work, I have video footage of the arresting officers using what I would consider to be excessive force."

"They were a bit brutal," Jackson agreed, rubbing his wrists.

"Do you want to press charges? I'm sure you have a case."

"Not really. I'm sure they thought they were doing what was necessary, and I'm in one piece. Believe me, I've survived worse."

Lucy shrugged, "That's your choice. I'll be back in a moment." She opened the door and left.

Jackson sat back down in the chair again and waited. He was alone in the room now, not even a silent Constable Smith for company. It was quiet but for the buzzing of the strip lights set into the ceiling. Just as he was becoming lost in his own thoughts, he heard the door click open again as somebody entered.

He looked up expecting to see either Lucy or Jacobs returning to tell him he could go. Instead, he saw a man in his early fifties wearing a black suit. He had short greying hair and the aura of a man that you did not mess with. He was tall and solidly built. Jackson felt his adrenaline building as he wondered if the man was here to threaten him or to do something far worse.

"Jackson Clarke?" he asked in a thick Yorkshire accent.

"Yes?" Jackson replied hesitantly.

The man smiled and nodded, "Of course you are, lad. You look just like him."

Jackson relaxed a little, only to go from uncertainty to confusion. "Like who? Also, who the hell are you?"

The man chuckled and nodded, "Direct and to the point. Yep, definitely just like him. I'm Detective Chief Inspector Cole. I worked with your father back in the 80s."

Jackson was glad that he was seated as he felt sure that his knees would not have held his weight otherwise. He stared at D.C.I. Cole for a long moment, trying to come to terms with this revelation. It made perfect sense. Cole was about the age his dad would have been, and his dad was a police officer in Leeds. He just did not expect this conversation.

"You... knew my father?" he finally stammered. He felt embarrassed by the ridiculousness of the question as soon as he asked it.

"I did, yes. In fact, we were very good friends."

"What do you want?" Jackson asked, finally feeling as though he was getting his thoughts together. "I doubt you are just here for a catch up with me, as you've had nearly thirty years for that."

"I will get to the point, Jackson," Cole replied. "I was surprised to see your name on my desk this morning. I had to check it twice just to be certain you were the correct Jackson Clarke. I was even more shocked when I saw why you were there. Arrested for attempted assault? However, we now know from Miss Silverman that you, in fact, saved her from a very serious attack."

"That's exactly what I told your arresting officers last night. But rather than chase down the real culprit, they brought me in instead," Jackson pointed out, clearly annoyed. "Makes me wonder why I pay my taxes."

"That is being investigated. We got a very good description of the man in question," Cole assured him. "But what I would like to know is, how did you come to be there?"

"Just in the right place at the right time, I guess."

Cole nodded at that, "I also found out that you were the person who reported finding the... remains... of Michael Johnson."

"I gave a statement to one of your guys at the time. I was just out for a walk when I found him."

"Yes. I read the statement," Cole replied. "Here's the strange thing, Jackson. I remember Martin, your father, during the riots in Chapeltown in 1987. He was based at another station and shouldn't have even been there. Wasn't his patch. Yet there he was, helping out. He was responsible for saving a lot of lives during that unfortunate event. Mine included. He just always seemed to be in the right place at the right time. It really was uncanny. Almost as if he knew what was going to happen!"

Jackson kept up his poker face. He had heard the rumours about his dad when he was growing up. How he always seemed to know about things in advance. Always rushing off, sometimes for days on end with his strange friend Freddy. Now, Jackson was getting an idea as to how his dad had known.

"I'm glad that you saw my dad as a hero. But I'm not quite

sure what any of this has to do with me. Or why you felt the need to come and see me."

"You really are very direct, just like he was. He never liked wasting time."

"He didn't like sticking around, either."

Cole looked sad at that as if he wanted to jump to Martin's defence. But then he seemed to decide that it was not productive to do so and pressed on with the reason he had come to see Jackson.

"Ok, I will get to it. The man who was killed two days ago."

"Michael Johnson?"

"Yes, well there is something unusual about his death."

"I overheard a paramedic saying that it looked as though he had been dead for weeks."

"That was at the scene. By the time the autopsy took place, which was yesterday morning, he looked as though he had been dead for years." Cole paused. "Decades in fact!"

"How is that even possible?" Jackson asked, his curiosity getting the better of him.

"It isn't," Cole admitted. "Or at least it shouldn't be. Believe me when I say some of the best medical minds out there are as stuck as we are. It's also surprising that you were the one to find the body."

"Surprising how?"

"What I am about to tell you is classified, Jackson. I could lose my job for passing on this information, but I think you have a right to know. There were a series of murders about thirty years ago. Your dad was involved with the case and was obsessed with finding the murderer. At first, the victims were mostly undesirables. Drug dealers, sex offenders, people like that. But soon they became almost anybody. The only thing that seemed to connect them was the corpses themselves. All of them had been aged by several years."

"Was the killer ever caught?"

"I'm afraid not. Around the time your father disappeared, the attacks stopped," Cole said sadly.

Jackson thought for a moment and did not like where those thoughts were taking him. He wished he could avoid asking the question, but he had to know the truth. "Be honest with me, Detective. Is there a chance my dad was the killer?"

"Oh, God no, Jackson," Cole said shaking his head. "Your dad's whereabouts were verified for almost every single killing. Although some on the force speculated that he knew who was responsible. Which is why he disappeared."

"How come I've never heard about any of these killings before? You'd think something like that would have made the local news at least!"

"There was a media blackout. The last thing anybody at the top wanted was a story about a killer that somehow aged his victims. Every death was recorded as either accidental or unsolved. Much to your father's objections."

"And then they just stopped?" Jackson asked.

Cole hesitated a beat before answering, "There was one more victim. Except this one didn't die. Though she did age."

"A survivor? Was she able to give a description?"

"In a manner of speaking. All she said was it was a girl with glowing eyes."

"A girl? To mention she had glowing eyes, though. That's a

strange thing to say," Jackson remarked. "Was this after my father left?"

"Some time after. It was over fifteen years ago."

"So, the victim may still be alive?"

"It's possible, Jackson," Cole replied, clearly uncomfortable with where this was headed.

"Where is she?"

"She was not in good mental health, as I'm sure you can imagine. The last I heard she was in a hospital somewhere for her own safety. If she's even still alive."

"What was her name?"

"I'm sorry, lad. I've told you all I can. Too much in fact. I can't say any more."

"Well, I guess thank you, for telling me as much as you have."

"Hope it helps you in some way." Cole smiled, "You clearly have your father's sharp mind. Have you ever thought about joining the force?"

"Once," Jackson admitted. "A long time ago. But that was his thing. I had to find my own."

"I can appreciate that. Now, I believe that your lawyer is causing quite the storm. Let's get you out of here."

***

After disconnecting the phone call, Allister sat back in his office chair. Chloe had called to tell him the girl she was having difficulties with at school, Nicola, had been badly beaten the night before and was currently in hospital with some serious injuries. She suspected that the attacker was her stalker, and he was inclined to agree. Though if he had not been with her at the time, he probably would have suspected Chloe. She certainly had the motive, and he was ashamed to admit that he thought her capable in the right circumstances.

He let out a sigh. He could not believe how much had happened in the last forty-eight hours. It was beginning to shape up to be a strange week, and it was difficult to put it altogether. The newspaper reports about future events made no logical sense at all. Obviously, he now had to accept that they were real, and what they foretold was, in fact, coming to pass. But why were they being sent to Jackson, though? Sure, he was a good guy, very capable in his job and he was one of those that always tried to do the right thing. Surely, however, there were better qualified people to deal with them? Like the police. What connection did his friend have to the sender, if any?

Allister had been right to suspect that they may be trouble too. Jackson had called him from the police station just before one in the morning, to report that he had been arrested. He was not able to tell Allister much, except that he had been successful. Which he took to mean Lucy was safe.

A *ping* came from his computer indicating the arrival of an email. Opening his inbox, he saw the new mail. It was from an unknown address with **ENCRYPTED** in the description. He knew from previous experience that this was a temporary address set up solely for the sending of this message, and had almost certainly already been deleted. His contact was meticulous about internet security and demanded the same from Allister, though no explanation had ever been forthcoming as to why. He clicked on the envelope symbol to open it and waited several seconds as his computer's encryption software got to work on deciphering the content. A tone sounded, indicating it was done, and a page of text appeared on the monitor.

Data package received. This may be a match. Do not attempt to interact with subject. Assume that she is very dangerous. Await further instructions. Gates.

P.S. As always, delete this message when read.

Allister immediately deleted the mail as instructed, then used a programme of his own design to purge it from all areas of his computer permanently. It seemed like overkill, but he knew that it was not a good idea to let them down. He did not know what their overall plan was, but he believed them when they had told him it was important. Life and death important. He had neglected to tell them about the messages that Jackson had been receiving. Something told him in the back of his head that it was best to keep Jackson out of it for now.

His phone began ringing; he glanced at the display and saw that it was Jackson. *Think of the devil and he calls.* He picked it up and swiped the screen to accept the call.

"They let you out then?" he asked upon answering. "I have to admit it's a lot quicker than I was expecting. I was sure they would have had you in there for at least seventy-two hours due to uncooperative behaviour," he quipped.

He heard Jackson laugh on the other end of the line. *"Sorry to disappoint you, Al. It turns out that I have a pretty good lawyer."*

"You do?"

"Lucy showed up while I was being interviewed. She was able to sort everything out in almost no time. She even got me an apology."

"That was lucky, and it was also good of her."

"I spoke to a detective who worked with my dad back in the day. Before he disappeared. He shared some very interesting stories about the past. Can you pick me up? I think we need a working lunch."

"Sure, I have some new information myself," Allister checked his watch. "I'll be outside the police station in about twenty minutes." He ended the call.

Picking up Jackson's car keys from the desk, Allister grabbed his laptop, set the office burglar alarm, and headed out of the door. He closed it behind him and locked it with a heavy deadbolt he had insisted upon having fitted for security. As he walked away, he didn't see the two blue glowing eyes in the shadows that observed him leave.

The girl watched as Allister got into Jackson's car and drove away. Seeing him gave her a brief pang of loss and regret in her chest, she had not seen him this close in so long. But it passed. Once upon a time, she may have had second thoughts about what she was about to do here, but not anymore. Guilt, like the rest of her emotions, died a long time ago. All that remained now was fear and rage.

She stepped out from her hiding place and approached the office. She could have walked straight through the door to enter, but she needed to do this without leaving any evidence that somebody as observant as Jackson would be sure to spot. Thanks to an accident some years ago, every time she came into contact with the physical world, she left marks. They were almost invisible, but they were there all the same. This task required more sensitivity. She could not be discovered or suspected. Not yet at least. She still needed more time to bring everything together.

Standing before the doorway, she raised her hand. Closing her eyes, she concentrated on the intricate lock inside the office door. She flicked her wrist three times and smiled when she heard the lock click open. She then bent her fingers slightly, and the door swung inwards.

As she walked into the office, she glanced at the alarm. It was an advanced system, but she managed to disarm it easily before it reacted to the door opening. She looked around; everything was where she had expected it to be. It was neater than the last time she was here. Less cluttered. This was good, it would make searching easier. She looked at the filing cabinets and the simple locks that held them closed. Pointless. She couldn't imagine there being anything of use in those. She was certain that what she wanted would be protected. Not left for just anybody to find easily.

Looking at Allister's desk, the girl saw the impressive computer setup he had there. If the information she wanted was anywhere, it would be there, buried beneath firewalls, security software and encryptions. It was going to be tough, but she loved a challenge, and maybe this time she would be successful. Standing in front of the computer, she held her hand steady over the keyboard and concentrated. The computer began to whirr into life and the monitor lit up. She bypassed the login passwords swiftly, and the screen filled with what looked to the untrained eye like random numbers and letters scrolling up from the bottom. She smiled as she realised Allister used the reverse spelling of his sister's middle name as his password. He always was sentimental.

The girl's eyes flashed through a full spectrum of colours as she searched the hard drive. The security software that had been installed was unbelievable. She had known Allister was good at what he did, probably among the best, but this certainly went beyond what she had expected him to be capable of. It definitely complicated things but did not make them impossible. Over the years she had had time to learn and develop many of her own skills. She scanned through the millions of files that were within the hard drive, searching for what she was after.

Then she found it. As suspected, it was hidden behind a number of security protocols. It was essentially the digital equivalent of Fort Knox. She frowned. She had only ever known one person who was capable of this sort of programming. Her mind drifted for a moment to the past she had lost forever. No. She could not allow herself to think about him right now. She had to be focused and not let the hurt in or the rage out. This was going to be hard enough to do already without giving in to the pain that still lurked inside her, searching for a way to assert itself. *Maybe my emotions are not as dead as I thought.*

She closed her eyes and doubled her efforts. If this was the work of who she suspected it was, it could take even more time to find a way in. And time may be something she might not have much left off.

***

Opening the passenger door, Jackson climbed into the car beside Allister. He was aware he looked tired and felt even more so. No doubt a consequence of not having been able to sleep the previous night. After his conversation with Detective Chief Inspector Cole, he had been released quickly. Thanks in no small part to Lucy hurrying things along and making sure Jacobs knew she would hold him personally responsible for every minute Jackson spent inside the station.

Allister began driving, then asked, "How was your night in the big house?"

"Disappointing, I'm afraid. It would seem that television

has been lying to us all this time," Jackson replied with a wry smile.

"Why doesn't that surprise me?" Allister said without humour. "Do you mind if we head back to the office first? I need to collect something I forgot to pick up on my way out."

"That's fine. I could do with changing my shirt while we are there at the very least."

"So, what's this new information you've managed to gather even while incarcerated?"

"This morning I met a Detective Chief Inspector Cole. Apparently, he and my dad were friends thirty years ago," Jackson explained. "It turns out that Dad used to have a knack of showing up and saving people. Almost like he knew what was going to happen in advance."

"So, you think that he was being warned about future events as well?"

"It stands to reason; I guess. I remember Mum often talking about that 'bloody pager' of his, and how he'd rush off the moment that it beeped."

"A pager?" Allister asked with a chuckle, and then he shrugged. "It was the 80s I suppose. A different time."

"It was thirty years ago, Al," Jackson pointed out. "Hardly medieval times."

"Trust me, mate. When it comes to technology, medieval describes the 80s exactly."

"Anyway, it would seem that whoever or whatever was contacting him, is now contacting me."

"I guess that trail of logic follows for the lack of a better explanation," Allister conceded.

"I've decided that this is a positive thing. I mean, it does kind of connect me to my dad as well."

"Seriously? You do realise that if you are right, then your dad disappeared around the same time he was receiving these future messages?"

Jackson eyed him in clear annoyance, "Of course I realise that. But from what I've been able to gather, he also saved a lot of lives before he did. Which means so can I."

"All I'm saying is, don't get too excited that this is happening. We don't know where those messages are coming from or where they may be leading us. This is already proving to be a very strange week, and we're only on Wednesday." They continued to drive in silence for a moment. Jackson watched people and buildings as they passed them by. Finally, Allister continued, "Did this friend of your dad's tell you anything else?"

"Apparently around the same time, there was a serial killer in Leeds. However, as well as being killed, the victims had also aged by several years."

"Like the guy you found on Monday?"

"Exactly like him. Cole told me that by the time they conducted an autopsy on Michael Johnson yesterday, his remains looked as though he'd been dead for decades!"

Allister shook his head in disbelief. "How have I never heard of this? Killings like that would be huge news. Every paper and television channel in the world would be all over it."

"Cole says there was a media blackout to stop the public from panicking. The whole thing was covered up. The murders were simply justified with other explanations."

"How can they do that? It's not right!"

"I agree. It would seem that so did my dad. He was apparently very opposed to the decision. Do you think you could do some digging around? See if you can find out any information? I find it hard to believe that everything is gone."

Allister sighed as he considered the request. "I can try. But I wasn't kidding about it being medieval times for technology back then. If they wanted to cover it up, I doubt any reports or evidence ever made it onto a computer. It was literally mostly just paperwork in those days. You would have loved it. I'd be surprised if they've left anything to find."

"What about fifteen years?" Jackson asked.

"That would certainly be more likely."

"The final victim was sometime about fifteen years ago. Except this one survived."

"Survived? How do they know the attack is connected?"

"Because although she survived, her body was still aged."

"Wow," was all Allister could respond.

"She was able to give a description of her attacker. Somewhat, anyway."

"Somewhat?"

"Just something about a girl with glowing eyes."

Glowing eyes? Allister wondered. He had been expecting Jackson to say dark or black eyes. *Could they still be connected?* "Did this Cole fella say where the survivor is now?"

"Only that the last he heard, she was in a hospital somewhere. If she's even still alive."

"I can guess what kind of hospital, too," Allister said with a grim expression. "Fortunately, there are not too many of those left anymore. Did you find out her name?"

Jackson shook his head, "He couldn't, or rather wouldn't, tell me."

"Convenient."

"Exactly what I thought. Do you think that you can find her?"

"I'm confident that I can. If she's still alive and in state care, she'll have to be on a system somewhere, no matter how hard they try to hide her."

"Good. I think we need to pay her a visit."

"I agree."

Jackson blinked in surprise, "You do? I was sure you would say that we should stay out of it and leave them in peace."

"Normally I probably would," Allister admitted. "However, I recently found out some new information about Michael Johnson's death."

"Go on."

"In the newspaper report, it said a blonde girl was seen walking the canal path shortly before him. Do you remember?"

"Of course I do," Jackson replied, then he felt the penny drop, and he knew what Allister was telling him. "You're not seriously saying..."

"I'm afraid I am," Allister confirmed. "The girl was Chloe and Johnson attempted to attack her. She got away but then he cornered her. Her stalker intervened and killed him. Also, it would seem, aged him. So, if we can find this missing person, she may be able to help uncover the identity of who's tormenting Chloe."

The car continued at a steady pace. Jackson rested his head against the side window and thought over this new information. What was the deal with this Chloe? Why was she being followed? Who was killing and ageing people and what did it have to do with his dad? He had so many questions but no answers. He considered mentioning his meeting with Chloe, but for some unknown reason, it just did not feel worth bringing up.

He turned to look at his friend. "I have to ask you something," he began.

"Why am I so caught up in helping Chloe?" Allister replied, clearly expecting the question.

"Yeah."

"You know why."

"I assumed so. But you never talk about her. You've never told me exactly what happened."

Allister sighed. He looked so sad and Jackson instantly regretted bringing it up.

"Ruby was fourteen, Jackson. *Fourteen!* She goes to school one day and never comes home. Two weeks later my parents tell me that the police found her body, but they insisted that I was not allowed to see her. She's too badly injured, they said. Remember how she looked in life, they told me. Then a closed casket funeral and into the incinerator. I wasn't even allowed to say goodbye to my own twin sister!"

"I'm sorry, Al. I wish I could have helped." Jackson remembered Ruby's disappearance vividly. He had even gone out with other kids from their school to help look for her. He also remembered for years afterwards how much her death had deeply affected Allister. Jackson had gone to the funeral, but he did not recall much about it.

"The only thing that could have helped her was one of

those future messages. Sadly, they were in short supply at the time." He wiped his eyes quickly. "I couldn't help Ruby, but I'm damned if I'm going to let something happen to Chloe. She's a good kid. She doesn't deserve this."

"We will help her, mate," Jackson promised. "Is there anything else she's told you, about who's following her?"

"Actually, there is," Allister replied, pulling up outside their office. "She's seen it, and she doesn't think she's the only one!"

***

Her eyes opened and she smiled. It had taken every piece of ingenuity she possessed, but she finally cracked the digital safe. She began copying the information to her consciousness, reading it as fast as she absorbed it. They had done a good job of limiting a computer trail, but if you knew how to look for the clues, you could always follow them.

Unfortunately, she could only find an approximation of their whereabouts. They had used multiple IP addresses within a ten square mile radius in Birmingham. She already knew that she could not go there, and obviously, they knew it too. But maybe there was a way to bring them here. They needed to pay for what they had done to her.

She frowned for a moment. *What was that?*

"Ahhhh!" she gasped as she buckled forward at a bolt of pain shooting through her stomach. Pain? She did not feel pain. In fact, it had been so long that she had forgotten what it was like. How though? What was happening to her? She quickly scanned everything she had copied from Allister's hard drive.

It did not take long to find it. A virus. She had obviously set off some kind of security trap without realising and released it when she absorbed the data. She was not sure how it was meant to affect her, but she did know that it was not Allister's doing. She could see that it had been designed to infect her specifically, and she knew of only one person who could and would, make it.

"Damn you, Gates!" she hissed through clenched teeth as she was hit by another bolt of gut-wrenching pain. "I'll kill you for this," she gasped, knowing the statement was not really true.

She began to examine the virus, to see if she could find a way to dismantle it. It had to be possible. All viruses had a kill switch, it was just a matter of finding it, but the continued barrage of pain was making it difficult to focus and figure out where to start.

She heard voices getting closer from outside which caused her to freeze suddenly. She recognised Allister's voice immediately. She looked toward the computer and with a nod of her head, it quickly powered down, another nod and the alarm armed itself again. Glancing toward the door, she knew there was no chance of her locking it in time. She would have to hope that Allister would assume he had forgotten to lock it on his way out. She looked around the room once more to make sure she had not missed any evidence of her having been here, then she closed her eyes and turned invisible.

A key slipped into the lock and tried to turn. A moment later Allister spoke.

"That's strange," he said.

"What is?" Jackson asked.

"The door. The main lock was undone."

"Really? Are you sure that you locked it?"

"Yes," Allister replied, then, less certain, "At least I think I did. Sorry, Jackson. I've had so much on my mind lately."

"Wait here, let me take a look." The door creaked open slowly and Jackson stepped inside alone. Crossing to the alarm, he inputted a four-digit code and it deactivated. He looked around the office, identifying places somebody could be hiding. His gaze swept to where she was standing, still invisible. If she was capable of breathing, she was certain she would be holding her breath right now. Jackson seemed to look straight at her for a moment longer than anywhere else, before returning to the door. It was almost as though he had sensed her. Not the first time that had happened she admitted to herself. "Everything looks ok," he called outside.

Allister entered the office and crossed to his desk. He unlocked the top drawer and retrieved a memory stick and what looked like two credit card-sized pieces of plastic from inside. The girl felt like screaming. Of course. Allister was a hacker. He knew the importance of keeping anything you wanted to stay secret off a computer connected to the internet. No matter how well you protected it. She needed that stick, but knew it would need to wait. She could easily take it from them right now, but it was vital that Jackson and Allister lived. For the time being, at least.

Jackson opened a drawer in his own desk and took out one of the spare shirts he kept there. "So, you were saying this Nicola girl saw the person who has been following Chloe then?" he asked Allister as he began to unbutton his shirt.

"Apparently so," Allister replied, locking his desk. "She's currently in hospital. Last night somebody decided to give her quite a severe beating."

"That's awful. Do they know who did it?" Jackson asked, taking off his shirt.

"From what I've been able to find out, the police have no official suspects. However, she was apparently not very well liked. A bit of a school bully, so I doubt the list would be short. But Chloe seems to think that her stalker may be involved."

She found herself looking at Jackson, naked from the waist up and appreciating what she saw. The girl realised she was feeling... something. That was definitely not normal. She didn't have feelings like those anymore. She had done away with them when... well, a long time ago. She re-examined the virus. She guessed it was designed to bring out feelings as well as to cause her literal pain. That was not acceptable. She had to get rid of it, and soon.

Jackson put on the clean shirt, "We need to talk to Nicola."

"Visits are restricted to family," Allister replied.

"I'm sure that we can find a way past that. We need to know what we are dealing with, and I think Nicola could be our best witness." Jackson finished buttoning up his shirt and looked at his friend.

"It's funny you should say that," Allister held up the two plastic cards. "Fake police IDs. I made them some time ago, you know, just in case."

Jackson looked incredulous as he took his and examined it, "You are kidding. Al! Have you any idea how illegal this is?"

"I have some idea, yes."

"Then why did you make them?"

"I'm not entirely sure. I just had this feeling that we would need them one day."

Jackson appeared to waver slightly before pushing the fake ID into his pocket, "Are you ready to go?"

"Yes," Allister replied, holding up the memory stick.

"Then let's get out of here."

Allister left first. Before following him, Jackson looked around the office once more. Again, his eyes lingered on where she was standing. A look of uncertainty crossed his face before he closed the door behind them, followed by the sound of a lock sliding into place.

As soon as they were gone, the girl reappeared and fell to the ground with a gasp of agony. *What the actual fuck?* This thing seemed to be screwing with her abilities now. Making herself visible had not hurt since she had first learned how to do it. Even then, it was nothing like this. She had to buy herself some time. Closing her eyes, she concentrated. She built the mental equivalent of a firewall, severing the connection. She knew that it was only a temporary measure as *he* would have anticipated this response and built in a countermeasure. In time, it would find a new way to infect her. He had designed it after all, and he knew her better than anyone.

She instantly felt better. Holding her hand toward the filing cabinets, she pulled them toward herself. All of the cabinets fell forward together with a crash. She waited to see if she would feel anything. Nothing. Good, that was how she liked it. As she approached the door, she did not stop, but passed through without resistance and found herself outside. The wood and glass of the door now showed barely visible signs of warping from where she had made contact.

As she was heading away, she was already making plans. She needed to pay Nicola a visit and make sure she didn't tell Jackson or Allister anything about her. But first, she was going to need a distraction.

Chapter Six

Jackson drove toward the Leeds city centre hospital. He had a lot on his mind and not just the worry of speaking to the girl who had been attacked. Lucy had called as they were getting into the car to arrange to meet up later that evening. She reminded him it was so he could explain his sudden appearance the previous night. She seemed friendly enough on the phone which he took as a good sign considering the circumstances. Sure, she would almost certainly call him crazy when she heard what he had to say and walk away, but he guessed there was only one way he could find out for sure. He had to try.

Next to him in the passenger seat, Allister sat with his laptop perched on his lap, the screen lifted up. His fingers blurred across the keyboard as he worked. Jackson had always been quietly impressed at Allister's natural talent with computers. Jackson could just about compile an email or order food online, but to Allister, it was almost as though a computer was an extension of who he was, like an extra limb.

Letting Allister work in silence, Jackson thought about all that they had learned today. It would seem so much surrounded his father. Also, it all appeared to have started around 1987, the year before his birth. He now admitted to himself that he strongly suspected that things were connected to whoever was following Chloe. He hoped that this Nicola they were going to see could help shed some light on what they were dealing with.

Allister closed his laptop. "Done. I've informed the hospital that two detectives are on their way to interview Nicola Ritchie. As long as you can talk your way past the reception desk quickly and they are happy with our ID badges then we should be fine."

"Excellent. We need to be as fast as possible. The longer we are in there the more likely they may suspect we are not the real police," Jackson replied.

"Or the real police show up."

"That too!"

They came to a stop outside the hospital. Before he could even switch off the ignition to his ancient car, Jackson's phone beeped. He picked it up from the holder on the dashboard. Swiping the screen, he hesitated when he saw the multimedia message waiting to be opened. Surely this had to be some kind of joke? Taking a deep breath, he tapped it and the message opened. As he suspected, it was once again a newspaper article from the Leeds Daily News dated for the following day:

SCHOOLGIRL, 15, KILLED IN HIT AND RUN INCIDENT!

by Jane McArther

Police are today looking for witnesses, after Leeds schoolgirl, Jade Greene, 15, was hit by a car on her way home from school yesterday afternoon. The only witness at the scene, a friend of the Jade's who cannot be named for legal reasons, said that Jade was knocked down by a red saloon car, seen speeding in the area, at 3:17pm on Seacroft Road. The driver failed to stop at the scene. Jade was rushed to hospital by air ambulance but later died of her injuries. Police are hoping somebody can identify either the driver or the car involved.

There was a photo of Jade in the article. She was smiling at the camera and looked like any other kid her age. Hopeful and full of life. And Jackson was not going to let that change. Hoping they still had time to speak to Nicola first, he checked his watch. 2:59pm. "Dammit!" he said, slapping the steering wheel.

"What's wrong?" Allister asked looking concerned.

"Newspaper report. We've got to go!"

"Seriously? Now?"

"Just what I was thinking." He sighed, "There's a girl called Jade Greene who will be killed in a hit and run."

"How long do we have?"

"Less than twenty minutes."

Allister looked at the hospital, "We had better go then. After all, Nicola isn't going anywhere."

Jackson nodded in agreement and pulled away from the curb, turned the car around, and drove from the hospital grounds. Unseen by them and everybody else around, a faint shadow moved quickly, entering the hospital.

Jackson drove at exactly the speed limit, knowing that now was not the time to attract unwanted police attention. He followed the directions Allister gave him, which he was interpreting from the map application on his phone. They arrived at Seacroft Road and came to a stop. Jackson checked his watch. 3.16pm. Less than a minute to spare. Leaving the engine idling, they both began to look up and down the road for any sign of Jade or the red car from the article.

"Can you see anything?" Jackson asked.

"No, nothing," Allister replied. "What time is it?"

"Just turned 3:17!"

Jackson heard the sound of tyres squealing up ahead and the noise of a revving engine. A red car swerved around the corner and was travelling in their direction at what looked like top speed. At that moment he also noticed two girls walking along the path. He instantly recognised Jade from the newspaper photo, and she was already beginning to take steps toward the curb, clearly deep in conversation and unaware of the danger.

"What—" Allister began to ask.

Without giving him time to finish the question, Jackson stepped on the accelerator. The car lurched forward, and he cut across to the opposite side of the road and began driving directly at the other car while picking up speed. He pressed his hand down hard on the horn to make as much noise as he possibly could.

"What the hell are you doing?" Allister demanded in a clear panic.

Jackson did not reply, instead, he just kept driving. Everything seemed to happen in slow motion. The girl with Jade reacted quickly, pulling her to safety. The driver of the other car swerved onto the wrong side of the road and roared past them pressing on his own horn. Jackson barely heard Allister screaming in the seat beside him. He hit the brakes, and the car skidded to a halt with a squeal of brakes and the smell of burning rubber. He watched the red car disappear in his rear-view mirror, then just sat for a few seconds, gripping the steering wheel.

"Jesus Christ, Jackson!" Allister almost shouted. "Are you crazy?"

Without responding, Jackson opened his car door and ran to where the girls were. Jade sat on the pavement looking shaken but otherwise unhurt. A girl with blonde hair was crouched over her, making sure she wasn't injured.

"Are you ok?" Jackson asked, his voice shaking.

"Oh my God!" Jade screamed at him. "Who the fuck taught you to drive, man? You almost bloody killed me!"

"I'm sorry. I was just trying to..."

"Actually, Jade," the blonde girl said, helping Jade to her feet. "I think he may have just saved your life." She looked at him, and he realised he knew her.

"Chloe?" Jackson asked, surprised by the coincidence. She looked at him, confused for a moment, almost as if she did not recognise him. "It's Jackson," he clarified.

"Oh yes, of course," she said, the confusion lifting from her eyes. Smiling, she held out her hand, and they shook. "Sorry. I guess I'm a little bit out of it after that idiot almost ran Jade down!"

Jackson looked at Jade. "Are you sure you're ok?" he asked again.

"I'll live," Jade replied, clearly annoyed. "Which is more than I can say for that son of a bitch in the red car if I ever catch him!"

Allister appeared beside Jackson. His face switched from concern to surprise when he saw Chloe standing with Jade.

"Hey, how are you doing?" he asked stepping toward her.

"Allister, hey," she replied, giving him a brief hug.

"What the fuck is going on?" Jade asked confused, looking from Chloe to Jackson to Allister. "Are they your gay dads, Chloe?"

"No, they are not my gay dads," Chloe replied, rolling her eyes. "I don't even have gay dads!"

"Shame. That would have at least made you interesting."

"Wow. Thanks very much."

***

Nicola was sleeping deeply in a bed in a private hospital room. She had been given some powerful painkillers to help ease the throbbing in her arm, but they had left her feeling drowsy. The hospital staff had left her alone to sleep off the drugs, relieved that for once, she would not be complaining and making the atmosphere they worked in unbearable.

Slowly, the door creaked open, as if by itself. Nobody could be seen entering or leaving, and then it closed again. The noise barely disturbed Nicola, who just mumbled incoherently for a moment, then continued to sleep.

Her dressing gown was hanging beside her bed. It was bright pink with puppies on it, which, if anybody who knew her from school had been told, they would have refused to believe it. The gown moved slightly like it was caught in a breeze, but the windows were firmly closed and the heavy curtains drawn. It moved again. Almost inaudible to anybody else, a faint whisper could be heard filling the room.

The belt began to slide through the hoops as if under its own power. Gliding along it left the last hoop and dropped to the hard, tiled floor. It lay still for a moment then shook and gradually gained momentum. Like a snake, it started to rise up and climbed onto the bed. It slid slowly under the back of Nicola's neck then flopped back over the front.

It looped around itself, making a knot, and then pulled tight. Nicola's eyes sprang open, and she grabbed at the belt as she was dragged from the bed. She hit the floor with a bone-jarring thud, but she was unable to cry out in pain. She felt herself being pulled along the floor, finding it impossible to prevent the movement even as she flailed and kicked out.

Finally, the tugging stopped and her hands went to the belt around her neck and tried to undo the knot. She froze as she heard that voice. The voice she had prayed that she would never hear again. The intense pain in her arm did its best to encourage her to black out, but her fear had kicked in, adrenaline forcing her to stay conscious.

"Sorry, Nicola," the voice said, almost sounding sincere. "I wish there was another way so that I didn't have to do this. But I can't risk letting you talk to them!"

She tried to reply, but could not get air into her lungs. She felt her body being lifted into the air as more pressure began to build on her throat. Looking up, Nicola saw that the belt now hung over a sturdy-looking strip light fitting which was suspended from metal chains screwed firmly into the ceiling. The other end was seemingly tying itself to the end of her bed, the wheel brakes on each leg flicked on to keep it securely in place. She quickly realised what was happening and tried to scream, but nothing more than a whimper would come out. Her feet left the ground, and she began to dangle in the air. As her vision started to fade slowly to black, the last thing she saw were two red eyes looking up at her, and that hateful face.

***

After Jackson and Allister left, Chloe and Jade continued their walk to Chloe's house. Jade had insisted upon escorting her to her home. Her reasoning was that she was just following Nicola's orders and making sure Chloe was left alone by others. Chloe could not help but think Jade had missed the irony. Nicola and her friends had been the only ones to give her a hard time at school. Everybody else already left her alone.

Despite her initial distrust of Jade, and Chloe making it clear that she did not need help from somebody like Jade, she quickly found that she actually liked having her around. Under the tough girl act, she was really very intelligent and witty. Even kind of fun to hang out with. Chloe had forgotten how nice it was to have a friend. Assuming that was even what they were becoming. Part of her still worried this could be a setup.

Sadly though, Jade was the kind of teenage girl who loved to gossip, and since meeting Allister and Jackson, she would not stop asking Chloe how she knew them. It was as if she was on a gossip mission.

"Just tell me, ok!" Jade insisted. "Is one of them, like, your boyfriend?"

"Eww, no!" Chloe replied, appalled at the idea.

"Are you being groomed then? You have to tell me if you are. It's important!"

Chloe sighed, "I can promise you that I am not being groomed!"

"How can you be sure, though?" Jade asked seriously.

"First of all, Allister is gay. So, I wouldn't even be on his radar."

"*Meh*, the cute ones always are."

Chloe laughed, "Jesus, Jade. He's twice your age, you know!"

Jade shrugged then winked. "Sometimes old dogs know more tricks," she said.

Chloe laughed again. It felt good to be laughing. It felt like she had not laughed in too long. Which she supposed, she had not. "You are officially disgusting. Anyway, what was I saying? Oh yes, and secondly, I don't think Jackson is like that at all, though I've literally only met him once."

"But you've still managed completely to avoid answering my question!"

"Which is?" Chloe asked warily.

"Who the fuck are they, man?"

She realised there was no way of evading the question entirely, "Ok, ok. I guess you could say that they work for me."

"You mean like staff? You have staff? Is your family rich or something?"

"Nooooo." Chloe thought it best to choose her words carefully. She still did not know how much she could actually trust Jade. She seemed genuine, but yesterday she was part of the group who had made going to school hell for her. If she told her the truth, she risked it being spread around school tomorrow or used against her later. "They're private investigators. My parents hired them to look for family in the UK. We don't really know anybody here."

"Seriously?" Jade looked unconvinced.

"I swear. We are just trying to reconnect with people."

Jade's face screwed up in disappointment, "Well, that's boring."

"I'm sorry to hear that."

"It was more interesting when you were being groomed."

"OMG, Jade! I was never being groomed!" Her phone beeped. Saved by the bell! "One moment."

She dug the phone from out of her blazer pocket. Her heart dropped when she saw that it was from her mum. *What have I done this time*? For goodness sake, she had actually even managed an entire day at school. With some trepidation, she opened the message:

Hi Sweetie. Your father and I have spoken to your grandparents. If you are sure that you want to go back to Australia for a while, then we can arrange a flight for Monday. But only if you are certain. We just want you to be happy. We can discuss it when you get home. Love Mum xx

What the hell? Could they really be serious? They would let her go back to Australia? To get away from this awful city? It would be all her dreams come true. She didn't know whether to cry or scream with joy.

"Hey, Chloe!" Jade said, sounding insistent. "Are you even listening? You've gone quiet, man. Also, a very unfashionable shade of white!"

Chloe realised that she had not said anything or even moved since she had finished reading the text message. Her hand seemed to be shaking slightly. She looked up at Jade when she said her name again.

"Hello? Chloe?"

"Sorry?" she asked. "What did you say?"

"I said, are you ok?" Jade asked again.

"Yes! Absolutely, yes!" Chloe said with a beaming smile. "I

think I might be going back to Australia!" Caught up in the moment she grabbed Jade, giving her a hug.

"Whoa. Steady on, man," Jade said, trying to regain her balance for a moment. "You're very pretty but you're really not my type!"

***

Jackson and Allister arrived back at the hospital almost an hour after they had left. They entered the reception area side by side and approached the desk. As they reached the receptionist, she was just putting down the phone, and she looked sombre as she acknowledged them.

"Hello," she said. "How can I help you?"

"Hi," Jackson replied with a bright smile. "I'm Detective Inspector Jones and this is Sergeant Cooper from the West Yorkshire Constabulary. We're here to interview a patient." He held out the fake identification card Allister had given him. Doubt crept in as the receptionist gave it a quick glance, but Allister had assured him that as long as the real police did not check it, it would be more than adequate.

"Ok, and what's the name of the patient?" the receptionist asked, turning to her computer.

Jackson pretended to check his notebook for the details, "It's a Miss Nicola Ritchie. I believe she's recovering from quite a brutal attack. We just want to see if she remembers anything more."

She turned away from the computer and looked sad, "Oh, have you not heard? The poor girl was found hanging in her room. It looks as though she committed suicide."

"What?" gasped Allister.

"That can't be right," Jackson said, feeling as though he had just been punched in the stomach.

"I'm afraid it is," the receptionist replied.

"When was she found?"

"About twenty past three. A nurse found her. She hadn't been there long as she had very recently been given something for the pain she was in, so the nurse was able to cut her down and attempted to revive her. But unfortunately, it was just too late."

"Oh my God." Jackson closed his eyes. He suddenly felt very tired.

"Your colleagues are already up there now if you want me to let them know that you've arrived," she said, her hand reaching for the phone again.

"No! It's ok," Jackson replied a little faster than he should have. The receptionist looked concerned by the quick response. "We need to report this to the Chief. Clearly, there's been a breakdown in communication and he has not been informed yet."

"We'll just let uniform do their job for now," Allister added with a sad smile.

The receptionist seemed to relax visibly, "Of course. I understand." Her hand moved away from the phone.

"We will be in touch if we need to speak to anybody, though," Jackson said.

The two of them turned around and began to walk away. Once outside they stopped, both silent for a moment, coming to terms with the enormity of what they had learned.

"This isn't right," Allister said, mirroring Jackson's own

thoughts.

"I was thinking the same thing," Jackson agreed. "Something seriously messed up is going on here."

"Just as we arrive to talk to Nicola about her attack, we get a message sending us to save somebody else, and at almost exactly the same time as we save them, Nicola kills herself? That cannot be just a coincidence."

"You don't think it was suicide either, then?"

"No way. Everything about this just feels completely off," Allister said, shaking his head. "It's almost as if somebody wanted us somewhere else."

"But we had to be there," Jackson countered. "If we hadn't gone when we did, Jade would have been killed by that car."

"Maybe, maybe not. We'll never know for sure. It just seems convenient that we got that message when we did. I doubt Jade was the only person in Leeds who was in danger or needed help today. Yet she's the only one you received a message about when we needed to be elsewhere."

"What are you suggesting?"

Allister seemed to be getting angry. "I'm saying what I've thought from the start. I'm saying that these newspaper reports are bad news. We need to start questioning them. Think about why we are getting them when they arrive, instead of doing everything they say and hoping we are making the right choice!"

Jackson thought for several long seconds. "I think that you could be right. We may have been drawn away from the hospital intentionally. That changes everything we thought we were dealing with. I promise I will be more careful in future. This also means that what happened in there was murder. But if somebody wanted to kill Nicola, why make it look like a suicide?"

"Any number of reasons. I will try to do some digging into her past. But for now, we should probably get out of here, before any more real police start showing up."

They quickly walked away from the hospital entrance towards where they had parked. Deciding on discretion they had left the car on a street a short distance away, rather than in the hospital car park itself. But as they approached and saw the car, they stopped.

"No, no, no, no!" Jackson said, feeling nothing short of utter despair on top of everything else.

His precious car, the only possession he owned that had belonged to his father, the car he had spent so many years carefully restoring and maintaining, had been trashed. All the windows were shattered, and the tyres slashed. Large dents had been beaten into the bodywork, and the word 'TRAITOR' had been seemingly melted into the paint finish. It was clear somebody was sending them a message. But who?

***

The pain was becoming far too much for her as the virus began to force its way in again. The firewall was weakening, and she could not seem to generate the energy needed to rebuild it. She curled into the foetal position on the cold hard floor and waited for this new wave of agony to pass.

Killing Nicola had taken more out of her than she had expected. She should have been able to carry out such a relatively simple task with ease, but it had proven almost impossible to concentrate. If she had been capable of perspiration, she was sure she would be damp with sweat right now. It had been so tempting to just drain Nicola, but she could not. For the time being, she needed the death to look like a suicide.

As she watched Nicola hanging there, struggling for her last breath, however, she had felt something. She guessed that she could have called it guilt or regret. She did not like it, though. She was meant to be beyond such emotions now. Emotions complicated things, and she could not allow things to become complicated at this late stage of her plan. She needed to get this virus out of her before it did any more damage.

As these thoughts rippled through her mind, she looked around her. She was lying in the staff car park that was situated under the hospital itself. This made it isolated and also poorly lit, which she needed in her current state as she could not afford to let anybody see her. She let out a cry of pain as another bolt jarred her body and weakness spread through her limbs. It was obvious that the virus was not only designed to ignite her long-dead emotions, but also to prevent her from recharging herself the usual way. Without being able to tap into the electromagnetic energy from the air around her as she usually did, she would need to recharge herself from another source. It had been a long time, but she still remembered how to hunt.

The sound of footsteps echoing through the car park pulled her back to her senses, and she stood and looked around. A woman dressed in a nurse's uniform was heading toward a car nearby. The girl checked to make sure that the woman was alone then raised a hand, disconnecting the nearby CCTV cameras. Turning herself invisible, she crossed the parking lot toward the unsuspecting nurse.

As she approached, she reached out with her mind. She

had accidentally learned this ability a long time ago. It enabled her to see into somebody's past and see what kind of person they had been. Once upon a time, she had also been able to view their future, but that had waned as time went by. A warning sign that worried her about her own mortality.

There. Nurse Veronica Trent. Hard-working, dedicated, ambitious. Almost a perfect example of a good person. Except for the time she had given an elderly patient the wrong dosage of medicine, causing him to overdose. He did not recover and died two days later. It was a genuine mistake, but rather than coming forward and admitting to it, she had instead let a colleague take the blame, which led to them losing their job. It was a single selfish act on an otherwise spotless record, but proof positive that, as she had always told that traitorous bastard, nobody was innocent.

Without another thought, she reached out and placed a hand on Veronica Trent's back. That was all it took—physical contact—and as the sound of the woman's screams filled her ears, she fed.

Chapter Seven

Jackson loathed having his hand stamped. The thought crossed his mind as the bouncer applied the ink-covered rubber shape onto his skin. For the sole purpose of proving that he had paid to access this god-awful establishment. The fact he had paid to enter a club called Wendy's, the evening it was having an 80s themed night, was another issue he was not currently in the mood to deal with.

He entered the bar area, where he was immediately hit by the sounds of music from that miserable decade being pumped from the speakers. Synthesised noise with repetitive lyrics from an age of music thankfully hidden between the 70s and the 90s. It was times like this he realised just how much he actually hated the 80s.

It was without a doubt the kind of place he would never have entertained the idea of visiting, if not for Lucy suggesting that they meet here. Though why she would want to come to such a place, he could not be certain. In his humble opinion, it was far from being an ideal meeting place. It was loud, dire, and even though it was only a Wednesday night, still relatively busy. But she had insisted on this location. He could only assume she wanted as many people around them as possible. After what had happened to her, this did make sense.

With the shock of the damage to his car, he had considered cancelling the meeting with her, but as Allister had pointed out, she would almost certainly see it as an excuse. So, he had gone home, showered, changed into what he hoped passed for acceptable clothes for a date that probably was not a date and headed into town. Since he didn't want to be late, he arrived fifteen minutes early.

With nothing else to do in the meantime, he decided to get a drink. He crossed to the bar and got the attention of the bartender who he guessed was attempting the world record for the highest number of piercings in his face. *He'd never be allowed in the army looking like that!*

"What can I get for you, mate?" the bartender asked.

Jackson considered enquiring about what whiskies they stocked but decided that as he was meeting Lucy shortly, he should probably keep a clear head. It was going to be difficult enough to convince her he was telling the truth as it was, without throwing alcohol into the mix.

"Mineral water, please," he replied instead.

The bartender nodded in acknowledgement and turned away. He returned a moment later with an uncapped bottle of branded water and a glass with ice and a slice of lemon inside. "Three pounds please, mate."

"Three pounds? For water?" Jackson asked incredulously. He knew water was overpriced, but it never failed to surprise him.

The bartender shrugged as if to say that it was not his problem, then pointed at the glass. "And ice and lemon," he replied as if it explained everything.

"But I didn't ask for ice and lemon. In fact, I don't even want ice and lemon!"

"Still three pounds, mate. The ice and lemon are free."

Jackson paid but made it clear he was not happy about it. After filling his glass, he turned away from the bar and began to look around the club. Some people had dressed up for the occasion, with 80s hairstyles and clothes, however, the majority just appeared to have come as they were. All were dancing and seemed to be having a good time. He sometimes wished he could throw himself into a night out, like those around him, but it had never been his thing. Almost as if he was born without the gene required for having a good time. Even at school, he would avoid anything that resembled a school disco at all costs, and prom passed him by without notice.

"Leave me alone, Sean!" The voice of a woman shouting brought him back to the here and now.

He looked around the room, and saw two women with a larger man, standing in a corner. By the size of him, Jackson guessed he was possibly a rugby player. The women seemed to look distressed, while the man, Sean, appeared to be taking great pleasure in giving them a hard time.

Crossing the club, Jackson stood a short distance away. "Is everything alright here?" he asked the group.

Sean looked at him dismissively, "Get lost. It's got nothing to do with you!"

Jackson, now annoyed, looked to the ladies for confirmation. One of them shook her head.

"He's been hassling my friend. She's told him that she's not interested, but he won't leave us alone!"

He looked back at Sean. "I think you need to be on your way," Jackson told him.

Sean turned and squared up to him. Though they were about the same height, he was clearly several inches wider than Jackson and seemed to feel this gave him an advantage. "What did you just say?"

Staring him straight in the eye, Jackson did not blink, "I said, be on your way."

"Do you know who I am?" No reply. "I'm Sean Benson!" No reply. "Have you not heard of me?"

"No," Jackson replied simply, keeping his face impassive. He nodded toward the exit, "So, Sean Benson, off you go then."

Sean seemed to be unnerved by the whole exchange, clearly used to people being intimidated by him. "This isn't over," he said half-heartedly, before skulking away.

"Are you ok?" Jackson asked the two women.

"Yes, thank you," the lady who had spoken previously answered with a smile.

He nodded at them both, turned away, and came face to face with Chloe, of all people. He almost did not recognise her, as she was dressed in 80s fashion and her hair was frizzy from far too much hairspray. She even sported hoop earrings and a large bow in her hair. From the look on her face, she had clearly been watching the confrontation.

"Hey," she said with a smile. "Tell me, are you always the knight in shining armour?"

Jackson chuckled. "I just seem to have a bad habit of being in the right place at the right time I guess," he replied. Then added, "Should you actually be here?"

She shrugged, "I'm supposed to be meeting Jade. Her dad works the doors, so as long as we don't drink alcohol, then he's ok with us hanging out." She held up her hands, indicating the room, "Also it's 80s night, and I love the 80s!"

"What would you even know about the 80s? I mean, I wasn't even born 'til the end of it!"

"You'd be surprised," she replied with a laugh. "My parents grew up in the 80s. When I was young, this is the music my mum always listened to. Just old vinyl records and cassette tapes. I was practically weaned on it. To be honest, it kind of grows on you after a while."

"Well, I'm afraid it's yet to grow on me," Jackson admitted. "I hate the decade."

"It had its moments!" she said looking sad. "Back to the Future, leggings, hairspray, The Smiths."

"I do like The Smiths."

"Of course you do," Chloe said with a laugh.

"Meaning?"

"Al says you're a smart guy. You can figure it out." She grinned, "If you hate the 80s though, I'm afraid to say that you are missing out."

"I'm going to have to take your word for it," Jackson replied.

Chloe's face became suddenly serious. "Thank you for saving Jade today," she said. "I never got the chance to tell you at the time."

"No problem. I guess it was just lucky that Allister and I were passing and saw what was happening."

"Well, you being there helped me a lot. I don't know what I would have done otherwise," she said sincerely.

"Don't worry about it. I really hope she's ok."

"She acts all tough, but I think she was quite shaken by it. She'll be fine though, I'm sure. Her pride is what got hurt the most."

"Well, I'm relieved to hear she's alright."

"So, what are you even doing here if you hate the 80s so much?" The change of topic was so quick Jackson barely noticed.

"Just meeting a friend," Jackson replied. He looked around and saw Lucy coming through the door. She spotted him and started walking in his direction, "Actually she's just arrived."

Chloe followed his gaze, "She's cute. Anyway, Jade just texted me; she wants to meet somewhere else now. I'll see you around. Tell Al I said hi!" And with that, she walked away.

Strange girl, Jackson thought, not for the first time. Moments later Lucy appeared beside him.

"Hi there," she said with a smile. She was, thankfully, not dressed up in 80s attire, instead just wearing casual clothes, confirming it was definitely not a date.

"Hi there, back at you," Jackson replied, all thoughts of Chloe now gone from his mind. "How are you?"

"Good, thanks. Also, thank you for agreeing to meet me."

"Not at all. I do owe you an explanation after all."

"Well, that is true," she agreed.

"How about I get us some drinks, then we find somewhere quiet to sit, and I'll tell you the whole story?"

"Sounds good."

***

As soon as Allister opened the door to the office, he knew something was wrong. Very wrong. It was a feeling that only grew even more as he stepped inside. Scanning the office, he saw the filing cabinets were knocked over; many of the drawers had been ripped from the frames and the contents spread across the carpet.

"Shit!" he whispered to himself.

He immediately crossed to his computer and switched it on. At first glance, it looked fine, but as he worked through the database and ran his security software, it did not take long to confirm what he already suspected. Somebody had hacked him. It was not a nice feeling. He knew of only one person in the world who could have gotten through his firewalls and encryption programs in such a short time. Allister was confident that they were not responsible. Which meant only one other option.

He dragged his desk across the floor, then pulled up a section of carpet revealing a loose floorboard. Lifting the board, he reached into the space underneath and retrieved an old-style flip phone handset. He switched it on and searched for the only number stored in the contacts. Thumbs moving fast as his hands shook, he compiled a text:

I've been hacked! was all he typed.

He hit send then waited. Though he was adamant it would never be necessary, they had been insistent that this protocol needed to be in place for just such a scenario. If his computer had been hacked, then so too might his usual phone. He hated being wrong. Fortunately, he did not have to wait long for a response. Less than twenty seconds after sending the message, the phone began to ring. The display simply said UNKNOWN. Taking a deep breath, he pressed accept.

"Hello?" Allister said, not liking the nervousness evident in his voice.

"What did they get?" replied a voice on the other end. It was stern, all business.

"Almost everything."

"Was the virus activated?"

Allister cursed inwardly for not thinking to check first. He tapped several keys, searching for the answer.

"It was," he confirmed.

There was a pause, and he thought he heard a sad sigh. *"It was her. Is the memory stick safe?"*

"Yes. I had it with me."

"Good. Plug it into your hard drive and download any digital information that was not there before the hack."

Allister did as he was told. There was not much to transfer, so it did not take long. "Done. What now?"

"The memory stick will do the rest. Keep it safe at any cost. We will be there to collect it soon." There was another brief pause, *"Destroy this phone,"* and the line went dead.

Well, that was direct, he thought. They would be here soon? That was a sentence that did not make him feel confident. He opened the phone, took out the SIM card and snapped it in two. He would dispose of the handset later and check his smartphone for any signs of being tampered with. He looked at the mess in the office but decided he did not have the energy to tidy up right now. He stood and walked out the door, locking it behind him.

***

Sean Benson was on the prowl. That wanker in the last bar might have ruined his fun, but he would not let him ruin his night, far from it in fact. It had not taken long for somebody else to catch his attention. He was following her now. She was walking alone, well, stumbling, along the street after clearly having too much to drink.

The drunks were the easiest; he thought. Why else would she get into that state if she didn't want a man to come and take advantage of her? He knew a lot of his friends would disagree, but Sean Benson did what he wanted. Alpha male and all that. He had been that way ever since he grew to be the biggest kid in his class. The strongest got their own way. Law of the jungle.

He knew if he followed her for long enough, an opportunity would present itself. She would break a heel or take a tumble, and he would be able to swoop in to offer her a friendly arm to guide her where she wanted to go. Or rather, where he wanted her to go. He stopped suddenly and frowned. For a moment he thought he had heard somebody whispering. He shook it off and continued to follow her.

Ahead of him, the woman swore as she stumbled, possibly twisting her ankle in the process. Sean smiled a wolfish grin. Now was the time to be a good Samaritan. He began to speed up but then hesitated again. He was sure he could hear whispering once more, though try as he might, he could not make out any of the words.

"Hello," said a voice from behind him.

He frowned and turned to face whoever had spoken. He was surprised to find a girl standing a few feet away from him. Sean could not see her face as the lights all around them seemed to have gone out. *When the hell did that happen?* Even in the dim light that remained, however, she looked like she was probably cute. He could just make out her hair hanging past her shoulders. Most importantly though; she was petite. Just how he liked girls to be; easy to overpower. His smile returned. Best part was that she had approached him. Like a fly to a spider.

"Hello," he replied, his voice full of charm. "How can I help you?"

"I'm new to the area," the girl answered. She sounded sad, even a little scared. "I just need to get home. Can you help me find a taxi?"

"Of course I can, love. Follow me."

He led the way, and she stayed very close behind him like he was there to protect her. He laughed inside at the irony of that. She would soon learn a valuable lesson about trusting strangers, one he was looking forward to teaching her. He knew just the place too. It was nearby and ideal for what he had in mind.

A few short minutes later, they were alone in an alley that ran behind several pubs and restaurants. There was nobody else around, which was perfect. Sean looked up as all the lights suddenly went out, again plunging them both into darkness.

"What the fuck?" he asked, confusion taking over. He turned to face the girl.

Without any kind of warning, he froze. Literally froze on the spot. No matter how much he tried, he could not move a muscle. He tried to talk, but no sound came from his rigid lips. The girl was standing in his line of vision, but all he could see of her face were two green, glowing orbs, staring back at him. She held her hand out in front of herself, the fingers squeezed into a tight fist. Strips of purple light began to run along the length of her as if keeping time with a heartbeat.

"Allow me to teach you a valuable lesson about trusting strangers," she said as if mocking him, her voice no longer sad, but instead full of menace. "This is how it feels, you know? When a girl is attacked. Frozen with fear. Unable to run away or fight back. Not knowing if she is going to live or die. Did you know that, Sean? Have you ever even considered that?"

Momentarily shocked that she knew his name, Sean tried to reply, but still, no sound would come. He could not even manage an incoherent mumble?

"What's the matter? Nothing to say? Or can't you talk?" Her eyes changed to blue. "I'll answer for you, shall I? Of course, you knew that! Not that it matters, does it? Because it's what people like you get off on, isn't it? Fear. It feeds your ego."

Who was this girl and what was her problem? Didn't she understand? Men were hunters and fighters. Women liked to play hard to get, but they all loved the chase, really. He wanted to try to explain this, but still, nothing would come out. How could she do this, just freeze him in place like she had? Also, how did her eyes glow? He hated to admit it, but he was afraid.

"Still struggling are you, Sean?" she asked. "I know what you're thinking. Women, we're all just a prize to you, aren't we? Something to be taken because you're bigger and stronger. Well, tell me, what's it like to be held by somebody stronger than you? Somebody you're unable to fight back against?" Her eyes turned red. "Or is it because you don't want to fight back? Is that it? Do you like being overpowered like this? Do you secretly get off on it?"

Sean began to shake with fear. It was the only movement he could make, which he realised he could only do because she was letting him do it.

"Tell me, would you like it if I let you go?" She cocked her head as if listening for a reply, but none came. "I know. Have you tried screaming? Yes, go on. Scream for help!"

Sensing a chance to escape, Sean sucked in as much air into his lungs as he was able to, and then tried to scream. But no matter how hard he tried, all that would come out was a barely audible gargle. *What is happening? Where is everyone? Why is no one helping me?*

The girl leaned toward him, then whispered close to his ear. "Not nice is it? Not being able to scream? All those poor girls, whose mouths you covered so they couldn't scream for help. All that fear." She leaned back again and was quiet for a moment as if she was thinking. When she spoke again, it was no longer a whisper. "It never goes away you know? What happens. You get your kicks; she gets a lifetime of torment and fear. Hardly a fair trade. Trust me, I speak from experience!"

Is that what all this was about? Jesus Christ. It was only a bit of fun. Why do girls always have to take everything so seriously? They all enjoyed it really. Girls loved it when a guy took charge.

"No! We don't!" she snapped as if she had been looking inside his head. "Even after all these years, my attack haunts me. You should think about that. You should think about all the girls whose lives you've affected by raping them!"

What the fuck was she talking about? He wasn't a rapist. Sure, maybe he didn't get a definite yes or no from some of them, but seriously, was that what the world was coming to now?

She stepped closer, "Would you like me to set you free? Have you learned your lesson?"

He tried to nod, but could only manage the tiniest of movements. Yes, he wanted to be set free, and when he was, he was going to do all manner of painful things to her. Of that, she could be certain.

"Ok, Sean, you've earned this."

She slowly unclenched the fingers of the hand that she

held in front of herself. Then she reached out towards him as if she was going to caress his cheek. As soon as her fingers touched his face, however, white-hot pain exploded inside his skull, rendering all other thoughts inconsequential.

***

With the sounds of 80s music still blasting from all sides, Jackson returned to the table Lucy had found, with their drinks in hand. He had begrudgingly purchased another glass of mineral water for himself and a glass of white wine for Lucy. She thanked him as he handed her the wine, then he took his own seat across the table from her. It already felt more like an interview rather than anything romantic.

"So," Lucy said.

"So," Jackson replied, the awkwardness of the situation already becoming apparent.

"How was your day? Aside from waking up in a police cell, that is."

Jackson gave a small laugh, "Believe it or not, if I'm honest, that was possibly the highlight!"

"Really?" she looked concerned. "What's happened?"

"Where to start? Quite a lot, all of which culminated in the vandalism of my car."

"Seriously?"

"I'm afraid so."

"Oh my God, that's awful. Do you have any idea who did it?"

Jackson shook his head, "Not exactly. I have my suspicions that it may be linked to a case we are currently working on, but I have no proof or even a specific suspect."

"You should have said. We could have put meeting up off for another night, you know."

"I thought about it, but I figured it was important to explain things to you sooner, rather than later."

She nodded in acknowledgement, "Thank you."

"I'm just not sure where to start."

"I'd suggest the beginning is best."

Reaching into his pocket, Jackson took out his phone and opened the message containing the news report from the previous day. He paused for a moment, wondering if it was the best way to do this, then offered it to Lucy. She took the phone from him and began to read.

Jackson watched as her face quickly switched between emotions. Confusion to disbelief to worry to anger. It was the final one that showed in her eyes when she finally looked at him again. It was clear she was not convinced, or impressed.

"What the hell is this?" she demanded.

"What it appears to be," Jackson replied. "A news report dated today, that I received yesterday."

"Seriously? Is this the best explanation you can come up with? Or is it some kind of joke? Because I am not amused if it is!"

"It's the only explanation I can offer. Believe me, I wish it wasn't. If you check the other two multimedia messages, you'll find two more reports. Both were received the day before they were dated."

"So, what you are saying, and clearly want me to believe, is that you are getting messages about the future?" she asked, looking at him as if he was crazy.

He couldn't really blame her. "It's the truth," was all he could think to reply.

"Or, they're faked."

"And why would I do that?"

"Oh, I don't know. Maybe you paid somebody to attack me, just so that you could come to my rescue and earn my trust. Then you or even your buddy Allister, knock up some fake newspaper reports to make it look like you were destined to be there."

Jackson almost laughed at the absurdity of the accusation, but he kept his face neutral instead. Now was not the time to laugh. "Honestly, how likely do you think that is?"

Lucy sighed, "Probably not very. But if you compare it to what you're suggesting, it seems a little more believable."

"Once you eliminate the impossible, whatever's left, however unlikely, must be the truth," Jackson said with a shrug.

"Seriously? You're comparing yourself to Sherlock Holmes?" she asked with an amused laugh.

"If the deerstalker fits..."

"And I suppose Allister is Watson?"

"Watson wishes he was Allister."

She laughed again, this time a little more relaxed, "Ok, so assuming I believe you, and I am not saying that I do, what does it all mean? Who is sending you these messages? Why ask you to save me?"

"I don't know, I don't know and... I honestly don't know," Jackson admitted. "I would like to think that if I was making all of this up, then I would have come better prepared to answer any questions you might have."

"True. Or this bumbling private eye thing you're doing could be part of your master plan to manipulate me and convince me to trust you."

"Please, I often struggle to come up with a plan, much less a master one!" he said with half a smile.

Lucy's face softened slightly but gave no hint she was convinced just yet. "So why tell me all of this? You could have said you were visiting a friend, or you'd been to the campus bar to see a band and you just happened to see me. Why risk me thinking you were nuts?"

"You asked for an explanation. To tell you the truth, you seem like the type of person who would spot when they are being lied to."

"I'll admit you are showing none of the signs I'd expect from somebody who is lying. So, you're either very good, a sociopath, or you're telling me the truth." She took another sip of wine. "I have not ruled any of them out yet. If you are telling the truth though, what now?"

"I really don't know. I didn't expect this conversation to go beyond you throwing your drink in my face and storming out."

"Sorry to disappoint you."

Jackson smiled, "I am glad I told you. Whether you believe me or not, I'm glad I told you the truth."

She placed a hand on his knee, "Tell you what, as you've had such an awful day, how about we leave all of this for now, and enjoy the rest of the evening. I feel like having a dance."

Jackson groaned inwardly at the thought, but instead replied, "Great idea!"

***

Maxwell Solomon arrived back at the front door of the empty apartment he had been squatting in for the last two weeks. He had taken to hiding since the previous evening, convinced that the police would turn up at any moment to arrest him for trying to kill that girl last night.

He had hidden in an abandoned factory near a railway line and spent a restless night worrying. He was sure that Lucy would be an easy choice. He had spent the last week following her and learning her routine; waiting for just the right time. She was, after all, the sole reason he had been brought to Leeds. After all his hard work, that son of a bitch had come along and ruined everything. His wrist and head both still ached from where he had been hit. He did not know who her rescuer was, but he would find out, and he would make him pay.

The stranger he knew only as Alice, had sent him that first package with a promise of a fresh start and instructions to follow. She, or he, had never told Maxwell anything about themselves. Just a photo of Lucy Silverman, a key to his new home and a note telling him to come to Leeds. As soon as he saw Lucy's face, the part of him that became obsessed with women had locked in. It was not so much that he wanted to kill her; he needed to. It was almost like destiny. Alice's note was not much of a promise, but it was enough for him to travel up from London, where his face, easy to remember thanks to his distinctive birthmark, was becoming too well known.

After spending the day in hiding, he had received a message on his very old and slightly damaged phone where Alice told him it was safe to return to his home. Maxwell considered that it could well be a trap, but he felt in his gut that he could trust her. Something deep inside told him she would never steer him wrong. He had returned to the apartment after dark, and after spending over an hour watching, making sure there were no police waiting for him, he approached the door. He used the key she had gifted him and let himself in.

The door opened into a meagre kitchen area. The sink and the countertops were covered in grime and garbage. The small bathroom to his left was also in poor repair, dirty and the toilet missing its seat. Without working plumbing, it was filling up fast, and the smell was obvious. To say that he lived in squalid conditions was an understatement. As soon as he entered, he was hit with the stench of sour milk and urine, which seemed to cling to everything, himself included. He did not care that he stank, though. People stayed away from things that smelled, so they stayed away from him and his business.

It was dark inside. He picked up the torch that he kept by the door and turned it on. Moving around by torchlight was inconvenient, but as the utility bills had not been paid in some time, he was left with no choice. At least he had a roof over his head.

Entering the only other room in the apartment, he looked around. There was very little that could be called furniture. Just a threadbare armchair, a battered table covered with empty food containers and a dirty mattress lying on the floor against the far wall. Not even a carpet covered the exposed floorboards.

It was then that he noticed the package. It was a large A4-size envelope, the padded kind filled with bubble wrap. Just his name was written on the front in large black letters. It lay in the centre of the mattress where he could not fail to see it.

Maxwell picked it up, noting immediately how heavy it was. Tearing the package open, he reached inside. His fingers immediately found a thin piece of cardboard. With excitement growing, he removed it and saw his suspicion was correct: a photograph. It showed a young blonde girl sitting in a garden looking sad. She had the bluest eyes he had ever seen. The obsession was instant. He turned the photo over. A name, Chloe Winchell, followed by an address, written in a perfectly elegant handwriting.

Reaching into the envelope again, he took out the only other item it contained. There was no note and no instructions. Just the photo and a knife. His knife; that he thought he had lost the night before.

Chapter Eight

Chloe headed to school feeling more optimistic than she had for some time. Befriending Jade had really made a change to her overall mood lately. She never realised the difference in having even one friend made. Especially one who dragged you kicking and screaming out of the comfort zone you had built for yourself. The previous night had been beyond amazing, although the dull ache in her head now made her wish Jade had not brought the flask of vodka with her. She had never been much of a drinker, despite the parties after she first arrived, and since she now seemed to have been taken off all invite lists recently, she could consider it a dry spell.

She was excited about being allowed to return to Australia. After a very long chat with her parents, they had agreed that she could live with her grandparents until she finished school, then they would discuss it again. It was almost the end of the school year in Australia, but she was sure that she could use the last two months to catch up with the workload she had let pass while missing so much school and be ready to start the new year in January. Her dad called the airline right away and purchased a ticket for Monday morning. Just like that, it was as if the world had been lifted from her shoulders.

There was no doubt in Chloe's mind that she would miss her parents, but the truth was that nothing had gone right for her since she had moved to England. She had struggled to make friends and her grades had plummeted. Her school attendance had reached the point where she had been absent as much as she was present, and she knew that they were already considering kicking her out soon if things did not change.

And obviously not forgetting the small matter of her stalker. *It*, or was Chloe now supposed to call it a *she*, had been a near constant companion for the last eighteen months, and one she had no doubts she would not miss. At all. She could only hope that moving to the other side of the world was finally going to be far away enough to be rid of her.

They had been strange times for her living in Leeds. She had always hoped that eventually it would grow on her, but in the end, it never had. A crowded city which was too far from the sea and whose weather was persistently awful. Two more things she would be glad to be rid of. Chloe thought about all the early morning surfing she had missed out on over the years and her excitement grew.

She stopped suddenly as a feeling of being watched washed briefly over her. She had grown accustomed to the sensation of being observed. It had become a sixth sense after so long. But this was different. It was almost like she was being hunted, as though she were prey. Glancing around her surroundings, she tried to spot anybody out of the ordinary. There did not appear to be any.

Chloe saw people everywhere, as anybody would expect at this time of the morning. People driving cars, walking, inside cafes and shops. But none of them seemed to give her more than a passing glance, if they noticed she was there at all. She tried to shake the feeling, but it remained. Continuing on her way, she decided that she would mention it to Allister when they next met. One more thing to convince him she was definitely crazy.

A slight pang of regret filled her as she thought about him. They had not known each other long, but he had become the closest thing she had to an older brother. He had looked out for her and offered to help her when she had nothing to repay him with. She was glad that he had taken the time to speak to her that day and show concern. She knew she had been dismissive at first, who could blame her really, though now it felt good to have somebody looking out for her for once.

Chloe also knew that she could have learned so much from him as a hacker. It was a skill she had begun to teach herself after the move to try to help alleviate the boredom, only to discover that she had quite the natural talent for it. But whereas she was a beginner, he was clearly leaps ahead of her in the field. She guessed they could always keep in touch online. Plus, she was certain to come back to visit her parents during the holidays. The upcoming conversation about her leaving would be an awkward one, but she was sure he would be happy for her to have a fresh start.

As she neared the school, a figure stood waiting outside. She brightened again when she recognised it was Jade. Her dark hair covered her face, and when Chloe got closer, her heart sank as she realised the other girl had been crying. Their eyes met as Jade attempted a small smile but failed to maintain it.

"Hey, Jade," she said as she reached her. She placed her hand on her friend's arm. "What's happened? Are you ok?"

"Oh my God, Chloe!" Jade replied, grabbing her and pulling her into a tight hug, almost crushing Chloe's ribs.

"Not that I don't appreciate the show of affection, but

you're making it very difficult to breathe," she managed to croak out before Jade let her go. "Seriously, what's happened?"

Jade looked at her in confusion, "Haven't you heard, man?"

"Heard what?"

"About Nicola?"

"No, what about her?" Chloe grew anxious as she got a strong suspicion she already knew what was coming, as though she had heard the news before.

"She's dead!"

Somehow managing to stop her knees from buckling, Chloe was able to ask, "What? When?"

"Yesterday afternoon. When I was walking you home."

"But how?" Chloe struggled to make sense of what she was being told. She had never liked Nicola, hated her in fact. Dead though? It was more than she could comprehend right now.

Jade seemed to be struggling with the news too, not that Chloe could blame her. She had actually been friends with Nicola. Even if, as she claimed, it had been one of convenience.

"The doctors say she committed suicide. Hung herself in the hospital room with the belt from her bathrobe."

"I don't understand! Why would she do that? It makes zero sense!"

Jade looked at her for a moment, as if deep in thought. "It doesn't, does it?" she said earnestly. "You see, I know Nicola may have been a bit of a psycho, but she was not suicidal. No way. I'm certain of it."

"So, what do you think happened?" Chloe asked cautiously.

"I think she was murdered."

"Seriously?"

Jade nodded once, showing her determination, "Fuck yeah, man, and I'm going to find out who did it."

***

Jackson sat quietly in the taxi as he travelled towards the centre of town. He still felt upset at the damage done to his car, and what made it worse was that he had been told it would cost more than it was worth to be restored to its former condition. He still had no idea why it had been damaged in the manner it was. Vandalism was rife, yes, but melting the word TRAITOR into the paintwork was particularly confusing. To the best of his knowledge, he had never done anything that warranted that.

Spending the previous evening with Lucy had lifted his spirits somewhat, and they really did have a good time together. She even managed to encourage him onto the dance floor for one dance, which led her to agree quickly with his earlier assertion that dancing was not for him.

He actually surprised himself when he continued to stay on the water. Though he switched to tap after Lucy's insistence that he should be more aware of the plastic he used, and also that it was free. It did not go unnoticed, however, that the ice and lemon were still provided. They were still unwanted, but now he felt he deserved them. He was starting to feel the benefits of keeping a clear head. It was good to wake up in the morning feeling ready to go, instead of suffering from a hangover.

The night had ended well enough. As it turned out, she had brought a group of friends with her who was sitting elsewhere in the bar, just to make sure she was safe. After midnight she left with them to return to their accommodations on campus.

Jackson could not but help admire her precautions as he returned to his own apartment. He went to bed feeling content in a way he had not felt in some time and slept well.

Sadly, the feeling did not prevail into the next morning. He found himself overwhelmed with more questions than he could answer. Who was the killer from the 1980s, and why had they made a return with the killing of Michael Johnson? How were they connected to Chloe and her alleged stalker? How much had his dad known about the killings and the killer? From what he was told by DCI Cole, Jackson's dad was not only familiar with the case but outspoken about the cover-up that followed the strange deaths. Could his disappearance be linked to him having found out too much? If so, was he simply missing by choice, or had his vocal opposition toward his superiors led to a fate worse than Jackson had previously believed?

Jackson was still waiting on Allister to find out what he could about the attacks with his own particular brand of technological skills, and strangely he was beginning to see the appeal behind those methods. But Jackson still felt he needed to be out there trying to find answers himself. Especially about the messages from the future. Taking all this into consideration, he realised there was only one person who may be able to help him now.

***

With that in mind, the taxi pulled up outside the small coffee shop named George and Son's. He considered asking the driver to just drive on, thinking that there was no way this strange man could possibly help him. After a quick internal struggle, he knew there was no other real choice. He paid and climbed out of the car. Jackson examined the outside of the shop with a critical eye. It appeared so innocuous when you looked at it, almost as if it did not want to be noticed. Blending seamlessly into its surroundings.

As he approached the coffee shop's front door, the shop itself looked closed. He checked his watch. 10:38am. They should certainly be open by now. Jackson could not imagine a coffee shop anywhere in the world that would not be open at this time of day. He shrugged, pushed the door open, and stepped inside. Likewise, he also found it difficult to believe that one could be vacant too, but that was exactly what confronted him. Every table was empty and strangely enough was set for only one person, though none showed evidence of having been recently vacated. As a result, the cafe positively sparkled. George really needed to work on his advertising if the lack of customers was anything to go by.

"So, you return," a voice announced as George appeared from the kitchen, the man looking as pristine as his coffee shop.

Jackson was surprised by the sudden appearance and took a moment to reply. "Ermm... yes. It would appear I have. The last time I was here, you said to come back if I needed help," he said, and then shrugged. "I guess I need help."

"I will assist you in any way I am able to. But first, may I offer you a hearty breakfast?"

"Can you actually refer to a vegan meal as hearty? It seems a little ironic."

George looked confused for a moment, "Well... I suppose... I mean..."

Although Jackson was enjoying watching the other man search for an answer, he decided there was no need to prolong the visit, so chose to move on. "Don't worry about it. I was joking. I'll pass on the breakfast, but I wouldn't mind a coffee, thank you."

"Of course." And George was gone again.

Jackson could not help but wonder about this place. It had a strange, relaxing feel to it, almost as though separate in some way from everything else in life. An oasis of calm in the middle of chaos. Maybe there was something to this Zen nonsense worth considering. Again, he wondered why nobody else had discovered it. It seemed like the kind of place millennials would flock to.

Moments later George reappeared holding a steaming mug of coffee that he passed to Jackson. "How can I help you?" he asked.

"I was wondering what you could tell me about receiving messages from the future," Jackson asked, deciding it was best to get straight to the point.

George thought about this for a moment, crossing his arms and resting his chin in a hand. "I can tell you that it's theoretically impossible."

"Theoretically?"

"Correct."

"It is also possible then?"

George nodded, "From one perspective you could say that. To answer your question, yes, it is also theoretically possible. Though I am not a scientist, so I couldn't begin to explain exactly how in detail. But many theories suggest energy can travel in a non-linear way, so maybe information can too."

"Let's say I was to receive such a message, about future events, what do you suggest I should do?"

"Think about it."

"Think about it?" Jackson asked confused. "Is that the best advice you have?"

"It's the only advice I have. Simply put, think about why you have been given the information. Has it been sent to benefit you, the person in the message or the person who sent it? Who has the most to gain from you acting upon the information?"

"I would imagine the person whose life I'm saving."

"Once maybe. In the beginning. But power often sets even the best of us down the wrong path," George said sagely. "Somebody's reasons for giving out warnings of the future may no longer be as pure as helping others."

"Previously, you told me that I should influence somebody's destiny if it was the right thing to do. If it made their life better."

"I did, and if you followed that advice then I hope only good will come from it. But sometimes changing somebody's destiny just passes that destiny onto somebody else. Only time will tell what the consequences will be, sadly the power of seeing the future is not one I possess."

"None of this is exactly helpful, you know."

"Not everything comes with an easy answer. I'm sorry. But can you really expect that changing the future would not carry consequences?"

Jackson frowned as he considered this, "Allister did try to tell me something similar, but I didn't want to hear it, I guess. I really need to think things through more."

"Deep down you already know the answer. Whoever sent the message about Lucy, knew who they needed to use if they wanted a reaction from you," George explained. He tilted his head to the left, "Is there anything else I can help you with today?"

"Well, there is something you can tell me. Something I've been curious about since I was last here. I'd like to know what happened between you and Chloe?"

He watched as George's eyes hardened and his jaw clenched. There was definitely an intense hatred there. But he could not understand why. What could she have done to deserve it? How could somebody display such a strong reaction to a teenage girl, just at the mention of their name?

"She is... complicated," George said, at last, his voice hard. "Not everything is always as it seems with her."

"Now that one I had actually figured out for myself," Jackson replied lightly.

"Listen to me, Jackson, and take notice. She is heading for trouble. If she does not change her path, she is going to get herself killed!"

"What are you talking about?"

"Sadly, I cannot say much more. There isn't a lot of time left. Just be careful." George took Jackson's now empty mug from him. "Can I help you further?"

Jackson thought for a moment but decided the conversation was over. For now, at least. "I think that's everything. How much for the coffee?"

George smiled, "There is no payment here."

"Really, then how on earth do you stay in business?"

"Not everything in this world is about earning money. Sometimes making a difference is its own reward." With a small nod, he disappeared back into the kitchen as silently as usual.

Jackson turned and headed toward the exit, feeling more confused than he had when he arrived. Talking to George had done little but confirm that the future messages were real, well probably, and to be wary of Chloe. Though the reasons why were vaguer than he would have liked to hear.

Stepping back outside and onto the pavement, he squinted as the mid-morning sunlight hit him. As he began walking, Jackson decided he needed to see if Allister was having any more luck than him. He sincerely hoped so, otherwise, this whole investigation was going nowhere fast.

Realising he had spent a lot of time in the cafe, Jackson checked his watch. He immediately stopped walking and checked it again. Strange. It was working, as he knew it would be. Keeping a watch in working order was a habit Jackson had picked up while in the army. He was obsessive about it. Yet his watch still insisted that the time was 10:38am.

***

Allister's fingers flew over the keyboard as he navigated his way around various government databases. His morning had been far from fruitful. His search for Lucy's attacker had yielded hardly any results, apart from a couple of mentions in police reports submitted by two arresting officers in London. They depicted a man with a similar description and made mention of the red birthmark, but there was little if anything else. It was almost as though all mention of him had been erased from the system, and in a very professional way. Criminal history, court cases, eyewitness accounts, everything except those two reports were gone. Unfortunately, neither officer had been able to take a name.

Allister decided there was little to go on, so instead began looking for any information he could find regarding the bizarre murders Cole told Jackson about from back in the 1980s. Honestly, he already doubted he would find anything on these either, mainly due to the scarcity of computers in everyday use back then. He began the task half-heartedly, already expecting a dead end.

His suspicions were immediately validated. There was nothing logged at all from that time period on the West Yorkshire Police computers. He widened the search to include for later activity. It seemed that during the early 90s they began to use computers on a semi-regular basis at least. As he looked through the various files, one stood out and caught his attention. It was simply entitled *AL* and dated November 1998, almost twenty years ago. Intrigued, Allister clicked his mouse on the file and was confronted with an encryption algorithm. Within seconds of starting to crack it, he realised it was similar to one he had recently designed himself. Complicated to most people but relatively easy for the creator. It was almost as if he was supposed to find it.

As soon as he opened the file, his computer began to download the contents automatically. Concerned that he may be receiving a virus, he was moving to terminate the transfer, when a message appeared on his monitor:

Hello Allister. I know you are searching for this information. We have kept it safe until such time as we were able to store it for you to find. I hope it helps you in your investigation. Do everything you can to keep her safe and trust nobody. I mean nobody. Destroy this file once the contents have downloaded. Gates.

Allister reread the message, convinced he must have misunderstood it somehow. It could not be for him. It was not possible. It had been set up and left untouched since 1998, he would have been ten years old at the time.

"How the hell..." he began.

"What's up?" a voice asked from across the room.

Allister looked up to see Chloe watching him from the doorway. She smiled and gave a small wave.

"Hi there," he replied, "it's nothing to worry about. I just found something unexpected is all."

Chloe indicated the filing cabinets and the paperwork that still lay littering the carpet, "You are aware that this place is a mess, right? Also, why do you even have them? Who uses filing cabinets anymore?"

"Yeah, I'm waiting for Jackson to show up. He's so obsessed with being tidy; he'll clear it away in no time. As for why? Jackson wants paper copies of everything because he still thinks that computers are a phase people will grow out of."

Chloe wrinkled her nose, "Really?"

"No, but sometimes I do wonder."

"So, what happened?"

"No need to stand in the doorway, grab a seat." Chloe nodded, walked to his desk and settled into the chair opposite him. Allister leaned back in his own chair, "I think that we were broken into."

"Oh my God! Did they take anything?" Chloe asked, looking around. She looked confused as she saw several items you would expect to be stolen during a burglary.

"Nothing physical. They knew exactly what they were after. They hacked into my computer and downloaded almost everything on there."

"You got hacked?" she asked, sounding strangely excited by the notion.

"Errrm... sadly yes."

"Wow. That is virtually impossible to do. Your security is ridiculous."

"I know. I designed it." Allister eyed Chloe suspiciously. "I'm curious to find out how you know, though."

She looked sheepish for a moment before replying, "You are kind of a legend in the hacker community. The guy with an uncrackable computer."

"I see."

"Yeah. *AKRubies.* I realised it was you when I saw your gaming name on Facebook. There's even a competition to see who can do it."

Allister was annoyed at the information. He purposely avoided other hackers as it was more than just a hobby to him. Nor was he interested in bringing down society or businesses. He was involved in something far bigger than most hackers you found in these forums. The fact that they had made hacking him into a game irritated Allister greatly.

"Is there?" he asked. "Have you tried yourself?"

Chloe was clearly embarrassed and glanced at the floor. "Yeah..." she admitted. "But I didn't think I'd be able to do it. I was just curious if it was as good as everybody claimed."

"It's ok, I'm not mad or anything. To be honest, I would have done the same thing," he said with a smile, making a mental note to do a complete overhaul of his security in light of current events, and now this new information.

"I'm really sorry, though. It's not ok for me to do that. Especially after everything you've done to help. If there's anything I can do to make it up just say." She glanced around the room, "Like, I could tidy up those cabinets and papers. It shouldn't take more than a day or two."

"Nah, I'd hate to deprive Jackson of the pleasure." Allister thought for a moment then nodded to himself, "Actually, I think there might be something that you could do to help. See how good your hacking skills really are."

He could see her interest pique. It was clearly more than a hobby to her too. "Oh, yeah?"

"I've spent this morning searching for... some people. I've managed to track down most of them; do you think you can locate the last one?"

"I reckon," Chloe replied with a smile. Allister passed her his laptop, and she took it eagerly. "Who am I looking for?"

"I don't know."

She looked at him in disbelief. "You're kidding me, right? How am I supposed to find them if you don't even have a name?"

"I hope you don't normally give up this easily," Allister replied with a chuckle. Chloe responded by giving him the kind of unimpressed look only a teenager could master. "I can tell you what I do know. We're looking for a female of uncertain age and we don't have a name. But she disappeared after a particularly nasty attack between fifteen and sixteen years ago. Rumour has it that she was placed in a hospital. I'm presuming a psychiatric hospital. If she's still alive, then start there."

"Wouldn't it make more sense to search police records

relating to attacks at the time first?"

"Usually. But we believe that it was covered up due to the nature of the assault. We know that she was from Leeds, so look at local hospitals first, then work your way out to include any in the region. If she has any form of mental illness, then she'll be medicated, so that will give you a potential paper trail. Prescriptions need to be filled on a regular basis."

"Seriously? That's it? That's all you're giving me?"

"Go on, get started," he replied, flicking his hands toward her in a shooing motion. "It's ok, I have faith in you."

She pulled a face at him and got to work. Straight away, Allister was impressed at how fast she typed. Her fingers were almost a blur as they moved across the keyboard. She worked quickly, her blue eyes barely blinking as she stared at the screen.

Allister began to sort through the information he had downloaded from the police computers. He was still finding it difficult to believe that this file had just been sitting waiting for him to find. How did the mysterious Gates know he would go looking for this very list of people one day? He could ask, but he doubted he would get an answer.

"Shouldn't you be at school?" he asked eventually, just to break the silence.

"Shouldn't you be at work?" she replied without missing a beat.

He smiled at that, "Touché. I am serious, though. I don't want you getting into trouble."

"We've been given the afternoon off."

"Really?"

"Yep." Her eyes broke contact with the screen briefly to look at him. "A student committed suicide yesterday, so the school has closed for the afternoon as a mark of respect."

"Oh yes, Nicola," he said sadly.

"You've heard already?"

"I read something on the police database earlier," he replied, noting how quickly he lied to her.

"It's really sad, I guess. I mean, we were far from friends. Saying we hated each other wouldn't be strong enough to describe our relationship, either. But nobody should feel like suicide is the only option."

"You think she did? Commit suicide I mean?"

"Christ, Allister," Chloe said rolling her eyes. "Not you as well."

"I'm not the only person who thinks so?"

"No, you're not. Jade is convinced that the whole thing is a cover-up. She thinks somebody snuck into her room and killed her, then made it look like suicide."

"We could check the security cameras," Allister suggested.

Chloe shook her head, "I already tried last night to try to placate Jade. All the cameras in that wing were down at the time."

"That qualifies as suspicious."

"Not really. They were also down in the staff car park underneath the hospital too. It happens with those things. You know that."

Allister had to agree that often, especially in government-owned departments, CCTV was unreliable. Usually, they were out dated, damaged, or simply because somebody had neglected to turn them on. So, not working in a hospital shouldn't automatically point to foul play. But his instincts told him there was more to this.

"How did you even become friends with Jade, anyway?" he asked. "Wasn't she one of the girls who gave you a hard time?"

Chloe shrugged, "I'm still trying to figure that one out myself. She says that the only reason she was in Nicola's crowd was that it was better than being out of it. I think she's being genuine, though. She's actually really nice once you know her, and surprisingly funny."

"I remember. She seemed... lovely," Allister replied with as little sarcasm as he could manage. He continued looking at his own monitor as they worked, glad to be sharing the workload Jackson had passed onto him.

"Honestly, I think she only acts like that as a front," Chloe said with a laugh. "I have to say though, I think I'll definitely miss her when I leave."

Allister's head snapped up to look at her when he heard this, "You're leaving?"

"Shit," she muttered to herself. "Sorry, so not how I intended to tell you. My parents have agreed that I can finish school in Australia. All my acting up seems to have paid off; I guess. I go back on Monday."

"I guess that congratulations are in order. That's brilliant news!" he replied with more enthusiasm than he felt.

"You really think so?"

"Absolutely. I know how unhappy you are here, and it will be good for you to get away from everything that's been going on."

"I really think so too," she returned to her work, fingers

moving quickly again, "and I hope we'll be able to stay in touch."

"Of course, we will. The world's a much smaller place now. It's not the 80s anymore."

"Thank God. I'm glad I missed that one."

"Also, I think I've found my apprentice to pass on all my hacking skills to."

"I'm glad that you just said that," she replied, looking up at him with a smirk.

"Why?"

Chloe turned the laptop to face him, "Because I've found her, and she's not that far away."

Chapter Nine

Later in the evening, Jackson returned to the office to be greeted by the sight of paper littering the carpet. His gaze switched to the filing cabinets, all lying on the floor like fallen sentinels beside each other. The first thought he had was that Allister must be making some kind of point about his insistence on still using a physical filing system. But Allister had been so serious lately he doubted such a juvenile prank would have even crossed his mind.

Looking towards Allister's desk, he saw the other man working at his computer. In the glow of the office lights, he appeared tired and stressed. Two things Jackson could not remember thinking about his friend in a long time. Not since Ruby had passed away at least.

"What on earth happened?" he asked, pointing to the mess.

"We were broken into," Allister replied simply.

"Really? It doesn't look like they took anything."

"They were just after what was on my hard drive, it seems."

"Well, how did they get in? Did you forget to lock it again?"

Allister sighed and looked at Jackson in clear annoyance, "No, Jackson. I didn't. In fact, I remember you standing over me to make sure I locked it properly!"

"Did they force the door then?" He began to examine the door and its frame.

"It was still locked when I got here earlier. I opened the door and found the office like this."

Jackson's attention was drawn to the centre of the door. It looked odd. In a barely noticeable way, but it did look slightly different from the wood and glass surrounding it. As if it had been distorted somehow. Running a hand over the surface, he noticed it felt wrong too. Smooth, where the rest of the door was rough.

"Jackson?" Allister called, almost shouting. "Are you even listening to me?"

"Yes, sorry." He turned away from the door and regarded Allister. "What we appear to be looking at then, is somebody broke in, stole something from your computer, knocked over all of the filing cabinets, and locked the door on the way out?"

"As crazy as it sounds, that's what seems to have happened, yes."

"Unless..."

"Unless what?"

Jackson shook his head, "I'm not sure. When we were here yesterday, I had this intense feeling that we weren't alone. As though we were being watched."

"Watched?" Allister sounded sceptical. "By whom?"

"I don't know. Obviously, it's not possible. There's nowhere a person could hide in here without us seeing them. But I definitely had the feeling. I had it more than once when I was in Afghanistan." Jackson became self-conscious as he saw how Allister was watching him as if concerned for his sanity, so quickly chose to change the subject. "Couldn't you have at least tidied up?"

"You want to keep those things; you look after them,"

Allister replied, and then returned to what he was doing.

Jackson walked to his own desk and sat down. Opening a drawer, he took out the half-empty bottle of whiskey that was stored there. As he held it, he had second thoughts, so returned the bottle and closed the drawer.

"Any luck today?" Allister asked, pretending not to notice what had just happened.

"Not especially. I went to see that strange coffee shop owner, George. He ended up being more cryptic than helpful."

"How so?"

"Apparently, I need to consider who has the most to benefit from me changing the future, as well as the agenda of the person who is sending the messages."

"You might call that cryptic, but to me, it does make a lot of sense."

"I do see his point, but how was saving Lucy anything but a good thing?"

"I don't know, and hopefully that is all it will ever be. A good thing." Allister sat back in his chair, "Speaking of which; her attacker."

"What about him?"

"There is almost nothing about the guy anywhere online. I haven't even been able to find a name."

"That's unusual I assume?"

"Yes. Extremely. What I did find indicated he was wanted on at least two separate counts of sexual assault around London. However, that is all there is. No mention of any court appearances or jail time."

"So where has it all gone?"

"If I had to guess, I would say someone beat me to it and erased everything they could find."

"Who could do that?" Jackson asked.

"I can only suggest they would have to be a very talented hacker. Or a high-ranking person within the justice system."

"We have no way of finding him?"

Allister shook his head, "Very unlikely. He's clearly been keeping his head down since coming to Leeds. I can't find any reference of him. So, it's a dead end, for now, I'm afraid."

"Damn. That's very disappointing. I really hoped we could help get him caught. Make sure Lucy was definitely safe. I can't believe I tripped like that," Jackson said, his voice full of regret.

"On a better note, however," Allister continued, sensing that he should change the topic, "I've been able to find the names of everybody murdered by our mysterious killer in the 80s."

"Really? Didn't you say it would be highly unlikely?"

"I did, and in all honesty, it should have been. But it's the weirdest thing. Somebody had put everything we wanted into a file and left it for me to find."

"I don't follow."

"I discovered a file named *AL*. When I opened it, all the information we were after downloaded automatically onto my computer. The names and personal details of all seventeen victims killed over a two-year period."

"Somebody knew you were looking for them?" Jackson asked, clearly as confused as Allister.

"It gets stranger than that. The file was left on the police database in 1998."

"You mean..."

Allister nodded, "The file was left for me to find twenty years ago."

"It was definitely left for you? There's no chance it may have been a different Al?" Jackson asked, knowing the logical part of his brain was grasping at straws.

"It was protected by an encryption program very similar to one I designed myself. I'm one of the few people who could have easily cracked it."

"It just seems unlikely that somebody would know what you were looking for twenty years ago."

"More unlikely than receiving a newspaper report about Lucy being attacked? Or Jade being hit by a car? The day before either of them was actually reported? I think we just have to accept this is another strange thing in a week of strange things," Allister insisted. "Besides, I've already crosschecked the names on the list. All of them died or disappeared on the dates listed. Every one of them was attributed to natural causes, accidents or foul play by rival gangs."

"Seventeen you say?"

"Yeah. I have to be honest, it's more than I was expecting. It's a lot to cover up."

"Somehow they managed," Jackson replied. He leaned forward and his brow furrowed; his brain was working fast, trying to connect the dots. He could already feel the start of a headache coming on. "Is there anything to link them? Anything to suggest why they were targeted?"

"Nothing that I've been able to find. Some of them were pretty shady characters. One was a known drug trafficker, for example. Others though, they just appeared to be typical, everyday people. A bank worker, a waitress, a college student called Jenny, even a police officer. I found nothing on any of them that suggested they deserved to be killed in such a way."

"Does the file say anything about the real cause of death?"

"Exactly as Cole told you. Rapid ageing, cause unknown."

"What about the survivor? Anything on her?"

Allister smiled proudly, "Not in the file, though she was attacked after it was uploaded. However, Chloe visited earlier, and she was actually able to find her. Very quickly in fact. I think she's a bit of a computer prodigy. She picks things up fast and can really think outside the box when finding solutions."

Jackson considered telling him of George's warning about Chloe; that he should not trust her. But the time felt wrong, they needed to stay focused on what they were doing, and he doubted Allister would take kindly to criticism of his new friend. He rubbed his head, trying to ignore the dull ache forming there. Besides, could he even say she was not worthy of trust? Every time he had met her, his instincts told him she was a decent person. Also, it was as if he already knew her somehow, though he was certain they had never met before.

"That's positive news, at least," Jackson said instead. "What do we know?"

"The patient is listed as a Rachel Smith. Admitted to Wakefield Psychiatric Care Unit in 2009. Prior to that, she bounced around various hospitals and clinics."

"How did Chloe find her? Can we be certain she is the right person?"

"She discovered only one person admitted under strange circumstances in the time frame we suspected who was attacked in the West Yorkshire area. Rachel Smith just suddenly appeared on medical records nearly sixteen years ago. She has no family, no previous address, and no other online presence. Although fifteen years ago that would be normal since social media did not take off until a couple of years later. There is no National Insurance number or even a birth certificate. Until she was placed under medical care, she did not exist."

"It's definitely her, though?" Jackson pressed. "We can't afford to get this wrong."

Allister nodded, "I was able to access a previous doctor's assessment. She insists she's fifteen years younger than she appears, and she talks a lot about the girl with glowing eyes."

"I guess that confirms we have a match then."

"I'm certain of it," Allister agreed. "She also insists her name is not Rachel Smith, which seems obvious. But any mention of what her real name actually is has been removed from every record I can find."

"Can we go and see her?"

"I'm trying to arrange a visit for tomorrow morning, but it isn't easy. It's a secure unit, and if she has a fake name, I doubt they'll believe we are family, nor will they be keen to allow reporters in."

"Let me have a word with Lucy. Maybe she will be able to think of a legal way for us to see this Rachel Smith."

"Good idea."

"We have a person who seems to have disappeared from existence and another who has appeared from nowhere. What have we gotten into here, Al?" Jackson asked a headache in full bloom now.

"I wish I knew," Allister replied. His phone started ringing, and he reached for it, swiping to take the call. "Hello? What? Wait, slow down." He paused as he listened to a reply. Panic quickly showed in his eyes, "Ok, stay where you are." He ended the call and looked at Jackson, "We have to go, now!"

***

Chloe sat on her bed trying to finish a pile of homework. Her parents had gone to a work function at her dad's office, so she had been left home alone. There was some random emo band playing on the docking system, and her stalker seemed to be staying away. She had heard no whispering for a couple of nights now and was not sure if she should be happy or worried.

The homework frustrated her. Not because she was unable to do it, as a rule, she found most lessons far too easy, but tomorrow was hopefully to be her last day attending this school, so what was the point? But she also knew she would want an incident-free final day. The last thing she needed was to be called to Mr Howard's office before she was out of the god-awful place.

After finding Rachel Smith, Allister had spent time teaching Chloe how to use some pretty impressive hacking tools. She was correct about how much she could learn from him. After asking if he would allow her to try out the security on his desktop system, he quickly declined. The excuse was that he had confidential client information stored there and the need for data protection, though she suspected the real reason was more likely that she admitted to trying to hack him. *Not that I can blame him,* she thought.

Chloe had read the doctor's report that Allister had located, and she was left shaken, to say the least. What stood out was Rachel's statement claiming to be years younger than she appeared. After Michael Johnson had tried to attack her and was killed, she hacked into the coroner's office computers to see how he had died. Aside from the brutal wounds he had sustained, the autopsy also stated he appeared to have been dead for decades.

Just before Chloe had begun her homework, she again searched for the report. She found it with ease, although now it simply said that he had died from wounds consistent with a blunt weapon. She could not help but wonder if Rachel Smith, or whoever she was, had been a victim of her stalker. Could this be the fate that awaited her? To be aged by years, then locked away in some government facility like a lab rat? She shuddered at the thought of missing out on so much life in such a sad way.

The video chat app on her computer began to chime, and she saw that Jade was trying to contact her. Smiling, she clicked her mouse on the call accept icon.

"Hey, mate," Chloe said as Jade's face appeared on the monitor.

"Hey, bitch," Jade replied in a friendly tone.

"Oh, so I'm a bitch now?" she laughed.

"I figured you were due a promotion."

"Thanks, I think."

"Welcome. What are you doing anyways?"

"Homework."

"Fuck that, man. Come meet me."

"I wish, but I have conditions to fulfil before I go back to Oz, and being up to date on my schoolwork is one of them. I'm not allowed out the house until it's finished."

"Oh my God! Your parents are worse than prison guards."

Chloe laughed again, "They are not that bad!"

"Agree to disagree?"

"No."

"Come meet me. I'm bored!"

"I'm free the next couple of nights, ok? We'll meet up then I swear."

"We better."

"Promise."

"And I want free holidays to Australia," Jade added.

"I will see what I can do."

"Going to hold you to that. I'll see you at school tomorrow. Laters."

"Bye, mate," Chloe replied, just before the chat window closed.

The friendship with Jade still surprised her. Chloe made it clear when Jade had offered to walk her to her home, that she did not trust her. Despite the assertion, however, the trust had built quickly. She only wished that they had become friends two years ago. With a friend like Jade, things might be different now. Who knew really? Sadly, she could not go back in time.

She stood and crossed her room to fetch a textbook from the desk. As she passed the bedroom window, she froze. There was that feeling again, the feeling of being watched.

The curtains were open as it had only recently begun to grow dark, and the street lamps were yet to be illuminated. However, as she looked down to the road that ran past the front of her home, she could make out a figure in the twilight, watching her.

At first, she guessed it must be her stalker, not as absent as she had initially believed, though quickly realised this was not the silhouette of a girl, but the shape of a man, and a tall one. He did not attempt to conceal himself, just stood and watched. Chloe's heart skipped a beat as she felt, rather than saw, their eyes meet.

Backing away from the window, she could now feel her heart had recovered and resumed pounding in her chest. She realised that she had been right this morning; there was somebody following her. She cursed herself for not telling Allister today, feeling too self-conscious that he would think she was having some kind of emotional breakdown or just being overly paranoid.

Looking around for her phone, she spotted it lying on the desk across the room. Typical; the first time it was not practically glued to her hand.

"Fuck," she whispered to herself. There was no option but to pass the window again to reach it. Not something to be relished. Taking a deep breath, she ran the short distance. As she passed the window again, a quick glance down to the road was enough to confirm he was still there, still watching.

Picking up the phone, Chloe pressed herself against the wall and searched for Allister's number. She guessed she should really call the police, but she knew that Allister would come fast, and without several questions. She pressed dial.

The phone rang, and he answered almost immediately.

"Hello, Allister, it's Chloe. I need your help." She paused as he responded. "There's a man outside. He's watching the house. I'm here on my own and I'm scared." She waited as he replied again. "Ok, I'll stay in the house. Thanks, Allister!"

After ending the call, she looked towards her desk. Sitting there discarded was an old stuffed kangaroo toy. It was chewed in places and slightly threadbare. *Kanga.* She picked him up and held him to her chest. Sliding down the wall to sit on the floor, she drew her legs up to her chest so she could rest her chin on her knees. For the first time, she found herself wishing that the stalker girl would come and help her.

***

Allister pushed the hire car faster than the allotted speed limit. He stared through the windscreen, trying to keep the fears at bay. He did not know what was happening at Chloe's house, but he knew she had sounded terrified on the phone which in turn scared him. The satnav on the dashboard gave directions to the address Chloe had provided after he agreed to take her case.

Jackson sat silently in the passenger seat, which Allister appreciated immensely. The last thing he needed right now was to be talking, and his friend had said nothing since he explained what was going on, not even a suggestion of calling the police. Instead, he looked as though he was eager to get there and do something. Allister guessed he was hoping to make amends for Lucy's attacker getting away on his watch.

"We're almost there," Allister announced as he turned a corner, following the automated directions, the sound of squealing tyres almost drowning out the electronic voice.

Jackson nodded. "As soon as we stop, you go check on Chloe, I will confront whoever is hanging around," he replied.

"Are you sure you don't need back up?"

"No offence, Al, but I can handle things better on my own."

Allister accepted that was most likely true. As much as it

hurt his pride to admit it, he had always been the peacemaker, while Jackson was the fighter. He knew deep down he would just be in the way if the confrontation turned physical.

The car's headlights illuminated a figure standing by the side of the road. As soon as the car screeched to a halt, the figure took off running in the opposite direction. Jackson pushed open the passenger door and immediately jumped out to give chase.

Allister switched off the engine and then stepped out of the car. After closing and locking the door, he crossed the road and opened the gate to Chloe's yard. As he walked down the path toward the front door, it was suddenly pulled open and Chloe rushed out to grab him in a tight hug. Her body shook as she sobbed against his chest.

He listened to her cry, but said nothing, choosing to let her get it out of her system. He felt lost for words as he was taken aback by her reaction to what had happened. She had always seemed to keep everything under control, acting as though she could cope with whatever fate sent her way, and then some. But now, he felt as though for the first time; he was seeing how deep the cracks he had glimpsed in the photo her mother had posted, truly ran. He was beginning to doubt she could honestly cope with much more, whatever she insisted to the contrary.

The sound of footsteps approaching along the pavement behind them caused Chloe to tense up against him.

"It's ok," he whispered in an assuring tone, "that'll just be Jackson coming back. You're safe now."

"He disappeared down some back alley and over a fence before I could catch up with him," Jackson announced, reaching them. "I doubt he'll be back tonight, anyway."

"Thank you, Jackson!" Chloe said, breaking away from Allister and hugging him instead.

"Errrrm... you're welcome," Jackson replied, looking uncomfortable, but also confused by her actions.

"Did you manage to get a look at him at all?" Allister asked.

Jackson, still looking awkward, eased Chloe away, so she was standing sheepishly between them. "No, I only saw him briefly from behind, then he was over the fence and gone by the time I had climbed it."

"Damn it." He looked towards Chloe, "Did you see his face at all?"

She shook her head in reply, "No, sorry. He stayed out of the light. Also, I was a little busy being scared and wondering if I should hide under my bed."

"You wanted to hide under your bed?" Jackson asked.

"Yeah, so?"

"Nothing, I just didn't realise that people did that in real life."

She shrugged, "I guess I didn't get that copy of the script."

Allister smiled slightly as he saw some of her attitude and spark coming back. "Do you know when your parents will be back?" he asked.

"Not for a couple of hours at least I think."

"Do you want to call the police?"

She shook her head emphatically, "No way. If they think I'm not safe, they won't let me out of their sight, let alone go home to Australia!"

"I'll ring them," Jackson said. "I'll tell the police I saw

somebody suspicious hanging around the area. I'm practically on first name terms with most of them now, anyway."

"Good idea," Allister agreed. "Try not to get yourself arrested this time, though."

Jackson smiled at the joke, "I won't. I'll also drive around the area, see if he's still about."

"Thank you again, Jackson," Chloe said. She looked at Allister, "Can you stay here? At least until my parents are almost home?"

"If you need me to, of course I will," Allister replied. He handed the keys to Jackson, "Stay safe, mate."

"I always do," Jackson replied, then turned and walked away, taking his phone from his jacket.

Chloe walked to her front door and indicated for Allister to follow. As he entered the living room, he was taken aback by what he saw. Everything from the decor to the electrical goods indicated that her family was more than a little well off. He was secretly pleased Jackson had not seen this, as he would certainly wonder why they were not being paid for helping her.

She sat on a sofa while Allister chose a seat opposite her, keen to keep distance between them. She pulled her legs under herself then picked up an old stuffed animal that she subconsciously held against her as she looked up at the ceiling.

"So that would be Kanga, I take it," he asked, indicating the toy.

She looked down as if noticing it for the first time and looked briefly embarrassed. "Yeah," was all she said.

"How are you feeling now?"

"Better, I guess," Chloe replied, then sighed heavily. "Still more than a little shaken, though."

"I'm not surprised. I'm sure on top of everything else going on at the moment, it was a lot of added stress to process."

"Yeah, you could say that. Thank you for getting here so fast."

"Don't mention it. Anytime you need us, we'll be here."

She sniffed, her eyes filling with tears, "I can't believe how lucky I am that you guys are helping me like this. Especially Jackson."

"Why would you be surprised by Jackson?"

"He's only met me twice, but he's out there searching for that guy who was here, risking his life for me. I've done nothing to earn it."

"You don't need to earn our help, Chloe. Jackson thinks you're worth helping, and so do I."

"Are you sure I'll be ok?" she asked in a small voice. She had never looked so fragile.

"Yes!" Allister said firmly. He looked her straight in the eyes, "Whatever happens next, Jackson and I will not let anything bad happen to you. I promise you that."

***

Letting the aged remains of her latest victim fall to the ground, the girl sighed in relief. Draining people was a temporary reprieve from the pain of the virus that still spread inside, but it helped her to focus once more. Or it would for the few hours it took for the virus to take hold again, and she would need to search for somebody else. A time that was growing shorter after each kill.

ECHO

Looking down at the body, she contemplated whom she had ended. His name had been Aiden Wallace. Not only a case of being in the wrong place at the wrong time but also that he was the wrong kind of person. He had been another police officer and another rotten one at that. Not that anybody knew or was ever likely to have found out, so he would almost certainly never have been punished for his crimes. Probably anyway. Sadly, for him, she was unable to see more than a few days into his future, but she had witnessed his past all too easily.

The girl took a moment to examine her surroundings. She had been here many times over the last thirty years or so. Stood in this exact spot more often than she could remember. Now she was just standing quietly on an empty road lined on both sides with orange street lamps. On the left was a sign announcing that you were leaving Leeds. It irritated her greatly. Yeah, as if she could just walk past it and never look back. Not likely, and she had tried more than once.

The sound of an approaching car could be heard heading toward Leeds. She walked into the middle of the road and waited. Raising her hand, she dimmed the street lights on her side of the sign, unable to influence those beyond. They faded in colour until each went out, leaving the surrounding area in relative darkness. As headlights appeared around a distant corner, she turned herself invisible while remaining in the centre of the road.

The car drew closer and began to slow as it neared the transparent barrier that held her here. When it was close to the sign, it pulled to the side of the road and came to a stop. The engine was turned off and her surroundings returned to near silence. The girl could just make out the driver sitting behind the steering wheel.

After what felt like several long seconds had passed, the driver opened his door and stepped into the evening air. There was a thud as he closed the door, made louder in the quiet. He continued forward on foot in her direction, footfalls echoing around him. He was tall and still incredibly skinny, dressed in a perfectly fitted dark grey suit that looked as though it had cost more than most people earned in a month. A black shirt and tie finished the outfit. He looked to be in his late forties, flecks of grey beginning to spread throughout his red hair. He had aged in the twenty years since she had last seen him, but God, he still looked good.

Stopping on the opposite side of the sign, keeping himself outside of the city's border, he looked directly at her. This was something he had rarely done, yet it still gave her chills, even after all this time.

"Hello, Alice," he said in that soft voice he used. His gaze flicked down toward the floor where she knew it would most probably remain. The sound of his voice drew a pang of regret from deep inside her, and she knew it had nothing to do with the virus he had infected her with.

"You can still see me then, Gates," she replied.

"As I told you then, I'll always see you."

Thirty-two years ago, that line had stolen her heart, or whatever it was she had now. It was when she knew she had fallen for him. A lot had happened in the intervening years, but it still had an effect on her, if not as fully as it once did.

Gates indicated the body a short distance away from her, "You've killed somebody."

"It was unfortunate but necessary. Just like the three others I've been forced to kill since you infected me with your virus."

"That was not my intention," he replied. Subconsciously he began to click the fingers of his left hand. It was a nervous habit he always displayed which she had once found endearing. She was the first person to realise that he was on the autistic spectrum when they met. He was just eighteen at the time and misunderstood by many people around him. But she always saw there was so much more to the quiet boy.

"I knew that one day you would inevitably hack Allister's computer to find out where the two of us had disappeared to," Gates continued. "It was the only way I could think of to get your attention." He smiled, "It's not as though you have a mobile phone I can call."

"Not the time for jokes, Gates," Alice replied, trying to stay focused. She could already feel the pain returning. "So, you infected me with a virus that makes me feel like I'm being eaten from the inside just to get me here?"

"I didn't want it to be like this. We need to talk, and it's just been so long since I've seen you. You stopped coming to meet me here."

That was true. Ever since their last argument, she could not face being here again. Not just because it hurt to see him, but because the pain was even greater when she had to watch him drive away yet again. To know that she could not set one foot past that damn sign to follow him. Being reminded she was trapped within the borders of this city that she loathed so much.

"Can you blame me?" Alice asked, her voice held a note of ice and her eyes shone red briefly. "You told me you couldn't love me anymore."

"No, I said it was becoming harder to love who you were becoming!" he defended himself.

"It's the same thing."

His eyes flicked briefly to meet hers before he dropped his gaze to the floor again. "It isn't. I didn't stop loving you, Alice. I still haven't."

The words pushed her off balance, but she recovered quickly, "Then why did the two of you leave me? Abandon me and go somewhere you knew I couldn't?"

"You killed all those people. I couldn't watch you do that anymore. It wasn't right."

"You sound like him!" she hissed.

Gates cocked his head to the side, "Nobody deserved what you did to them. It's not for you to decide who is guilty and innocent."

"As I always told him, nobody is innocent, Gates. You have no idea what they did, or what they were going to do. I did the world a favour. You talk about what people deserve; I did not deserve to be abandoned by the only people I trusted."

"You tried to kill his son!" he all but shouted.

Alice shrank back from this, in part from the anger, which Gates rarely exhibited, but also from the memory. She had not exactly forgotten what she had attempted to do, but she had worked hard over the decades to block it out. It was one of the few things she still regretted.

"I know," she said quietly.

"I still tried to protect you, even then. I promised to find a way to make things right between the two of you."

She snorted, "You also promised to find a way to get me home, to get me away from this place, and yet, here I am."

"We are getting nowhere talking about the past," Gates

said with a finality she was not used to hearing from him. He seemed to have finally found the voice she had tried to encourage.

"Then why did you want me here?"

He reached into his jacket pocket and pulled out a memory stick, very similar to the one she had seen Allister take from his desk. Gates held it toward her.

"First, a goodwill gesture," he said.

Alice eyed it suspiciously, "What is it?"

"The anti-virus. If you download the code stored on here, it will destroy the virus and permanently remove the infection. I will give this to you, but I need you to agree to listen to me."

"How do I know it won't kill me?"

"You know that I would never do that."

"There are a lot of things I thought you'd never do. Like giving me a virus in the first place."

He sighed sadly, "Assuming you can even be killed, if it was my intention, I could have set such a trap on Allister's hard drive for you to download."

Alice conceded he had had the opportunity to finish her if that was his intent. Looking at the cure, she wondered what strings were attached to it. He had already told her there was something to say, and he expected her to listen. She reached out with her mind to see if she could simply take it from him, but as expected, the influence of her abilities also ended at the border. She was confined here, Leeds was her prison, and that damn sign was her warden.

"Fine," she said at last. "I'll listen."

Gates smiled and tossed the stick towards her. As soon as

it had passed the border, she 'caught' it in mid-air. Levitating it in front of her, she carefully examined the content. It appeared to be what he had said it would be and nothing more. Alice looked at him and sensed no malicious intent. Though even if he had stood on her side of the city limits, she would get the same reading. He had been the only person whose past and future she had never been able to see. It was one of the many things that made him different to almost everybody else she had ever met, and why she had never seen his betrayal coming.

Choosing to trust him this time, she began absorbing the content of the memory stick. The effect was immediate, and she could already feel herself getting stronger and more like her old self. She searched her 'body' and could find no sign of the virus. By all accounts, she appeared to be cured.

Alice looked to Gates, "Out with it then, what did you get me here to discuss?"

"I know what you're planning," he said simply.

"Do you?"

"Yes, and you can't!"

"I think you mean that I shouldn't because we both know that I can."

"You shouldn't. Whatever you believe, she's a fifteen-year-old girl; she has done nothing to deserve to die."

As she looked at him, she made her eyes glow a soft green, which had always been his favourite colour. "What about me, though? What happens to me if I don't go through with this? Have you thought about that?" she asked. He did not answer, his clicking fingers the only sound in the night. "If she lives, then I'm as good as dead. Or possibly worse than dead if I go back *there*."

"You know that's not true."

"Ah yes, as the old man used to be so fond of saying, it's all perspective, isn't it? So, tell me, Gates, what does happen to me afterwards?"

"I don't know," he admitted, his whisper barely audible.

"So, you think that I should chance it? Risk my entire existence?" she looked away. "Risk us, what we had?" she added quietly.

"It's not right," Gates replied sadly.

She walked towards him, then stopped where she knew the border that kept her there began. She raised her hand and placed it against the invisible barrier. It was hard, smooth and ice cold. She lowered her own gaze to the road between them.

"I will think about it," she said softly.

Gates raised his own hand and held his palm millimetres from hers, but still safe from being touched, "Thank you, Alice."

"You do remember that my name isn't even Alice, don't you? Any more than yours is Gates."

"Yes, you know I do."

Alice took several steps backwards and away from him, "I have to go now, please stop coming here, I won't be returning." She turned her back to him and began to walk toward the lights of the city.

Gates watched her go and then sighed, "I know you won't."

Chapter Ten

The car came to a stop in the grounds of the Wakefield Psychiatric Care Unit. Jackson and Allister examined the large building from their seats. Jackson was not sure why, but he had expected it to be some kind of derelict dump with crumbling walls and boarded-up windows, but to his surprise it looked... nice. Better than nice in fact. Instead, it was a modern construction, surrounded by well-maintained gardens.

After a phone call to Lucy, they were advised that everybody was entitled to legal representation, even if they were considered to be mentally impaired. Off the record, she suggested informing the hospital that it had come to their attention Rachel Smith did not have such representation. As a result, they would be visiting to ensure all her lawful needs were being met. The irony of having agreed to impersonate a lawyer had not been lost on Jackson.

Allister had compiled and sent the relevant email the previous night, indicating that if they were denied access to Rachel, then they would have no choice but to take the matter to court. They were rewarded with a reply instructing them that a meeting with Rachel had been arranged for eight thirty this morning. It all seemed to be finally going their way for once.

"Ready to do this?" Jackson asked.

"As ready as I'll ever be," Allister replied with a shrug.

They exited the car and headed toward the main entrance. The door was secured with an electronic lock, but after a brief conversation with a security guard through an intercom connected to the side of the entrance, the door was unlocked and they were allowed to step inside.

The interior of the building was as impressive as the exterior. Bright and clean, with a large reception area and several orderlies and nurses striding about the corridors, some with patients and others presumably rushing to see somebody or be somewhere. It all looked like an extremely professional and well-run establishment.

"I expected something more, I don't know, dark and dingy," Allister whispered.

"You're not alone," Jackson replied, glad he was not the only person making prejudgements.

The reception desk was in the centre of the room and was small but welcoming. It was clearly designed to make visitors feel comfortable as they approached it. When they reached the desk, Jackson smiled to the friendly looking member of staff seated on the opposite side.

She smiled back. "Good morning and welcome to Wakefield Psychiatric Care Unit. How can I assist you?"

"Hi there," Jackson replied. "I am Steven Samuels and this is my colleague, Peter Croft. We represent Camball and Blackwell law firm. We are here for a meeting with Rachel Smith."

Without another word, the receptionist began to check her appointments on the computer. As well as the email, Allister had also put together fake IDs for each of them and a website. Jackson had felt it was too risky to use the name of a real firm. If anybody googled their supposed employers, they would find a link to the website. It would not stand up to intense scrutiny, but Allister assured him it should pass a cursory glance.

"Ah, yes," she replied. "Doctor Beeston has been advised of your arrival, and she should be here shortly."

"Thank you very much," Allister replied. They stepped away from the desk, and he turned to Jackson. "How do we get rid of the doctor?" he whispered.

"Leave that with me," Jackson whispered back. "I'll think of something."

"Mister Samuels and Mister Croft, I presume?" a voice asked from behind them.

They turned to see a woman in her early fifties walking toward them. She wore a white doctor's coat and gold-rimmed glasses. Her hair was cut very short, which made her look just like their old headmistress. She had a pleasant smile and a friendly demeanour, again being a contrast to what Jackson had expected. He decided he needed to stop basing opinions on movies that Allister insisted he watch.

"That's correct," Jackson answered, shaking the offered hand.

"Doctor Beeston."

"I had guessed."

Beeston looked slightly taken aback by his directness, but recovered quickly, "I understand that you are here to see Rachel Smith?"

"We are. Thank you for arranging to see us so soon. We would like to get things squared away as quickly as possible." He looked at her with a serious expression, "For Rachel's benefit."

"Of course, I fully understand. Though I must say, I was surprised when I read your email. She hasn't had any visitors since she was admitted."

"This is just a preliminary visit. To ensure she is getting what she needs. From a legal representation point of view."

"I appreciate that," Beeston said with a nod. "Follow me; her room is just this way."

As the Doctor led them through a maze of corridors, each identical to the last, Jackson could not help but reflect on how well this was going. He had initially been concerned that they would be caught in their lie, but so far, the staff had been more than willing to help. Allister had been right, impersonating a lawyer got results, even if it was morally questionable.

They stopped outside of a white door that was identical to every other door they had passed. "She's just inside," Beeston announced. "Before we go in, however, I would just like to remind you again, that she might not respond to any questions you ask her since she is unaccustomed to visitors. These days she mostly sits quietly in her room. We are no longer sure how much she is even aware of anymore."

Jackson nodded and then pointed to a file under his arm, "We understand. But we would still like to try. Just so we will be able to fill out the relevant paperwork. Dot the i's and cross the t's if you will."

With that, Beeston pushed open the door to a small room. It was, like everywhere else they had seen in the clinic, immaculate and sanitary. A single sized bed ran along the length of one wall, with a table, chair, chest of drawers and wardrobe occupying the rest of the room. Sitting on the bed was a lady who looked to be in her mid-forties. She wore a dressing gown, and she was staring blankly at a television on the table which remained switched off.

"Rachel?" Beeston said in a soft voice. "These gentlemen are Steven and Peter. They are lawyers who are here to check up on your legal day-to-day needs." Rachel continued to stare and did not respond. "It'll just be a quick chat if that's ok. Rachel?" There was still no response. The doctor turned to Jackson and Allister, "I'm really sorry, but I'm afraid she hasn't said a word in over a year."

"Could we possibly talk to her in private?" Jackson asked. "Perhaps she will respond if she doesn't feel as though she is being assessed."

The doctor looked uncertain, "I don't know if I should leave her alone."

"We just need to make an unbiased assessment of our client," Allister replied. "We have to confirm she is unwilling to speak as part of her condition. You being here may be making her reluctant to engage."

Jackson was immediately concerned that Allister may have pushed the issue too far. Beeston now looked more hesitant, even a little concerned. But clearly, the worry of legal action being taken against the clinic on her watch was enough to sway those worries. She finally nodded her consent.

"Very well," she replied stiffly. "You have ten minutes." She looked at her patient, "Rachel, I'm going to leave you to chat with these men, ok? I'll just be right outside if you need me." She left, and the door clicked into place behind her.

As soon as she was gone, Jackson crouched in front of Rachel so that they were eye level, and smiled, "Hello, Rachel. I'm Jackson. I was hoping I could ask you some questions." There was again no response. "We know how you ended up here and we believe you. We know about the girl with the glowing eyes." Still nothing. "Can you tell us anything about her?"

"I don't think that we are going to get a response, Jackson," Allister said. "I'm not sure there is even anybody in there anymore."

Standing, Jackson turned to face him, "I think you're right, Al. We should probably go." They began to walk the short distance to the door.

"Allister?" Rachel suddenly said, looking at them with very clear eyes. "Oh my God, is that really you?"

Allister turned and stepped forward, examining her closely. His face was a mixture of confusion and shock and then slowly recognition dawned. He gasped and had to steady himself against the chair.

"Ruby?" he asked.

***

Chloe stood on her own outside the school waiting for Jade to arrive. After the events of the previous evening, she had insisted on her mother driving her there this morning. Her mum was curious as to why she did not get the bus like every other day, but Chloe told her she wanted to spend as much time together as they could before she left for Australia on Monday. This was though, to be fair, at least half true. She was very aware of how little time they had left together.

Allister had stayed with her the previous evening for about an hour before Jackson returned to pick him up. Jackson filled them in by saying the police were in the area and looking for whoever she had seen from the window. After saying their goodbyes they left and as soon as she was alone once more, she felt sad. Clearly, any hopes she had held for a quiet last few nights before she left, had been crushed by the creepy guy outside her window.

Looking down the road again for Jade, she spotted him. He was leaning casually against a lamppost, eyes watching her. He was too far away to make out many of his features, but she could tell that he was tall, skinny and appeared to have a red birthmark on the left side of his face.

"Hey, man," Jade said, suddenly appearing behind her.

Chloe literally jumped in surprise. "What the fuck, Jade?" she snapped, more harshly than she would have liked. "Don't do that!"

"Wow, somebody needs to go back to bed and wake up again. What is wrong with you?"

Still feeling shaken, she looked around and noticed the man was still there, focused on the two of them now. "That guy over there, I think he's been following me."

Jade followed her gaze, "Him there? The trampy looking bloke?"

"Yeah, that one."

"Are you sure that he's actually following you, and not a random perv who hangs out near schools?"

"I'm positive. I saw him last night too. He was standing outside my house."

"For real?" Jade looked shocked and then annoyed. "I'll deal with this." To Chloe's horror, she began striding with determination directly toward him.

"Jade, wait. Don't..." Chloe tried, but her friend was clearly not going to listen to reason.

"Oi, weirdo!" Jade shouted as she approached. "Have you

been following my mate?"

He slowly straightened and tilted his head slightly as he observed Jade getting closer, almost as if she was an object instead of a person. However, as he realised that her shouting was beginning to draw attention to him, he took one last look at Chloe, turned, and began to walk away quickly.

"Hey! Don't you dare run away from me! I want a fucking word with you!"

Chloe was quickly becoming worried about Jade's safety but was relieved when she saw her turn and begin heading back. She could not help but think Jade was crazy, but at least she was crazy and on her side now. *How have I gotten through the last eighteen months without this weirdly amazing girl?*

"That got rid of him," Jade said with a grin when she returned.

Chloe grabbed and hugged her, "Oh my God, you are so crazy. You should not have done that, but thank you so much."

"It's what friends do. Are you sure you don't know him? Because he was looking at you as though he knew exactly who you were."

"I swear, until last night, I've never seen him before in my life." She let go of Jade reluctantly and looked back down the road to where he had disappeared. "It's all too weird for words."

"That guy?"

"This entire week. It's almost as though the world has decided to send every nutcase out there my way."

Jade looked momentarily deep in thought, "Do you think he may have had something to do with Nicola being murdered?"

Chloe sighed and placed a comforting hand on Jade's arm. "Mate, Nicola killed herself," she said as gently as she could.

"I know that she didn't. She wouldn't have. I definitely think he could be connected in some way."

"What are you thinking about doing?"

"I'm going to call the police at break time. I got a good look at him. I reckon he would be easy to spot."

"I did notice that he had some kind of red birthmark on his face."

"Yeah, and that's not all I noticed, either," she looked Chloe straight in the eye. "He stank. I mean, he really, really smelt bad."

"Like sweat or something?" Chloe asked, wrinkling her nose.

"No, it was worse than that. He smelt like sour milk."

***

Allister felt as if all the air had been knocked out of his body. It could not be possible that this woman, this lady who looked to be in her mid-40s, was his dead twin sister. But when he looked into her eyes and examined her face, the truth was undeniable. It was Ruby. Which could only mean that a large part of the last fifteen years of his life, had been nothing but a lie.

His parents must have known, and he now understood their insistence on a closed casket. One that he hoped had in fact been empty. Then for whatever twisted reasoning, they had presumably shoved her in here, or at least a place very much like it, and thrown away the key. He just could not think of any conceivable reason why.

The silence began to stretch as he struggled to think of what to say to her. In the end, he knew there was only one response, and he wrapped his arms around his long-lost sister and hugged her as they both broke down in tears.

"Al," Jackson began as diplomatically as he could, "we don't have long here, mate."

Allister let go of Ruby and sat down on the bed next to her, still feeling dazed. He took her hand. "I don't believe it. Rube, what are you even doing here?" he asked. "I thought... Mum and Dad told me you had died!"

A dark shadow crossed her face at the mention of their parents. "I bet they did," she said coldly. "Our loving father certainly told me I was dead to him when he sent me away."

"But how? What happened to you?"

"It's a very long story, Ally. I wouldn't know where to start."

"Maybe start at the beginning, Miss Kelwick," Jackson suggested. "How did you end up being prematurely aged?"

Ruby looked at Jackson with the sly smile Allister remembered so well, especially when aimed at his friends. "Jesus Christ, Jackson, you haven't changed. Still as direct as ever. Also, I'm the same age as you so cut the Miss Kelwick crap and call me Ruby!"

"Sorry," Jackson replied, turning visibly red.

"As for your question, it started when I met a girl called Alice." She looked at her brother, "Do you remember her?"

"Alice?" Allister thought for a moment. "I don't think so."

"You only met her a couple of times. She was about our age and beautiful. Long blonde hair, a sweet smile and the strangest eyes I have ever seen. Some days they were green, other days blue. I swear, once when she was angry, they were red."

"The girl with the glowing eyes," Jackson said.

"That's her. As for Allister not remembering her, well, she was not exactly his type." She looked at him and smiled again, "You might have had Mum and Dad fooled, but it was always obvious to me you liked guys."

"Well, they know now," Allister replied.

"I can only imagine how they took it, too," she chuckled, but there was very little humour behind it.

"You were telling us about Alice?" Jackson interrupted, as he attempted to keep them on topic with the short amount of time they had remaining.

"Of course. Well, you may not remember her, but she certainly knew who you were. Always wanted to know where you were, what you were doing and if you had mentioned her. Sometimes I wondered if the only reason she had befriended me at all, was so that she could see you."

"It's so strange that I don't recall her at all, though." Allister looked at Jackson, "Do you?"

Before Jackson could reply Ruby spoke again, "For some reason, she wanted to avoid Jackson like the plague. If she knew he was going to be somewhere, she would refuse to go or insist on us going somewhere else. Though she would never say why. Just always wanted to stay away if she knew he was nearby."

"Like most girls when I was fourteen," Jackson muttered to himself dryly.

"Did she attack you, Rube?" Allister asked, squeezing her

hand gently.

"No, no. Nothing like that. It was my fault really; I guess," Ruby continued. "Alice wasn't at all like most teenage girls. She hated touching and avoided every sort of physical contact. She wouldn't hug or hold hands. Always kept me at arm's length. But I was besotted with her. I just hoped she was playing hard to get. One day we were standing outside talking, and I took a risk. I leaned in and kissed her." Her eyes began to water at the memory.

"Doesn't like touching?" Jackson muttered to himself. Allister waited a moment to see if he would continue, but he seemed lost in thought.

"What happened next?" Allister asked his sister.

"I'm not sure. I just remember this white-hot pain rush through me. Like every cell in my body was being electrocuted at the same time. I was lying on the floor and when I could open my own eyes enough to look at Alice again, her eyes had turned black and she looked terrified. I honestly don't think it was her intention to hurt me." She wiped a tear away from her cheek with her free hand, "She asked if I was alive and seemed surprised, although relieved when she realised that I was. Alice ran to fetch help and then disappeared. Literally, right in front of my eyes she just vanished. I know it sounds crazy, and I was in a lot of pain at the time, but it's what I saw."

"After the last few days I've had, Sis, I have no trouble believing you."

"So, is that when you started to grow older?" Jackson enquired, returning to the conversation. "After the kiss?"

"I guess so," Ruby replied. "They first noticed it when I was in the ambulance. By the time Dad saw me, I looked thirty. Fortunately, that seemed to be as old as I was going to get for the time being. I was terrified I was going to go straight to old age and die." She shrugged, "I've often wished that I had."

"I'm glad that you didn't," Allister said firmly, then asked, "What did Dad say?"

"He wanted to know exactly what happened, and I told him the truth. He got angry and told me that Alice was clearly the devil, and I had been punished for giving in to sin. Just because I kissed a girl. He said I was dead to him, and he just walked away. It was the last time I ever saw him."

"Just wait until I get my hands on him," Allister almost growled. "Did you ever see Alice again?"

"At first. She somehow found out which hospital I was in and every so often would just turn up in my room. I was scared in the beginning, but she seemed so sad. I know she felt guilty for what happened to me, so she stopped by every few months for the first five years. But she never seemed to be getting any older, and that always surprised me."

"Have you seen her recently?" Jackson asked.

Ruby shook her head slowly, "Not for a long time. According to a previous doctor, some charity known as the Gates Foundation heard about my case and moved me here. They said I would be better off outside of the Leeds area. But Alice has not visited since I moved here." She turned to Allister, "Why all the interest in her?"

"It would seem that she has taken to terrorising another girl, and by the look of it, all unprovoked. We are looking into different angles to see if we can spot a weakness, something we might be able to use against her."

"She mentioned some guy who hurt her once. Just the thought of him seemed to cause her physical pain, but she never gave me any details. Not sure if that's a weakness, though." Ruby thought for a moment, "Did you say she's terrorising somebody now? That really doesn't sound like Alice. She always seemed kind and sweet, even a little lonely. To me anyway." She sighed, "I wish I could be more help."

"You've been plenty of help, Rube." He checked his watch and saw the ten minutes were almost up, "We have to go, but trust me, now that I know where you are, I will get you out of here."

She squeezed his hand, "I know you will. But for now, please don't tell them that I've been talking. I need them to believe I'm still taking their disgusting pills."

The door creaked open behind them and Ruby immediately returned to staring into space, almost as if it were a mask she could put on at will. Doctor Beeston entered the room and looked from Ruby to Jackson.

"Any response?" she asked.

"Nothing," Jackson replied, the lie coming easily. "You were right."

"I wish that I could tell you I'm surprised, but as I said, she hasn't spoken for a very long time now. I'm not sure if we'll ever get her back."

From the corner of his eye, Jackson saw Allister's jaw begin to twitch, and concerned he was about to say something they would regret, he quickly responded, "We will report back to our office and let you know if there's anything else we require."

"I look forward to it," Beeston said, her expression clearly stating the opposite. As she showed Jackson and Allister out of Ruby's room, she closed the door behind them, "I do wish your trip had not been a waste of time."

"We got some of the information we needed, so it wasn't a complete waste. Thank you for your help, Doctor," Allister replied with as much sincerity he could manage.

***

After the bell for morning break sounded, Jade headed straight from History toward the girls' restroom. She had promised Chloe she would meet with her, but she intended to call the police first, and knew her friend would try to talk her out of it. It was nice that Chloe showed so much concern for her, but she still liked to do things her way.

As Jade walked down the hallways, she purposely ignored everybody she passed. She had friends, but none of them was particularly close. With Nicola gone and Danielle still away from school with an injured eye, she was enjoying not having to play the role of school bitch. Befriending Chloe was really having some positive influence on her, and she had to admit she kind of enjoyed it.

Pushing open the door to the restroom, Jade stepped inside. Two small groups of girls were already in there, talking and fixing their hair and make-up. As soon as they saw Jade arrive all chatter stopped and silence filled the room. The other girls watched her warily as if they were afraid to be in her presence. Jade was not sure if she should feel sorry for them, or herself.

Taking her phone from her bag, she looked around the room. "I need to make a private phone call," she announced. There was no response. "Fuck off then!"

Without a word of protest both groups of girls gathered up their belongings and quickly filed out through the door. Yes, she was trying to be a nicer person but had to admit it felt good that her reputation still seemed to stand even when she was alone.

Using a fingerprint to unlock the phone, she began to search the internet to find the non-emergency number for the police. She stopped suddenly and cocked her head to one side. What was that whispering she could hear?

"Hey! If there's still somebody in here, you better get out now, or I'm not going to be happy, man!" she called.

Walking along the row of cubicles and pushing each one open, she found them all empty. Shaking her head in confusion, she glanced around the restroom, only to confirm that she was definitely the only one in there. She returned to her phone, found the number she was looking for and tapped it to start dialling.

The whispering returned and her phone shut down; the screen turning entirely blank. A moment later, the lights in the room flickered as one, then switched off, plunging the room into near darkness. All that remained was the meagre sunlight allowed through a small frosted glass window near the ceiling. She looked around at everything now obscured by shadow.

"What the hell is this?" Jade asked, more in frustration than concern. "If someone is messing about, I'm warning you now, man. I'm not in the mood!"

"Hello, Jade," a voice said from behind her.

Jade spun around, hands clenched into fists and ready for a fight. She stopped as she was confronted with a girl who appeared to be slightly smaller than herself, and possibly about the same age, though she could not be sure. The poor lighting meant she could not make out the girl's features. Jade tried to convince herself that the faint blue that seemed to glow in the girl's eyes was in her imagination. She jumped a little as purple light suddenly threaded through the girl's hair.

"Who are you?" Jade demanded, her voice sounding more shaken than she would have preferred.

"My name is Alice, but that's not what's important here," Alice replied. "What we need to talk about, is what you are about to do."

"Yeah? So, what am I about to do?"

"Make a huge mistake by calling the police. It would be very inconvenient for me if you do."

"Whatever. That weirdo has been following Chloe, and I think he was involved in murdering Nicola. Screw what you say, I am going to call the police," Jade replied defiantly.

"I'm going to level with you, Jade," Alice began. "I actually kind of like you. Despite what other people say, you're a decent person and you could have a decent future ahead of you. I want that for you. So, listen to me. Let this go, ok?"

"Is that a threat?" Jade raised her fist but suddenly found herself frozen in place, unable to move at all. "What the fuck, man?"

"You really do not want to touch me, Jade!" Alice held a hand in front of her, the fingers outstretched. Her eyes glowed a deep red now, purple travelling along the length of her hair again. She released her hold on Jade, "It never goes well for the other person. I do not say that as a threat either, just as advice you should pay attention to."

"You're that girl from the park!" Jade gasped, feeling her knees wobble at the realisation. She was ashamed to admit even to herself that those events had caused a couple of nightmares for her.

"You do remember me! That's so sweet. Tell me, how is Danielle?"

"She almost lost her eye you evil, psychotic freak!"

"Let's not get into name calling and instead get back to why I'm here. Forget about calling the police. The guy with the birthmark had nothing to do with Nicola's death."

Jade heard somebody push on the door from the other side, but it remained firmly shut somehow. This was followed by a kick, then Chloe's voice shouting through the wood.

"Jade? Are you in there?" she called. "Are you ok?"

"Don't answer," Alice said, pressing a finger to her lips. "I don't think you want her involved in this."

"You killed Nicola!" Jade hissed as quietly as she could.

Alice simply shrugged, "Allegedly."

"I'll make sure everybody knows what you've..."

Before Jade could say anything more, Alice flicked her wrist toward her, and she felt herself pushed back against the tiled wall, her head slamming against it hard. She let out a yelp of pain, then slid down to a sitting position on the floor. She reached round to the back of her head and felt something warm and sticky spreading in her hair. She examined her fingertips and could see the blood, even in the dull light.

Outside in the corridor, she could hear Chloe's shouts and frantic pounding getting louder, but still, the door held fast. She had no idea how, as there was no lock attached to it.

Alice stepped closer and squatted down before her, somehow her eyes were now shining blue. When she spoke again, her voice sounded sad, "This is your last warning, Jade. I really have no wish to hurt you further, but I will if you push this. I'm not a bad person; I'm just trying to survive. Leave it alone, and you have my word nobody will get hurt who doesn't need to. Do you understand?"

"Yes," Jade replied, fighting back tears and sounding beaten.

"Good. Do not tell anybody about this. Not even Chloe. Believe me, I will know if you do. Don't make me have to come back, ok?"

"Ok."

"Thank you," Alice replied. She lowered her head and whispered, "I've really missed you," then vanished.

An instant later the lights flickered back on and the door opened. Chloe rushed in and spotted Jade sitting on the floor with blood on her hand and shirt. She went to her and sat down too, putting a comforting arm around Jade.

"Are you ok, mate?" she asked gently. "What happened?"

"Bloody slipped, man. Banged my head against the wall," Jade replied, voice still shaking. "I'll be fine."

"You sure?"

"Totally." She tried to sound more confident.

"Alright," Chloe said, obviously not entirely believing her. "What the hell was the deal with the door?"

"It gets stuck sometimes."

"Yeah, but not like that, though."

Sensing Chloe's curiosity getting the better of her, Jade struggled to her feet, "Get me out of here, man. The bell's going to ring soon and I should probably get to the nurse before everybody sees."

Chapter Eleven

The drive back to Leeds had been a quiet one with barely a word spoken between the two friends. Jackson sensed Allister needed time to think and process his emotions and did not want to interrupt him until he was ready to talk. The visit had been far more informative than either of them had been prepared for. Not to mention far more surprising.

The revelation that Rachel Smith was, in fact, Allister's supposedly deceased sister Ruby, had also completely taken Jackson by surprise. He struggled to understand how Allister's father could have possibly done such a thing to his own daughter. He had never liked the man, seeing first-hand how Allister had been treated growing up. But this went far beyond the cruelty he thought the man could be capable of.

Now, sitting alone in their office, Jackson typed up the conversation with Ruby as best as he remembered it. He hadn't wanted to risk taking a recording device into the hospital in case it was discovered. At least now they had a name for one of Chloe's tormentors: Alice. Another surprise. It seemed too innocent a name for a person who was clearly as dangerous as she had proved to be.

He listed the little they knew about her: a girl whose touch was essentially lethal, who could turn invisible and apparently lift objects with her thoughts; if Chloe was to be believed. What they didn't have was a means to make her stop. How could they possibly battle something like her, the soldier in him asked repeatedly?

Jackson heard the office door open, and Allister stepped inside, looking slightly better than the last time Jackson had seen him. It was clear the time alone had helped some, at least. Although he could not begin to imagine how his friend must be feeling right now.

"How are you feeling, Al?" he decided to ask.

"You couldn't even begin to imagine, mate," Allister replied, confirming his suspicions.

"I know we are both more than a little shocked and this probably sounds harsh, but we still have a job to do. I think the best thing we can do for now, is talk about what we've learned. See if we can figure out a way to help Chloe."

"Agreed," Allister replied, looking relieved to have something to focus on. As he sat down at his own desk, his face looked deep in thought, "I guess we first need to discuss Alice. What do you make of her? Do you think that Ruby remembers events correctly? She's my sister and I don't want to doubt her, but with all she has been through, she's given us a lot to take in."

"Logically, I want to say that she's wrong. How can somebody like that possibly be real? Life isn't a comic book after all. But how else can you explain all those people who have been murdered and their remains aged? Also, we have Ruby in the flesh, who is clearly older than she should be."

Allister sighed, "We then have to ask, and I'm not saying I'm not grateful, but how did she survive? Why did she only age around fifteen years, when the bodies of the other victims appear to have aged at least twice that?"

Jackson leaned forward, placing his elbows on the desk and considered the question, "If I had to guess, and it is only a guess, I would say it's possibly because the contact was brief.

Perhaps the longer the contact with Alice is, the more severe the ageing caused."

"I guess that makes as much sense as anything else," Allister agreed. "What do you make of Alice disappearing?"

"At first I thought Ruby may have been delusional with the pain she was in."

"The same thought crossed my mind."

"Then I remembered the feeling I had when the office was broken into and I thought I was being watched."

"I'm almost certain that this Alice is the one who hacked my computer, though don't ask me how. It would also explain the door being unlocked. That she was here and we didn't realise is a worry, Jackson. She could be anywhere and there would be no way of us knowing."

"Whatever we are dealing with, I'm starting to think we may be out of our depth. How can we confront something we cannot touch or even see?"

"I don't know if we can, and honestly I don't know if we should," Allister replied. "All I want right now is to get Chloe on that plane on Monday morning, and hopefully out of Alice's reach. After that, Alice can rot."

"There would be nothing to stop her going after somebody else, though," Jackson replied.

"I don't care. We can't save everybody," Allister snapped.

"This doesn't sound like you, Al."

Allister groaned and rubbed the bridge of his nose. "Sorry. You're right. I'm tired and feeling useless. Let's just get Chloe to a safe place, then we can decide how to deal with Alice."

There was a sudden, heavy knock on the office door

followed by it swinging open. The large form of Detective Chief Inspector Cole, dressed in a perfectly pressed suit, entered with the confidence of somebody who belonged there. As he looked around the office, he seemed to be taking in the layout of the room.

"Can we help you?" Jackson asked remaining seated and sounding irritated.

Cole looked at Jackson and smiled, "Just having a look at the setup you've gotten yourself here, lad. Very nice. Your dad would be proud."

"Who is this guy, Jackson?" Allister asked, examining the new arrival.

"This is DCI Cole," Jackson replied. He turned to Cole, annoyed by the unannounced intrusion on their conversation. "This is not a good time, what do you want, Detective? Because I have a suspicion, you're not just here to tell me how proud my father is of me."

A grin spread across Cole's face at Jackson's response. He looked at Allister, "Direct and to the point as always. He's so much like his dad, you know."

"Actually, I don't," Allister replied simply, "having never met the guy."

"Again, what are you doing here, Cole?" Jackson asked.

"Right, yes, of course," Cole replied. "Well, I thought I'd pop by because it's been brought to my attention that somebody visited a Miss Rachel Smith this morning. That somebody, being the both of you. Please do not deny it as the head of security at the hospital knows to contact me directly if anybody attempts to make contact with Rachel. He emailed me the CCTV footage of you as soon as he clocked on today.

Unfortunately, he was not on duty when you arrived or he would not have allowed contact."

"Would this be the same Rachel Smith you told me you didn't know the whereabouts of, her name or even if she was still alive?"

Cole smiled again, "You have to understand that she is the only witness to a particularly nasty killer. It's in the police's interest to keep somebody like her out of the way and safe from harm."

"By placing her in a mental institute?" Allister asked, his tone full of accusation.

Raising both his hands in a sign of defence, Cole continued, "You misunderstand me, Allister. Rachel was placed into medical care by professionals who agreed it was the best course of treatment for her. The police have simply kept her whereabouts secret from the public for her own safety."

"I see," Jackson replied, feeling he should intervene in before Allister said too much.

"Now, as this is an ongoing investigation, we can skip over how you found her for now, but I need to know why you went to see her. Because I know it wasn't to offer legal support."

Jackson knew denying they had gone to see her was now out of the question. Cole had made it clear that he had the evidence and would not be in their office if he was not certain the facts were watertight. This did not mean, however, that he could not bend the truth a little.

"We felt that she may be able to assist us in helping a client," he replied.

"Can you elaborate?" Cole asked, raising a sceptical eyebrow.

"Not without breaking client confidentiality."

"I could get my officers to search your office."

"On what grounds? We've broken no laws."

"How about impersonating a lawyer?"

"Not actually illegal," Allister said. "If you check the law on it. Not that I'm saying I have."

"Well, are the police not able to assist this... client?"

"No actual crime has been committed against them, so it would be a waste of your men's valuable time. I'm sure that they have enough to do."

Cole looked far from convinced, but Jackson got the impression he was purposefully holding back. "That's very considerate of you, Jackson. But if somebody is in danger, then you need to let the police do their jobs."

"If we need you, then I'll be in touch. For now, I think we can cope."

Without being offered, Cole sat in the chair opposite Jackson, "As I'm here I may as well ask, was Rachel able to help you? Did she talk at all?"

It was very fast, but when Cole mentioned Rachel, his eyes briefly flicked in Allister's direction. Jackson could not help but wonder if he knew her real identity and if he had played a part in faking Ruby's death. Sadly, he could not ask without revealing more than he was prepared to.

"Unfortunately, she didn't. She remained completely unresponsive for the entire visit," Jackson replied.

"That is disappointing. Especially right now," Cole said with a sigh.

"Is there something you would like to share?"

The police officer seemed to consider his answer before replying, "It would seem our killer has made a comeback."

"I remember you saying so. They killed Michael Johnson."

"They have not stopped there, however. Over the last two days, four more deaths have been discovered by the police. All with the same cause of death as Johnson."

"Four?" Allister asked in surprise, then began tapping the keyboard before him. "I've not seen anything about them on the news."

"We've been able to keep it out of the media," Cole explained. "To avoid a panic, of course."

"Of course," Jackson replied dryly. "Were the victims connected?"

"Not that we've been able to find so far. It looks as though they all just happened to be in the wrong place at the wrong time."

"That certainly is disturbing."

"I just cannot understand why they've resurfaced after all these years." Cole looked at Jackson as though he thought he might be able to provide an answer.

"Thank you for letting us know," Jackson said instead, deciding that it was time to wrap the conversation up. "Obviously if we hear anything of interest during our own investigation, we will be sure to be in touch."

If Cole had any reaction to being dismissed in such a manner, he kept it to himself. Instead, he reached into his jacket pocket and retrieved a business card which he placed on Jackson's desk.

"That's my direct number. If you find out anything you

think might be helpful, day or night, call me." He stood and looked at Jackson with an unreadable expression, "Good to see you again, Jackson."

"Ok," Jackson simply replied.

Cole nodded to Allister and left, closing the door firmly behind him. Jackson picked up the business card and tossed it into the wastepaper basket without examining it.

"Well," Allister began. "He was kind of a dick."

Jackson nodded in agreement, "I don't know what to make of him. He acts as though he wants to help but my gut is starting to say don't trust him. I mean. He seems remarkably keen to give us information."

"Maybe he feels he owes your dad something."

"Possibly, but that doesn't feel like enough. Something else must be going on." He decided to push the thought to the back of his mind to consider later and focus on what needed to be done now. "Do you think you can find out who Alice's recent victims are?"

"I should think so," Allister replied confidently. "If the attacks have all happened in the last forty-eight hours, I doubt anybody will have been able to bury all information about them completely. Yet."

"Thank you." Jackson picked up his coat and car keys, "I'm going to head over to Chloe's house. I emailed her this afternoon and said I'd be outside to see if stalker number two shows up again."

"Good idea. I think she needs to feel safe right now."

"Let me know if you find anything out about Alice's latest victims and see if you can find a pattern," Jackson said opening the door. "I have a terrible feeling she isn't done yet."

Leading Jade into her room, Chloe immediately jumped onto the bed and pulled her feet up so she was sitting cross-legged. Jade sat down at the opposite end of the bed, but was quiet and mostly just stared at the floor. She had barely said a word as they travelled back from the hospital to Chloe's house.

Chloe was becoming increasingly worried about her friend. Ever since she had found Jade on the floor in the girl's restroom, Jade had remained withdrawn. At first, Chloe thought it may be shock, but she was starting to doubt that assessment. She had a growing feeling that insisted more had to have taken place than a simple slip today. No matter how she approached the subject though, Jade refused to speak any more about it. *Is she just embarrassed, or scared?*

After reporting the fall to the school nurse, Mr Howard had insisted upon driving Jade to the hospital for a check-up. Likewise, Jade had insisted Chloe accompany her too, and clutched her hand tightly the whole time they were in the Accident and Emergency waiting room. She seemed terrified of being in the hospital, and after what had happened to Nicola, Chloe guessed that she could not blame her.

After she selected a song on her phone, Chloe sent it to play on the docking station that sat on the desk. She looked at Jade. The cut on the back of her head had needed to be glued. After several tests, and only when the doctor had been certain she would be fine, would he allow her to leave. Even though she had assured Chloe she would be ok, she still continued to sit staring quietly at her feet.

"Are you alright, mate?" Chloe asked.

Jade shrugged her shoulders, "I guess."

"Seriously, is everything ok?"

"You mean apart from me having a crack in my head and probably being the laughingstock of the whole school?" she snapped.

"Hey, settle down. I'm asking because I'm worried about you."

"I know you are. I'm sorry." Letting out a deep sigh, Jade looked at Chloe and tried to smile, "Just a hell of a day, I guess."

"I can honestly say that you made my last day at school memorable. Which I was trying to avoid, I might add."

Without any warning, Jade leaned forward and kissed Chloe on the lips. It was brief, no more than a peck, and lacked any passion, but still left Chloe stunned. Jade leaned back and returned to staring at her feet.

"Errrmmm... what was that?" Chloe asked, clearly confused.

"A kiss," Jade replied simply.

"I got that. But I didn't think that I was your type."

"You're not, and I'm not yours."

"So, why kiss me?"

"It was the only way I could think of to say thank you. You know, for being there for me today."

"Saying thank you would have worked just fine," Chloe replied, clearly flustered.

Jade looked at her with a mischievous grin, the spark almost returning to her eyes, "Aww, man. Did I make you blush?"

"No. I wasn't expecting it. I guess I'm not used to people finding me irresistible."

"I would not go that far, man," Jade said with a bark of surprised laughter.

"You're the one doing all the kissing, not me, mate."

"I really am going to miss you when you go," Jade said suddenly, voice sombre again. "I wish we had become friends sooner."

"I had the same thought too," Chloe replied. "I could have used a friend like you."

Jade returned to studying the floor, "Instead I was a total bitch toward you."

"Lots of people were. No worries, ok. I kind of got used to it. Besides, we became friends eventually."

"Yeah, right before you're due to fly to the other side of the world."

"Perfect timing, aye. Story of my goddamn life."

"Anyway, have you got any booze here?" Jade asked, switching the subject. "This is supposed to be a party!"

"It is?"

"It should be."

Chloe stood and walked to her wardrobe, "It just so happens that I do. I swiped some from the liquor cabinet. By the time my parents realise it, I should be out of the country and safe from any repercussions."

"Chlo," Jade said suddenly, her voice full of concern.

Chloe turned to see Jade standing by the window, looking down onto the street. She felt her stomach drop as she suspected what Jade was going to say next.

"Y-Yeah?" she asked slowly.

"I don't mean to alarm you, but there's a guy in a car parked outside your house."

She felt relief flood through her, "Oh, thank God. Don't worry, that will be Jackson."

"Who's Jackson again?"

"From the other day? He saved you from being run down by that car."

"That's right, I remember now. One of the guys looking for your long-lost family."

"That's him," Chloe confirmed.

Jade looked suspicious, "Is he looking for them outside of your house, at night, when it's dark? I'm not being funny, but that seems unlikely."

Chloe closed her eyes as she realised Jade had caught her out in her lie, "I'll be honest, he isn't looking for our family. He's keeping an eye out for that weirdo from this morning. I appear to have a bit of a stalker problem."

"I had noticed. It's ok, I can see why you kept that piece of gossip to yourself."

"Sorry I lied. We'd only just started talking, and I wasn't sure I could trust you, yet."

"That's fair." Jade cocked her head, almost like a cat, "Do you feel like you can now?"

"I know I can trust you enough to keep a secret, though apparently not enough to keep your hands to yourself."

Jade laughed and gave her a gentle shove, "Jesus, Chlo. You're making far too big a deal out of one little kiss."

"Just setting boundaries," Chloe replied with a smile. "Also, please don't call me Chlo. It's lazy."

"I can go back to calling you bitch again?"

"Try it." Chloe was pleased to have the banter back, to have Jade stop worrying about having slipped on the floor. She held up the vodka bottle, "So, are we drinking this or not?"

"Does a bear..." Jade began.

"Just a yes is fine, mate."

***

Allister sat in the now darkened office, working on locating the identities of the latest victims of the girl Ruby had called Alice. He had been correct about there not being enough time for the information to be buried and had located all four of them. A cause of death and photos were all included in the files. He downloaded the content and automatically set the computer to terminate its connection on completion.

As the info was being saved and filed, his thoughts turned to something else Ruby had mentioned as they talked. The Gates Foundation. With fingers moving easily across the keyboard, Allister did a Google search for the name which turned up zero results. Trying different combinations of words and phrases, he could find no organisation, charitable or otherwise, past or present, registered under the name.

It was far too much of a coincidence, however. Gates. There had to be a connection somehow, and if he could not find it online, he was left with no other option. Allister knew he was about to break the rules spelt out to him by his mysterious mentor and benefactor, but what else could he do?

Picking up his phone, he activated the encryption application. Once he was sure the phone was secure, he began to dial the number he had been made to memorise strictly for emergencies. The call connected and a familiar voice answered after the first ring. Efficient, as always.

"Yes?" Gates asked. *"What's happened?"*

"Do you know about my sister?" Allister asked, choosing not to waste any time.

There was an annoyed sigh on the other end of the line, *"You know that this number is for—"*

"Screw you, Gates!" Allister snapped angrily. "This is important to me so cut the crap. After everything I've done for you over the last twelve years, no questions asked, you can tell me what I want to know."

There was a silence that stretched on for so long, Allister began to suspect the call had been ended. *"Fine,"* Gates said eventually.

"How long have you known about Ruby?"

"I found out about her around twenty years ago. When I started tracking you down, I was surprised to find out you had a twin sister. When I learned of her death, I had my suspicions there was some kind of cover-up but I could not find any evidence. At first."

"So, you did find some though?"

"Yes, 2009. I was able to find out what had really happened to her, and where she was being kept."

"How did you find out?" Allister asked.

"It's irrelevant."

"Not to me."

"Trust me, Allister," Gates said with a tone of finality, *"it is. You do not want to know. I also discovered who had been visiting her. There was no other option but to move her outside of the Leeds area."*

"You mean Alice. She was the one visiting Ruby."

There was another stretch of silence. *"Yes,"* was all Gates said.

"So, you knew all about my sister being alive and where she was for nine years, but you chose to keep that information from me?"

"I had no choice. If I had told you, then you would have almost certainly tried to get her out and bring her back to Leeds."

"Of course, I would. Ruby is my sister, and she's not crazy."

"Exactly. But a girl returning from the dead looking years older than her supposed age would have drawn media attention, and Alice would have then seen Ruby as a threat. Believe me when I tell you, she knows of only one way to deal with threats to her existence. Your sister was safer kept secret from you and outside of Leeds."

Allister wanted to argue, but it appeared that Gates had really been acting in Ruby's best interests. Without more information, he could not be certain and even though it went against his instincts, he chose to trust Gates, for now.

"What is Alice?" Allister asked instead. "What exactly are Jackson and I dealing with?"

"I have many theories, but I'm not entirely sure," Gates admitted. *"I spent many years learning about her and her abilities, but I was never able to pinpoint precisely what she was. To be honest, I don't even think Alice knows what she is, not entirely."*

"Do you at least know how to stop her?"

"Not yet. But we are working on it. Again, all I have are theories. Nothing concrete."

"We?"

Dodging the question, Gates asked, *"Is there anything else?"*

"Yes. How did you know to leave a file on police computers twenty years ago containing everything I was going to be looking for?"

"I have to go."

"Will there be a new emergency number in case I need to reach you?" Allister asked, realising he was not going to get all the answers he wanted.

Gates was briefly silent again, as though choosing an answer, *"No, I do not think we will need one."* The line went dead as the call was disconnected.

Allister could not help but wonder what that could possibly mean. Was he now out of the loop, or were things about to come to a head? Although unsure of the answer, he had a strong feeling in his gut they were all going to find out, and soon.

Chapter Twelve

The first thing Chloe realised when she woke early on Saturday morning was that her head hurt. A lot. The thudding ache only increased as she tentatively opened her eyes and was hit by sunlight filtering through the curtains. Groaning, she rolled over and came face to face with a still sleeping Jade, who looked surprisingly harmless with her eyes closed. The tough girl persona was gone, replaced with the fifteen-year-old teenager she was.

Jade had rung her mother the previous evening, to tell her she was spending the night at Chloe's house. There had been the briefest of exchanges, ending with Jade hanging up and announcing her mother was fine with it. Knowing that her own mum would have wanted Chloe at home under close observation if she had spent the afternoon in A&E, she was surprised. She suspected that Jade was left mostly to her own devices, which made Chloe feel sad for her.

Carefully extracting herself from the bed, trying hard not to wake Jade, Chloe tiptoed to the window. Squinting, she parted the curtains and peeked outside. It was no surprise to see that Jackson's car was no longer there. She had slept well knowing he had been close by, though.

She tried to think of some way to thank Jackson and Allister for everything they were doing for her. Chloe felt certain that without both of them, she would almost certainly have gone mad by now. There was a little over a thousand pounds in her bank savings account, and she decided she would transfer it to Jackson's business account that afternoon. It was the least she could do. As it was a weekend, it would not clear until Monday, by which point she would be on her way to Australia and they would be unable to return it to her. After all, she could not begin to imagine how much money she must have cost them this week.

Picking up her phone from the desk, she put on a dressing gown and crossed to the bedroom door, creaking it open gently. Sneaking out, she headed downstairs to the kitchen. Chloe knew that her parents were unlikely to be awake before eleven on a Saturday. It may be her last weekend here, but she still wanted them to sleep in as they both worked hard.

While deciding on what to make Jade for breakfast, she felt her phone begin to vibrate in her pocket. Retrieving the handset, Chloe checked the screen to see that it was Allister calling. She swiped right to accept.

"Hi, Allister," she said brightly, pleased to hear from him.

"Hey, Chloe," he replied.

"How are you?"

"I'm good. Just a quick call, really. I need to ask you something."

"Ok..." Chloe answered slowly.

"Does the name Alice mean anything to you?"

"Alice?" she thought for a moment, but nothing came to mind. "No, not at all. Why?"

"We are still putting all the pieces together, but the name has come up in our investigation."

"Really? That's strange."

"Are you sure the name doesn't mean anything to you?"

"Certain. I'm pretty sure I've never even met an Alice."

"Ok." Allister went quiet for a moment and she heard him tapping on his keyboard. *"Jackson and I have a few things to follow up on today, but we do need to meet up before you leave, agreed?"*

"Definitely agreed," Chloe replied.

"I'll see you later, then."

"Bye, Allister." She ended the call and returned to searching the cupboards. "Alice?" she whispered to herself. She could not help but wonder who this Alice was, and how she was connected to everything. The name did not ring any bells. At least she did not think so. Chloe was so lost in thought, she did not notice when Jade appeared in the doorway.

"What you doing?" Jade asked.

Chloe jumped, dropping the box of cereal she was holding, spilling wheat shapes across the tiled floor.

"Jesus, Jade!" Chloe almost shouted, her heart pounding in her chest. "How many more times? Don't sneak up on me! You know what I'm dealing with!"

"Sorry, man. My bad."

Taking a deep breath, Chloe tried to settle her nerves, "To answer your question, I was making you breakfast in bed."

Jade pulled a confused face, "Why?"

"Because you are a guest and I want you to feel welcome."

"Seems more like something you'd do for your wife."

Opening a cupboard door, Chloe retrieved a dustpan and brush and began to clean up the mess she had made. "Then I'm glad I didn't," she replied, feeling more than a little hurt.

"Hey, man," Jade quickly responded, picking up that she had upset Chloe. "I didn't mean anything by it. I'm just really not used to friends who do nice things for me. Or are even that nice in general, if I'm completely honest."

"It's ok. I haven't exactly had a friend sleepover in a few years. I guess I'm a little out of practice."

"Some breakfast would be nice, though."

Chloe smiled, "Coming right up."

"And some coffee. I have a hangover like you would not believe."

Chloe began to put the request together, already starting to feel better about the day again. She handed a steaming mug of coffee to Jade.

"Who was on the phone?" Jade asked after taking a sip.

"Just Allister," Chloe replied. "He wanted to know if I knew anybody called Alice."

Chloe saw a dark look cross Jade's eyes before she replied, unusually quickly, "Alice? Means nothing to me. Like, who the fuck is Alice anyway?"

"Intentional pun?" Chloe asked with a laugh.

"Huh?"

"You know, the song?"

"What song?"

"You are kidding me, right?"

The blank expression on Jade's face told Chloe she honestly had no clue. She shook her head slowly in genuine exasperation, "Am I the only one who listens to music in this city?"

"Whatever, man," Jade replied with a shrug and then changed the subject. "What are we doing today?"

"I need to start packing for my flight. Do you need to go home? Won't your mum be worried about you?"

"Not usually. Tell you what, finish making me breakfast, we'll eat it watching Saturday morning cartoons, then I can help you pack."

"Cartoons? Really? Are we going to braid each other's hair too?" Chloe asked with more than a hint of sarcasm in her voice.

"I like that idea, so yes, we are now," Jade replied with a grin.

***

Jackson was woken mid-morning by the sound of his phone ringing. Sitting up, he stretched then reached for the handset lying on the bedside table. He saw the call was from Lucy and immediately hit accept.

"Good morning," he said brightly.

"Morning, Jackson," Lucy replied, sounding serious. This was obviously not going to be a social call.

"Is everything ok?"

"I've been doing some digging. Can we meet later? I'd rather not discuss this over the phone."

"Sounds serious. Of course. I'm free all morning, I think. Where did you have in mind?"

"The bar where we first met. In about two hours?"

"I need to go to the office first, but I'll definitely be there."

"See you soon," Lucy said before disconnecting the call.

Jackson could not begin to guess what she wanted to see him about, but he was glad she did. First, he would need to make himself presentable, though. *I definitely need more sleep.*

He had remained outside Chloe's home until six in the morning but had seen nothing to give him cause for concern. That meant either the man she had seen from her window had moved on, or he had spotted Jackson first and stayed away. Whatever the case, it was a night Chloe had been safe.

Glancing at his phone again, he saw he had received five messages from Allister during the night. He wondered how much sleep his friend had gotten. He had never seen Allister so committed before. Opening the most recent message, he saw there were several picture files attached to it.

Jackson, I don't know if you are awake yet, but I've found information about all four of Alice's most recent victims. They include autopsy reports as well as photos. Allister.

Jackson read the names on the list, not recognising any of them. Veronica Trent, Sean Benson, Joseph Wilks and Aidan Wallace. He quickly scanned through the information relating to their untimely deaths.

Finally, he opened the attached file to view the photos. Initially, nothing really caught his eye until one of them jumped out at him. *Sean Benson.* He would recognise that arrogant face anywhere. The guy from the bar who had been pestering those women. He checked through the details of his death: killed after a violent beating. Found shortly after 10pm, Wednesday.

That would not have been long after Jackson and Chloe had seen him. Could Alice have been following Chloe and also seen his exchange with Sean? It was possible, Chloe had always referred to Alice as her stalker, and she had the ability to go around unseen. But what was her motive for killing Benson? Was it simply because she had seen him alone? Or was there more to it than that? Did she even need a motive for what she did?

Jackson realised that Sean had only left the bar at his insistence. Had he inadvertently sent him to his own death? He knew he could not blame himself for what had happened, but had to at least consider the possibility his own actions may have caused it. *I can't say I knew the guy, but he probably didn't deserve to go that way.* Perhaps Alice had known something he had not?

Placing his phone down, he headed for the shower, his head already spinning with questions for which he had no real answers.

***

Allister was already back in the office, on a Saturday of all days. He was struggling to remember the last time he had spent so many hours behind his desk. Normally he would do everything possible to stay away from here. But, for the first time since joining Jackson in this business venture, he actually felt as though he was doing something worthwhile. Like he was making a difference to somebody's world, instead of wasting his time catching cheats and fraudsters.

He honestly had not meant what he said about only being interested in getting Chloe out of the UK and to safety. Allister knew that even when they managed to succeed in doing that, he had a suspicion Alice would remain a very real problem for Jackson and himself. If she had started up another killing spree, then they needed to figure out how to stop her. Something the police had been unable to do for over three decades.

The door opened and Jackson entered the office. Allister expected him to look worse for wear after staying outside Chloe's house the previous night. Instead, he looked refreshed and ready for the day. He had shaved and dressed as though he was ready for an evening out.

"Bit flash for work, aren't they?" Allister commented.

"What are?" Jackson asked, looking confused.

"Your clothes."

"Oh, I see. I'm meeting Lucy in a little while."

"Big date?" Allister checked his watch. "At this time of day?"

Jackson shook his head, "Not at all. She said she's been doing some digging and has some information for us."

"Really? Did she say what it was about?"

"No. If anything, she was very cagey and didn't want to say anything on the phone."

"That's probably wise if she's found something she shouldn't know."

"I suppose we'll find out." Jackson sat on the edge of his desk, "Anyway, the reason I'm here is those victims' photos you sent me. I'm certain I recognised one of them."

"You did?" Allister asked, surprised. He knew none of the pictures had meant anything to him.

"Sean Benson."

"How did you know him?"

"I didn't actually know him. At least not until the night he died," explained Jackson. "We had something of a confrontation in the bar before I met with Lucy."

"Are you worried that you may be implicated?"

"Not at all. I have several witnesses who can confirm where I was that night. I'm just curious as to why Alice chose to kill him. He was a big guy, if it was a random killing, there must have been easier targets."

"Does the size of a person even matter to something like her?" Allister mused, tapping a finger idly on the desk. He looked at Jackson, "I know that expression, what are you thinking?"

"My impression of Sean was that he was arrogant and disrespectful. I saw him getting more than a little pushy with two women in the bar, it was obvious he was not going to take no for an answer from them."

"I see."

"I remember Cole saying the first time Alice started killing, she targeted known criminals. I'm wondering if there is a similar pattern this time."

"Do you want me to see what I can find out about this Sean Benson?" Allister asked.

"All four of them if you can. See if they match her known M.O."

"I can definitely do that. It shouldn't take me long either."

"Thanks." Jackson headed for the door, "I'm going to meet Lucy, but call me if you find any kind of link between them."

"Just one thing I don't understand, Jackson," Allister said.

"What's that?"

"Ruby and Chloe. Alice took an interest in the two of them, and I cannot believe for a second that either would have done anything to warrant being killed by her. Can you?"

Jackson thought about this for a moment. "I agree with you. But don't forget, Alice hasn't killed them."

***

Arriving at the bar five minutes early, Jackson was surprised to see Lucy was already there ahead of him. As he looked at her outfit, he was relieved to see she had also decided to dress up. But then again, she probably always looked this good. After checking that Lucy had a drink in front of her, he stopped at the bar and ordered a coffee. When it was ready, Jackson crossed the mostly empty room and took a seat opposite her.

"You look stunning," he commented.

"Thanks," Lucy replied with a smile. "I'm meeting with some friends for a bachelorette party this afternoon."

"Oh, I see," he said, quickly realising his previous assumption had been a mistake. "Me too."

"You're going to a bachelorette party?"

"No. Out. Just out." His words were flustered, as he tried to collect himself. "With some guys from work!"

"Don't you only work with Allister?" she asked.

"Yeah... I do." Jackson decided on a quick change of subject, "So, how can I help? You mentioned that you had found some information?"

"That's right," Lucy replied, picking up her bag and taking out a file. "I contacted an old friend of mine who recently started working at a large law firm in London. They represent people from all over the country, and she was able to find out some information about my attacker."

"Seriously? Allister said everything had been wiped."

"He's not entirely wrong. It's information that hasn't been made public, hence my caution on the phone. All of this information was found offline, in the firm's physical filing system. My friend's firm was the prosecution for two separate cases of sexual assault allegedly carried out by him."

"Allegedly?"

"He was never actually convicted. Vital evidence disappeared before both hearings."

"Why does that not surprise me? What did you manage to find out about him?"

"His name is Maxwell Solomon, forty-seven years old with no fixed address. No history of further education or employment and was born and lived most of his life in London." Flicking through the file, she continued, "It appears he only recently came to Leeds. I do mean recently, too. A little over a week ago at the most."

Jackson leaned back in his seat, thinking hard, "I wonder why he suddenly came up here."

"I have no idea. It certainly appears to be a random thing to do. I personally have no link to London, so I doubt it was for me." She handed Jackson all the paperwork she had brought. "Whatever his reasons, I hope this helps you find him." After a pause, she added, "You understand the risk I'm taking giving you this information? I could get into serious trouble if anybody was to find out I did this."

"Of course, I shall be very discreet."

"Thank you, but I want him off the streets so I can sleep at night again. I appreciate you keeping this to yourself."

"I'm sure it will be incredibly useful in tracking him down.

Also, don't worry. I will make sure all of this is destroyed after I've read it."

"As long as it gets this guy caught. Not only so I can sleep better at night but also before he goes after some other poor girl."

"I promise I will do everything I can to put him in police custody," he assured her. "I'm the reason he got away after all."

"Don't think like that! You're also the reason I'm still alive, remember? I literally owe you my life, Jackson."

"I understand where you're coming from, but until he's caught, I don't think I will be able to forgive myself for that one." After finishing the last of his coffee, he asked, "Do you have time for another drink?"

Lucy looked disappointed, "I'm really sorry, but I have to meet my friends." Then she brightened, "But I would like to see you again. Maybe you could cook for me?"

Jackson laughed, "Why would you want me to do that? Trust me, I can't cook, and I'm not exaggerating."

"Didn't you say you were a chef in the army?"

"Ah, yes. Actually, Allister said that. He likes to tell people I was a chef to annoy me."

"Can I ask what you actually did in the army?" Lucy enquired, now obviously intrigued.

"This and that."

"Does that mean that you can't tell me, or you won't tell me?"

"Yes," was all Jackson would give by way of a reply.

"Are you trying to make yourself more attractive by being mysterious?"

"No, but if I were, would it be working?"

Lucy smiled and stood, picking up her bag, "I have to go, Jackson." She leaned over and kissed his cheek. "Call me soon, though," she said, before leaving.

Chapter Thirteen

Allister entered the park just after the sun was beginning to set. He was both glad and a little annoyed Chloe had texted him to meet her here, but only annoyed that she was not staying safely in her house until it was time to catch her flight. He knew she was her own person and would do her own thing, but she made protecting her a full-time job.

As always, he found her sitting on one of the swings, gently rocking backwards and forwards. She smiled at the sight of him approaching, which he immediately returned. As he got closer, though, Allister noticed that something looked different about Chloe. It took him a moment, but then he realised. It was her hair, and he struggled not to laugh.

"Is that a braid?" he asked, a smirk breaking out across his face.

Chloe looked embarrassed, "Yes. It's my own fault and I don't want to talk about it."

"Let me guess, Jade?"

"Yeah... the worst part is she's made me promise I won't take it out until I'm back in Australia! Which is going to make washing it a real pain."

"I'm beginning to think she is a bad influence on you."

"Me too," Chloe sighed. "But God, am I glad she's in my life now. Which makes leaving even harder."

Allister sat on the swing beside her, "How are you feeling

about going?"

"If you'd have asked me this time last week, the answer would have been easy. Over the moon. But last week I had no friends, and I was lonely. Now I have Jade and you. So even though I'm still excited, I'm sad I'm leaving you guys."

"I'm especially sorry that you are going, but I'm also glad you will be away from everything here, and most importantly, that you'll be happy."

"There is that, too." She suddenly put her feet on the floor to stop her swing moving, then looked at Allister. "Are we just going to small talk or are you going to tell me who Alice is?"

Allister considered the question as he tried to think of the best way to answer and finally decided to go with the truth, "She's your stalker."

Chloe's brow furrowed, "Really? Her name is Alice?"

"Yes."

"I have to be honest, I really expected something a little scarier than Alice."

"Don't let her name fool you. She's not any less dangerous, she's already killed more than once, remember."

"Oh, I do remember. Believe me, hearing her kill isn't something you forget, whatever her name is," Chloe replied with a shudder.

"Have you seen or heard her recently?"

"Strangely, no. I've not been aware of her presence for a couple of days now."

"Let's hope she stays away for a couple more, then," Allister said. He decided it was best to try to change the subject, "Do you have any plans for the remainder of your time here?"

"My parents are expecting me home shortly," Chloe replied. "They want us to have a last meal out as a family tonight."

"That should be nice."

"It will be dull and mundane, but I know I'm going to miss them both so much when I leave, so I'll endure it. Tomorrow we will be shopping for anything I might need for Australia."

"When do you need to be back?" Allister asked.

Chloe checked her watch and sighed, "Now, I guess. Sorry we didn't get to spend more time here."

"It's ok. But I'm going to walk you home."

"You don't have to. It's not far, remember."

"No offence, Chloe, but you have a habit of attracting the wrong kind of person. I'm getting you home safely. End of discussion."

Chloe smiled and seemed to look relieved, "You're right, I guess." She looked at him again, smile gone but blue eyes piercing him like the first time they met, "Allister?"

"Yeah?" he asked.

"I think I'm going to miss you the most. I've not known you long, but you're like the big brother I never had."

"I know," he replied, aware that the reverse was also very much true.

***

Detective Chief Inspector Cole sat watching some mindless Saturday night television show. It was a clear waste of his

237

time, but after the difficult week he had been forced to suffer, he did not have the energy to change the channel right now.

For many cities in the United Kingdom, five murders in one week were a regular occurrence, but not Leeds. Already people higher up the ladder wanted explanations and results. Right now, Cole could not provide either. At least not any that would make him look sane. If he did not come up with something fast, however, then his bosses may start to think it could be time to give somebody else a chance. Somebody younger and more ambitious. Where would that leave him? On the scrapheap, that's where. Forced retirement. After everything he had done for this city.

No. He had worked too hard and given up too much to be put out to pasture now. He had missed out on marriage and starting a family; instead, living alone in this house with nobody to share his achievements with. Some could even say he had sold his soul to get to where he now was. They may even be right. He picked up the bottle of expensive brandy and poured a large measure into a fancy-looking glass. When had he started drinking so much? Probably when his conscience had needed to be drowned. May as well have another, just to help himself sleep. *What would that naïve young copper you used to be, think of what you've become? Probably shame.*

Cole jumped slightly as he heard three sharp thuds on his front door. He groaned as he pulled himself to his feet, head already light from the alcohol. He had always tried to stay in shape and was as strong as a man half his age, but slowly, old age was beginning to creep into his joints. Heading toward the door, he heard three more loud thuds.

"Alright, alright," he shouted. "I'm on my way!"

Reaching the door, he pulled it open and intended to use his size to intimidate whoever was trying to break his door from its hinges. Instead, what he saw made him freeze in place, fear rising from a dark memory he had tried to keep buried for thirty years.

In front of him was a man dressed head to foot in black combat clothing. He was slightly shorter than Cole, slim, but obviously muscular. A hood covered his head with a scarf obscuring his mouth and nose, leaving only his cold, hard eyes showing.

Eyes that Cole knew well and had spent many years praying he would never look into again. Trembling slightly, he opened his mouth to speak, but the man moved too fast. Cole barely saw the club before it slammed against the side of his head. Feeling his knees give out beneath him, he first saw the floor coming up to meet him, and then nothing.

***

Jackson pulled up outside George and Son's coffee shop with great reluctance. He had received a phone call from George, which surprised him as he did not recall giving the man his number. George had asked him to go to the cafe as soon as possible. Apparently, there were things he needed to know.

He already doubted George could actually help, since all his previous encounters with the man had left Jackson with more questions than answers. But right now, he felt so lost as to what to do next; he knew he needed to grasp at any straw that presented itself.

Opening the door to the coffee shop, he was unsurprised to find it virtually empty. Just two customers occupied the place, each sitting at different tables and with only a cup of coffee before them. Neither said nor did anything, just stared forlornly into their drinks.

"Thank you for coming, Jackson," George said, appearing as always from the kitchen.

"Your call sounded important and apparently I didn't have anything else to do on a Saturday night," Jackson replied. "So here I am."

"Before I start, can I get you anything?"

"The point, maybe?" Jackson knew he was being unnecessarily harsh, but at the moment, his patience was as short as the time left to put everything together.

George smiled in response, despite his obvious irritation at being spoken to in such a way, "I understand you are searching for information on the girl known only as Alice."

This immediately caught Jackson's attention, "You can tell me who she is?"

"Unfortunately, I cannot. However, I can tell you what she is. At least, what we suspect she is."

"I'm listening."

"Have you ever heard of a stone tape?"

"I can't say that I'm familiar with the term."

"It's ok, it's not a common myth. It is possibly the best way to describe how Alice came to be," George explained. "You see, sometimes, when somebody suffers a traumatic or violent death, part of their psyche is transferred to something nearby, almost like a recording. Usually a house, rock or even stone. Hence the phrase."

"Like a ghost?" Jackson asked, his logical side clearly dubious.

"They could be what started the ghost stories, certainly. But in reality, it's more of an echo of who the person was. In the right conditions, it is possible to witness this psychic recording. Most people call them hauntings."

"From what I've heard of this Alice, she is not a recording anchored to one rock."

"That is true. Normally, a stone tape will repeat the same event to itself, usually their final moments, until he or she finally find peace, then allow themselves to pass over."

"Are many of these stone tapes psychotic murderers?" Jackson asked.

George chuckled at that, although there was no humour to it, just sadness, "Not at all. Most are just harmless imprints. Again, just an echo left behind, not the actual soul of the person. It has no conscious thought."

"Alice is not just an echo of somebody left behind and is in no way harmless. She has killed; I can't even guess how many people," Jackson pointed out.

"Again, that is also true. However, Alice is... different," George explained. "Something happened when she died. Something that changed everything we previously thought we understood."

"Do you know what happened?"

"We are not sure. We know she suffered a traumatic death when she was still young, but instead of a small part of her being imprinted in one place, somehow all of her ended up imprinted on the entire city."

"So, nothing of her passed to..." Jackson rolled his eyes at the thought of completing the sentence, "the other side?"

"No, she has remained entirely 'anchored' here. She can move anywhere within the borders of the city, but she cannot leave them."

"Are you saying she cannot leave Leeds at all?" Jackson asked.

"That is correct," George confirmed.

"No wonder she's so angry." Jackson thought for a moment, "To check that I understand you, thirty or so years ago, Alice was killed in a violent and traumatic way?"

"Depending upon your perspective, yes."

"Perspective?"

"Everybody has one, and it often differs from person to person. But yes, Alice has been dead for thirty-two years."

"I see. Anyway, she died and rather than going to the other side, assuming such a place exists..."

"It does," George insisted.

Jackson looked unconvinced, "Really? Heaven is real?"

"I didn't say heaven."

"Ok, perhaps a conversation for another time."

"Perhaps."

"Assuming, then, that the afterlife does exist, Alice didn't go there. Instead, she stayed here. Why didn't she pass over?"

"As I say, nobody knows. Something prevented her from doing so. She's almost a unique case, so we do not have a lot of information to go on."

Jackson picked up on one word in particular, "Almost... a unique case?"

"We have heard rumours of others, my father and I. But Alice is by far the most powerful. Sadly, she never found peace. Perhaps given time, she would have," George shrugged.

"Except?" Jackson pressed, sensing there was more to the story.

"Except she met somebody who made her want to stay in this world. He made her everything she has become. Both good and bad. Both intentionally and unintentionally. You see, Jackson, you said she is not an echo. In a sense you are right, but in many ways, that is exactly what she is."

"This is all very interesting, but can you tell me how to stop her from killing anybody else?"

"There is no easy answer, I am afraid," George said with a sigh. "There is only one way we know that can stop Alice. You have to stop her from dying."

Jackson stood still, his mouth slightly open in disbelief, "What? How do we even do that?"

"I never said it would be easy."

"It doesn't even sound possible," Jackson replied in irritation. "Ok, since I cannot save a girl who died over thirty years ago, can you at least tell me that there is a plan B?"

"You need to convince her that it's time to pass over."

"And how do I do that?"

"Each person is different. But if you can convince her to come here of her own free will, then I can help her."

"What exactly is this place?" Jackson asked looking around. "I'm guessing it is more than a shop for buying coffee and vegan food. And why doesn't my watch work here?"

"It is a coffee shop. But mostly, we are here to help lost souls find their way."

"How did I find my way here? I'm not dead." A terrible thought suddenly crossed his mind, "Am I?"

George laughed at that, "No. You are not dead. But you do not need to be dead to be a lost soul trying to find their way. As for your watch, it works fine. Things are just a little different here. Time is precious, you should not lose it needlessly."

"You don't like to give straight answers, do you?"

"Are there any?"

Jackson shook his head, thinking there could be a headache coming if he did not leave soon. "Have it your way. Can you tell me how I find Alice?"

"That should be the easy part. You've already met her."

***

Cole awoke in total darkness. He could feel a fabric hood of some kind over his head, and his hands were bound securely behind his back. A professional job, not that he expected anything less from his abductor. The surface beneath him rocked gently, and the sound of a car engine confirmed his fears that he was being held in a car. Almost certainly inside the boot.

The side of his head pounded from the blow he had received. One hit had knocked him unconscious, and he would have been embarrassed had he not known who was responsible. That alone was enough to terrify him.

Why he had been knocked out, tied up and bundled into the boot of a car he was not one hundred percent sure. He certainly had his suspicions, though. The detective found himself praying to a God he barely believed in anymore, that he was wrong. Because he knew if he was right, and the driver of this car knew what he had been doing for the last twenty-nine years, then his life was now possibly measured in minutes, at best.

Feeling the car beginning to slow, fear took over and he started to yell for help, kicking out at the side of the boot's interior. He knew it was a futile gesture since they would be in the middle of nowhere by now. The man who had taken him was a consummate professional, after all.

The car rocked more as he listened to tyres hit gravel, then the crunch of the car coming to a stop. Cole was shaking as he heard the door open then slam shut, followed by footsteps getting closer and finally the squeak of the boot being opened. Cold air suddenly rushed inside, causing him to shake uncontrollably, making it even harder to hide how scared he was.

A strong pair of hands grabbed hold of him then dragged him from the car, easily throwing Cole to the hard ground. With his hands still bound behind his back, he had no way of breaking his fall, and pain exploded in his shoulder as it took the brunt of the impact.

"I know who you are!" Cole said, figuring he could try to reason with his attacker. "You don't have to do this."

He was met with silence, instead, being roughly pulled to his feet, then shoved forward. Still wearing the hood and unable to see, he stumbled a few feet before tripping and making another undignified crash to the floor, gritting his teeth to prevent himself from crying out in pain. A moment later, he was pulled back to his feet, and Cole was prodded more gently in the direction he was expected to walk.

Moving slowly, the policeman was able to walk and stay on his feet this time, so again attempted to reason with his captor, "I'm serious. You do not have to do this. We can talk about it."

"Can we?" a familiar voice asked, one that now sounded

colder than he previously remembered. "What can we possibly talk about that would convince me to let you go?"

"For a start, I'm a very well-known and respected police officer. If anything happens to me, they will come looking for you."

There was a harsh laugh, but it displayed no humour. "Now there was a question that bothered me for some time. How did a second-rate cop like you end up getting promoted at all? Not only to such an esteemed position but also so fast? DCI? When you were barely into your thirties? It just seemed so unlikely."

"Hey!" Cole protested. "I'm damn good at my job."

"I'm afraid you're not. You were always average at best, Nathan," the voice replied in a mocking tone. "But then one day, it dawned on me. All those drug busts, the kidnappings and murders you solved time and time again. That terrorist attack you foiled that nobody else had seen coming. All the papers praising you and asking how you did it. The answer was so obvious. You had outside help."

"I did not..."

"Please don't lie to me. You went from being barely able to shine your shoes to super cop almost overnight. Almost as if... you could suddenly see the future. Do you see where I'm going with this?"

Any doubts Cole may have harboured about why he had been taken were gone now. He always knew this day might one day come. But he had always hoped he would have been warned in advance. It was clear she had no interest in what happened to him anymore. Strangely, that realisation did not surprise him in the slightest. Deep down he knew he had only ever been a means to an end. *I might not be sure if there's a*

God, but the Devil certainly exists!

"It's not like that," he replied, a note of pleading in his voice.

"The thing is, Nathan," the voice of his abductor continued as if Cole had not spoken, "we both know you cannot see into the future. There is, in fact, only one person who can predict the future."

Cole decided it was best to remain silent now, knowing there was nothing more to be said. The game was up. His biggest secret had been discovered. He chose instead just to walk; slow and careful footfalls now crushing damp grass underfoot, the growing sense inside that he was walking to his grave.

"There's something else I know for sure, too," the voice continued despite Cole's silence. "The days of her helping people out of the goodness of... well... I guess you would call it her heart, though personally, I've doubted she's had one for some time, are long gone. I could always see what was in your little arrangement for you, I just could never figure out what was in it for her."

"You misunderstand her," Cole replied. "She is not as evil as you make her out to be."

"I'm afraid that she is. She murdered seventeen people, Nathan. You should know, you helped cover many of them up!" the voice snapped. He was close, Nathan felt his breath on the back of his neck. "Seventeen is how many we know about. God only knows how many bodies were never found or not linked to her. She did not always follow the same M.O., after all."

"It was to protect the public. We couldn't risk the panic. You had the same brief I did."

"It was to protect her!" his captor shouted. "Back when some people in government still thought she might be able to be controlled. To be used somehow."

"I was just following orders."

"And when you had a poor girl committed for the best years of her life after she managed to survive an attack?"

"That was unintentional. She never meant to hurt Ruby. She just wanted a friend."

"Her intent is irrelevant. It's more proof that she quite literally, destroys everything she touches. You still hid Ruby away at the expense of her own sanity to protect her attacker."

They continued, both in silence. Cole was beginning to make out sunlight filtering through the hood, indicating it was now early on Sunday morning. He had discovered a rhythm to walking blindfolded, so he rarely stumbled or tripped. He considered making a break for it but knew he was unlikely to get far while both blind and with his hands bound behind his back.

Eventually the voice returned, "We had a few people under observation who could possibly be the killer. We could not be sure exactly who it was because we never had a name. She never knew who did it, after all. But just over a week ago, Freddy noticed one of them, Maxwell Solomon, suddenly leave London and head for Leeds. It made absolutely no sense for him to do that. He has no family here. No work. No reason."

"Maybe he felt like a change," Cole tried, although he knew it was not true.

"Homeless sex predator ups and moves nearly two hundred miles to a new city on a whim? Come on, Nathan, I thought you were supposed to be a good detective. How often does that happen? He was clearly drawn here, I just wasn't sure how."

The silence returned as Cole continued his blind, forced march to who knew where. He was glad of the pause in conversation as it gave him time to think. He knew there was probably little chance of him talking his way out of this, but he had to try something at least. Unfortunately, the silence was short-lived.

"As you and I both know," the voice began again, "she cannot leave Leeds, and Maxwell didn't have his own phone. He went to great lengths to keep himself off the grid, as Freddy would say."

"So, what do you think happened?" Cole asked nervously.

"I have to be honest, I wasn't sure. So, I decided to follow him here."

"Was that wise? You know what she would do to you if she finds out you're back in Leeds."

"What can I say, Nathan? Sometimes life is a risk." There was a brief pause before he continued, "Now, I already knew that Lucy Silverman would be his first target. So, you see, last Monday night I was there, at the university. My intention was to put him down when he turned up. Unfortunately, Jackson showed up first and intervened. I needed to remain hidden, hoping that he could deal with Solomon instead." Another pause. "Except she was there, wasn't she? As Jackson chased Maxwell down, she used her telekinesis to trip him, and the son of a bitch got away. I guess her priorities have changed since the last time I saw her."

"Fine, so Jackson screwed up, what does that have to do with me?" Cole asked, already knowing the answer. Which meant his fate was now sealed.

Suddenly his legs were kicked out from beneath him and he was again sent crashing to the floor. The hood was pulled from his head and he blinked from the light of the early morning sunrise. A powerful hand clamped around his throat and the face of his kidnapper was mere centimetres from his own.

"Because she was not the only person I saw there that night. Somebody took Maxwell's knife after Jackson kicked it away and that somebody was you!"

"It was a crime scene," Cole managed to croak out. "I was collecting evidence!"

"So, if I call the station to check, the knife will be bagged and locked away safely in the evidence room?" He waited for an answer, but Cole failed to reply. "Just as I thought." He released him and stood up straight.

"You can't stop her," Cole managed to wheeze. "She will go through with her plan."

"We still have to try, and I will do everything in my power to stop an innocent girl from dying. Which is what makes you, not only a bad copper but also a despicable human being."

"You think you're doing the right thing? You have no idea what could happen if you stop her!"

"Maybe not. But I know what will happen if I don't. That alone means I have to try something."

Cole took a deep breath. "What about me?" he asked.

"I think you've fulfilled your usefulness."

"You're not a killer. I know you're not capable of that."

The club smashed down on Cole's left knee, shattering something inside. He screamed in agony as pain flooded through him. A moment later, the club hit his other knee, resulting in another wave of pain. Cole felt warm tears flowing down his cheeks now, and he was not even ashamed that he was crying.

"Don't ever tell me what I am capable of," his abductor shouted. "Since she arrived, you have no idea what I have had to do!"

"You became a monster to stop a monster?" Cole asked through clenched teeth. "Is that what you're saying?"

"Something like that."

"My officers will…"

"Do nothing. You see, they are now my officers. At least once your body has been discovered."

"What are you talking about?"

"I never actually left the police. I've just been on assignment working directly with the government to find a way to stop her. For good. Something you have failed to even try to do. I've already been placed in charge of West Yorkshire Constabulary. As I said, you've served your purpose." His smile was sad but ironic, "I'll make sure it's reported as an accident. That's the usual story, isn't it? Anyway, as I'm sure you've already figured out, we are still within the borders of Leeds, and she knows where you are. I imagine she will be here soon to clear up any loose ends."

"No! Please no. Don't let her kill me. I don't want to die like that." Cole's voice was now past pleading, he was begging, "Martin, please. Not like that." He stared at the blood-stained bat that Martin still held, "Please, make it quick. For old time's sake."

Martin nodded and raised the bat above his head. "I'm

sorry it came to this, Nathan," he said, before bringing it down with a loud thud that sent Cole spinning into nothing.

Chapter Fourteen

On top of the tallest building in Leeds, Gates, real name Freddy, was putting the final touches to a device of his own design. It was the culmination of years of designs and calculations. He was working towards a theory he knew few people would even be able to hope to grasp. Unfortunately, he had never been able to test it, so he had no idea if it would actually work at all.

As a cold steady wind blew around him, Freddy had spent the entire night setting up a network of similar devices spaced throughout the city limits. All of them needed to be placed as high as possible to achieve the maximum coverage of the area. As a child, Freddy had always been terrified of heights, but over time and with experience, he discovered there were other things to be far more scared of. He learned to adapt, something he had struggled with as a child.

Connecting the final wire to a battery pack, he opened his laptop and ran a diagnostic. Once he was certain everything checked out, he entered a password and clicked an icon marked 'activate'. A red light on the device switched to green, confirming it had successfully linked to the other eight similar devices that surrounded them in a near perfect circle. He was surprised at how easily his hands worked as if they already knew what to do. *I wonder how many times I've done this?*

Content that everything was now functioning as planned, Freddy took in the view of the city where he had spent his entire life before being convinced to leave. He was certain the equipment would do as required but less than confident it would achieve the results he theorised. But he had done all he could.

His phone began to ring. He checked the caller ID then swiped to accept, "Hello, Martin."

"Cole's been taken care of," Martin replied, getting straight to the point.

"Understood." Freddy knew that many people may have been affected by the news, but to him, it was just information. Cole had once been Martin's friend, however, so he asked, "How are you coping with this?"

"Fine. Cole made his choice. At least he won't be a problem for us today."

"Agreed," was all Freddy responded.

"Is the trap ready?"

Freddy took a moment to double check the status of his setup, "Yes. Everything is running as expected."

"Will it work, though? Will it kill her?"

"As I have explained already, I do not know. We've never tried this before."

"I have faith in you, Freddy," Martin said. "I've never known you to be wrong."

Freddy was quiet for a moment before speaking again, "Remember your promise. We only do this if everything else fails. I still think I can get through to her."

"I gave you my word. Though we both know it is unlikely, we'll try it your way first." Martin paused before continuing, "But be assured, one way or another, she has to end. Tonight."

***

Jackson nodded to Allister as he entered the office. He looked exhausted, and Jackson could not blame him. He had never seen Allister so dedicated to a case before. He doubted either of them had been sleeping recently, and this was confirmed by the heaviness behind his own eyes. His expression became more alert when a steaming cup of coffee was placed on his desk.

"Thanks, Al," Jackson said, picking it up and taking a grateful sip.

"You're welcome," Allister replied as he took a seat at his own desk. He switched on his computer, which began to hum into life, "I did as you asked and looked into Sean Benson's history."

"Did you find anything?"

"It would appear your instincts were right. He's been accused of sexual harassment on multiple occasions. There were two separate charges of sexual assault also brought against him. Sadly though his dad is rich and connected. Both cases seemed to have been dropped before ever getting to court. Another example of money talking, I guess."

"Maybe that is what drew Alice to him," Jackson considered. "What about the other three victims? Anything in their pasts that may have made them a target?"

"Joseph Wilks used kids to sell drugs. He was on the police radar, but they were still building a case against him. The nurse, however, was a strange one. The only thing I could find on her was that she helped get a colleague sacked for medical negligence. Although the dismissed woman always maintained that she was innocent and Veronica was the guilty person."

"Maybe Alice knew the truth somehow."

"That's quite an assumption," Allister said. "I found nothing else to suggest she was actually the guilty person."

"I understand what you're saying. I'm just trying to consider all the possibilities," Jackson admitted. "What about the police officer?"

"I couldn't find anything on him. By all accounts, he was a good, hardworking man. Glowing record, up for promotion. Several letters of commendation in his file from our friend DCI Cole," Allister said with a shrug. "Maybe he really was just in the wrong place at the wrong time."

"Unless he's just been very good at covering his tracks. Until we know more, let's suppose that she looks for people she feels have slipped through the cracks of justice. From what George said, she may have good reason to want to play judge and executioner."

"It's a possibility, I guess," Allister replied. "How did your conversation with George go? More productive than last time?"

"Maybe," Jackson answered. "I'm still trying to put together a lot of what he said and what it means. The man seems incapable of giving a straight answer which means talking to him is infuriating. However, George did mention that Alice was murdered thirty-two years ago in Leeds."

Allister turned to his computer and began typing, "I'll see what I can find out. Most newspapers put their archives online, so if anybody ran a story about it, then we should be able to find it."

As Allister worked, Jackson considered telling him he had apparently already met Alice. Unfortunately, George claimed to be unable to tell him exactly when this supposed meet had taken place. Without more to go on, Jackson decided it was unreasonable to give his already burdened friend even more to think about. At least not until he had an idea who she could be.

Everything just seemed to lead to loose ends and unanswered questions, no matter what they did.

"I sometimes feel as though we are going around in a circle. Reaching the same dead ends over and over again," he said, more to himself than Allister.

Allister frowned and looked at Jackson, "I've just done a search for a girl aged between thirteen and nineteen called Alice who was murdered in Leeds during the 80s. There's nothing."

"Nothing at all?" Jackson asked. Allister shook his head. "Could it have been removed?"

"I don't see anything that could indicate it has. Either it wasn't reported, or it didn't happen."

"Could Alice just be a pseudonym? Maybe she went by a different name before her murder."

"If that's the case, then we have little chance of finding her. There are more than a few murdered or missing girls in that age group from the 80s in the Leeds area."

Jackson sighed in frustration, "Every time I feel like we are making progress, we hit a brick wall."

"Let's just focus on what we do know and what we can do."

Jackson nodded in agreement, "I'm going to drive by Chloe's house. See if I can spot anything suspicious. I may as well try to be proactive for now."

"I'll see if I can narrow down this list of names. Check if I can put a face to the mysterious Alice. Somebody somewhere must know who she is."

"Message me if you find anything more?" Jackson began

walking toward the office door.

"It's strange," Allister said suddenly.

"What is?"

"After the week we've had, this morning feels like the first we've actually been able to catch a breath. It almost feels calm."

"I agree. But don't get too comfortable. Remember what a calm normally comes before." He smiled solemnly at Allister, then closed the door behind him.

***

Alice found the body of Detective Chief Inspector Nathan Cole lying on the hard ground, clothes now damp from the early morning dew. His body had ended up in an uncomfortable-looking position in the same place he had probably met his particularly nasty end. A large puddle of drying blood pooled behind his head. His lifeless eyes stared toward the sky but now saw nothing.

It was somewhat unfortunate, really. He had been useful to her over the years, and may still have been, but for his undignified end. On a positive note, Alice mused with a slight smile, she had been saved the messy task of eventually killing him herself.

After Freddy and Martin had chosen to abandon her, leaving Leeds without a word, Cole had become a convenient means to an end. He had been one of the few people who knew about her. He had clearly been besotted with her, as evidenced by the creepy way she always caught him looking at her. That infatuation had proven useful in manipulating him into doing anything she asked. That, and her knowledge of the future, which quickly aided him in climbing the ranks of the police force to a position that benefited herself.

There was only one person she knew who would have killed Cole and left him for her to find like this. Martin. He was back. Just the thought of him drove an anger through her she could barely contain. She doubted it was by accident he chose now to make his reappearance. Freddy had told Alice they were aware of what she had planned to do, so he was obviously here in an attempt to stop her. His own sense of justice often mirrored hers in a strange way.

Truthfully, it would be a pleasure to see him again. She had waited too many years to crush the life out of the traitor. What she did to his car was nothing compared to what she had planned for the man himself. She was brought back from her vengeful fantasy by the sound of cracking wood. She looked to her left and saw she had inadvertently crushed the trunk of a nearby tree with her telekinetic power. A moment later it toppled over, showering Alice with splinters of wood.

She would let Freddy live. There was no doubt he would be here too. He followed Martin wherever he went, such was his loyalty to the man. But for all Freddy had done, much of it too painful for words, she knew deep down, she could never hurt him. They had shared too much for her to be able to cause him any harm.

Unfortunately, she could not say the same for Jackson and Allister. She had no real wish to harm them. They had done nothing to warrant it, and she tried to only kill those she decided were deserving. If they got in her way or tried to stop her through, then she would be left with no choice.

She looked up as if following Cole's empty gaze to the sky, watching the sun as it continued to climb the blue of a new day. She wished she could see what was coming, but her power to view the future was almost entirely gone now.

Events were no longer certain, which made her nervous for the first time in decades. Things had to go to plan now.

Clouds passed by overhead, followed by a bird, and for a moment she felt a memory stir, like nostalgia. Everything looked so peaceful and tranquil. Like her first day. She grinned and her eyes shone red. It was time to change that. It was time to cause a storm.

***

Jackson sat in the rental car, observing Chloe's street. He had seen little movement, which was to be expected for a Sunday morning. All the curtains were still drawn in the Winchell home, indicating they were most likely still sleeping. Nobody else appeared to be watching the house, though.

So much did not feel right to him at the moment. Jackson felt as though he almost had the answer, but it always seemed to remain annoyingly just outside of his grasp. Almost as if he was waiting for one more piece of the puzzle to drop.

Not for the first time, Jackson was feeling overwhelmed. He had been in difficult situations before, and he had always been able to trust his instincts and think his way through. This time though, he felt his instincts were off. He was not sure what to do next and it was a feeling he did not like.

Alice was clearly a massive threat. Not just to Chloe, but to anybody that she decided deserved to die. He had met people with such delusional ideas of grandeur before and had always dealt with them. But he felt certain it would not be in the same way he had dealt with threats in Afghanistan.

Jackson jumped slightly when he heard the loud beep coming from his phone. Cursing, he reached into his pocket and retrieved it. Tapping his pin number onto the screen, he frowned when he saw it was another multimedia message. He had hoped he had seen the last of these.

Opening the message, he found it was indeed another newspaper article from the Leeds Daily News that was dated for the following day. He froze as he registered the headline and felt as though he was going to be sick. Throwing the phone onto the passenger seat, he turned the key in the ignition and began to pull away to the sound of squealing tyres.

***

Allister had decided to give up on the fruitless search of finding Alice's real identity. He tried to feel positive about how everything was going. A part of him was starting to hope that they could do this. It had been a long and difficult week. But if everything went well, by this time tomorrow, he and Jackson could move on and deal with whatever came next, knowing that Chloe was safe.

As soon as he heard the office door burst open and saw Jackson's face, he knew getting his hopes up had been a big mistake. Jackson looked as white as a sheet and was opening and closing his mouth, but no words came out.

"What's happened?" Allister asked, the worry in his friend's face now contagious.

Holding his phone out to Allister, Jackson gulped hard and just said, "Read it!"

Taking the handset from him, Allister saw it was another newspaper article. He began reading and immediately understood Jackson's fear.

CITY SHOCKED BY MURDER OF TEENAGE GIRL!

By Jane McArther

This morning, the city of Leeds woke to the news of the brutal murder of schoolgirl Chloe Winchell. Chloe, 15, had moved to the area only two years ago from Australia with her family.

Sadly, her body was found by friends in the early hours of this morning behind the Gold Rush Casino on York Road. Police maintain she is believed to have died around 10pm last night. An exhaustive search of CCTV footage has so far yielded no clues as to the identity of Chloe's attacker.

Officers are attempting to piece together her final movements. If anybody has any information or may have witnessed anybody in the area, please contact West Yorkshire police on...

Allister stopped reading. He felt as though he was about to vomit. This could not possibly be real. Moments ago, he had been so close to believing they were going to succeed. It had to be some kind of sick joke. Hands shaking, he looked at Jackson.

"Do you think it's genuine?" he asked, knowing the answer and that he was almost certainly grasping at straws.

"I don't know," Jackson replied with a heavy sigh. "All the others were, so we have to assume this one is too."

"Then we need to stop it."

Jackson frowned, "Didn't we agree to think about them

from now on? Decide if acting on the information is the right thing to do?"

Allister stared at Jackson as if seeing him for the first time, "You're kidding me, right?"

"Think about it, Al. How do we know that this isn't just another distraction?"

"To hell with distraction. This is Chloe we are talking about. If there's even a chance that she is in danger, then we do everything possible to stop this!"

"When we received the message about Lucy, you were the one who advised we think about it," Jackson reminded him.

"Yeah, and you completely ignored me and saved her anyway. You did the right thing," Allister replied. He knew he was being hypocritical but did not care.

Jackson looked as though he was about to argue further but seemed to change his mind. With a heavy sigh, he continued, "You're right. What do you think we should do?"

"This should be relatively easy. We just need to tell Chloe to stay home tonight, lock the doors and then we stand guard outside the house until morning."

"Hmm..." was all Jackson said in reply.

"I don't think I like the '*hmm*' you just made."

"It just seems too convenient that that would be the answer. Especially as I already intended to be there tonight."

"You did?"

"Yes. There is no way I would leave anything to chance right now. I've already sent her an email telling her not to leave the house alone today."

"How did she take that?"

"Very well. I think she understands the gravity of what's going on."

"If you had already decided to stay close to her and she still..." Allister hesitated before continuing "... and the news report happens, then something must happen between now and then that we haven't thought of."

Jackson nodded his agreement, "Something makes her go to York Road on her own tonight."

"Then we tell her not to go."

"Which may be what makes her go."

"You think so?"

"Can we risk it? She may wonder what's so important and go despite what we say."

Allister almost growled in frustration, "What do you suggest?"

"I go to the Gold Rush Casino tonight before 10pm. If she shows up, I get her out of there."

"Ok, but I'm coming with you."

"Al, if there's a confrontation..."

"All the more reason for me to be there. She trusts me more than you for a start, and if there is a fight, I can get her out while you deal with it. It makes the most sense that we both go."

With obvious reluctance, Jackson conceded, "Very good points. Fine, we do this together."

Chapter Fifteen

George quietly mopped the floor to his coffee shop, even though he knew in reality, it never actually got dirty. But he was nervous and felt he needed to be doing something. Today was a day he had known was coming since he was five years old. He understood the enormity of the task ahead, but he could only hope he was up to it.

He had been handed his destiny at birth, just like his father before him. Part of a long line of men and women known only as George, whose sole aim was to help the lost find their way to peace. Most of the time it was a lonely existence, as his clientele were only echoes of who they were, searching for a way to move on to what came next.

He sighed and clutched his mop tightly as the lights above his head flickered, then went dark. He knew what it meant even before the sound of whispering surrounded him. This was followed moments later by footsteps coming closer from behind. She knew the whole effect would be lost on him, but she loved to make an entrance all the same.

"You can stop with the theatrics, Alice," he said, his voice firm and confident, even though he did not feel either. "I know it's you."

"Don't spoil my fun, George," she replied. "You know I enjoy the whispering effect. It really freaks people out. Also, it's very entertaining."

George turned to face her. As was often the case now, she kept her face hidden in shadow, but her eyes shone blue. A sign she was in a less sadistic mood than she was capable of. She was clearly in what passed for a good mood right now.

"What do you want?" he demanded.

"You know what today is, don't you?"

"Of course, you know I do."

"I'm here to request very politely that you stay out of it, George."

"I'm sorry, but I cannot do that. I can't just stand by and let you harm an innocent girl."

"She'll thank you for it. Maybe not at first. But one day."

"She deserves better than you!" George hissed.

Alice hissed back and her eyes turned red. She raised her hand, but nothing happened. She hissed again in annoyance, "You are lucky I cannot use all of my abilities here, or I would crush you where you stand!"

"There is no need for all the threats and acts of violence, Alice! Why don't you let me help you cross over?" George asked, his voice softening. "You can still find peace."

"I don't want peace, George. I've seen what's waiting for me on the other side, and I won't go back!"

"It does not have to be like that this time. It could be different, you just have to want it!"

"What I want, is to survive!"

"Alice, sometimes just surviving isn't enough."

Her eyes glowed an even deeper red colour, and her voice was part threatening but also part lost. "Maybe. But maybe surviving is all I have left!"

"How did you become so twisted? You used to be a good

person."

Her hair glowed purple, illuminating the walls around them, "Your father did a great job of destroying the good that was left in me."

"He was trying to help, to show you what would happen if you did not change your path."

"Brilliant effort, as you can see!" she replied, her voice dripping with sarcasm.

"Alice, you can still..." George began, but it was too late.

The lights flickered back on again with a soft hum, and he found himself standing alone, with no evidence she had ever been there. He took a deep breath and turned to continue mopping. He had tried. For a moment, he thought he might have been able to convince her to cross right now, ending this nightmare before it could really start. Unfortunately, it seemed he would have to venture out tonight and try to correct old mistakes.

Suddenly, he felt pain rip into his body, as though a white-hot poker had slashed through him, forcing him to cry out. Fighting the urge, he slowly looked down. He cried out a second time when he saw the point of a blade from a carving knife protruding from his chest begin to twist, and the pain became almost unbearable. George heard Alice's voice close to his ear as she stood behind him, her free hand grasping his shoulder tightly, keeping him from collapsing to the floor.

"You forget," she began, barely above a whisper. "I may not be able to use all of my power here, but I can touch things. If you cannot stay away tonight, then you can go and join your father."

Alice disappeared again, and George fell to his knees. He

instinctively reached for the blade, knowing there was nothing he could do, and his vision began fading with each breath.

***

Allister busied himself in the office, desperately trying to find something that would give Jackson the edge when they finally confronted Alice. He had Googled stone tapes, but like Jackson, he failed to see how they were anything like the Alice he had learned about from Ruby and Chloe. Instead, he searched for anything online which might help. Except for some vague social media comments and one vlog about a mysterious ghost girl, he came up with nothing useful. Certainly nothing to provide any clues that they could actually use to stop her. Given time he could find out more, but time was something they were fast running out of.

Crossing to Jackson's side of the office, he opened a panel in the wall that was almost invisible to the naked eye. Behind it was where Jackson kept his safe. It had taken Allister some time, but he had eventually figured out the code to open it. He was acutely aware Jackson would not be happy with him breaking into the metal box, but since he was back at Chloe's street watching the house, he was unlikely to be back anytime soon.

Turning the lock quickly left and right eight times, he heard the dull clunk of the electronic lock being released. The door swung slowly open revealing the only two items Jackson kept there. Most prominent was a Glock 17 handgun. It was the old service pistol Jackson had somehow managed to keep after leaving the army. Allister had been tempted to ask how he had been able to hold on to it but knew well enough by now that when it came to his time in the army, Jackson would almost certainly remain silent.

Allister picked the weapon up. It was cold and heavier than he would have expected. Taking a clip of bullets from the safe, he pushed it into the gun grip. He had seen this done several times on the YouTube videos he watched after first discovering the Glock. He held it up in front of himself, practising his aim. The barrel wavered uncontrollably as his hands trembled.

"That won't help you," a familiar voice said from the door. "Not against Alice."

Allister looked towards the speaker, and although the voice was familiar, the face was not. The man whose voice he had instantly recognised as Gates stood just inside the office. Allister had always imagined the mysterious Gates to be a confident, strong, take charge individual. That, he now realised, could not have been further from the truth. He saw a thin, red-haired man in his late forties who looked very uncomfortable. He appeared to be trying to look everywhere else at once, just so he could avoid looking directly at Allister.

"You would be Gates, I take it," Allister said.

"Yes. But my real name is Freddy," the man replied.

Allister placed the gun down on Jackson's desk, ensuring the barrel did not point toward either of them. "What can I do for you, Freddy?"

"I know that you and Jackson intend to confront Alice tonight."

"If we have to. To be honest, all we want to do is keep Chloe safe."

"Believe me when I say that I have the same intention. You have no idea who or what you are dealing with, though. Which is why I am here. I have to ask you both to stay away tonight.

Let us deal with Alice."

"You like to get straight to the point I see."

"I see no reason to waste time."

"So, can you?" Allister asked. "Because in our last conversation, I remember you saying that you did not know how to stop her."

"Not for certain. But I have some theories," Freddy replied. "We've known her for over thirty years. I spent much of that time studying her. This gives us an edge you lack."

"Who is this 'us' you keep talking about?"

Freddy hesitated a moment before answering, "My associate and I. Please, Allister, let us handle this."

"What exactly are we dealing with? Because you also told me that you didn't know what she is."

Allister could see that Freddy was becoming frustrated. He stared hard at the floor and began repeatedly clicking the fingers of his left hand. It was clearly a coping technique.

"I do not know exactly what she is," Freddy finally admitted. "I've heard George's explanation and disagree with it."

"I think you're right. Alice appears to think for herself and is not restricted to repeating the same actions over and over."

"Your last statement remains to be seen. I personally think of her more as a glitch in reality. She interacts with our world without actually being a part of it physically. She's really more electrical. She creates her visible presence with radiation, using red, blue and green wavelengths from the electromagnetic spectrum so she can be seen by others."

"Is that why her eyes glow?" Allister asked.

"Initially that was a side effect of becoming visible. Although I believe it to be more for effect now. She has been able to appear to look like an ordinary person for some years now. Once she learns something new, she masters it very quickly."

"Are you actually saying she is like a computer glitch?"

"Not entirely, but I do think it's the best way to describe her. She's almost comprised exclusively of high-frequency electromagnetic energy. This eventually made her touch lethal to humans, as it disrupts their cells, giving them the appearance of ageing. It also allows her to manipulate or control almost anything electronic. She can even interface with computers and download information for her own benefit. It's one of the ways she evolves."

"She can manipulate electronics? Like closed circuit cameras for example?"

"Yes."

"Did she kill Nicola?" Allister whispered.

"Most likely," Freddy answered. "She harboured a great dislike for Nicola Ritchie for as long as I can remember."

"How is that possible? Nicola was sixteen!"

"Alice can see the future in certain instances. She can predict what someone will do, or what kind of person they might become."

"Wait a moment," Allister said suddenly. "Can she send information to mobile phones?"

"Yes, I imagine that would be possible for her," Freddy replied.

"Is she responsible for the messages Jackson has been

receiving? The ones about the future?"

"Yes."

"Why would she warn us about Chloe being killed tonight? Isn't that what she wants?"

"I don't know. Not for sure, anyway. But you can be certain she has a reason. She doesn't do anything that does not fit in with her objective. Which is exactly why you have to stay away tonight. If she thinks either Jackson or you might stand in her way, she will not think twice about removing you!"

Allister considered what Freddy was saying. If true, it made sense that Alice wanted them there for a reason and that staying away might actually be the right choice for Chloe. But how could he be certain? How much did he even trust Freddy, anyway? He had certainly been responsible for keeping things from him in the past. After brief consideration, he knew there was really only one choice he could make.

"I'm sorry, Freddy, but we cannot do that," he said in a tone that indicated there would be no further discussion. His decision was final.

"Allister listen to me..." Freddy tried regardless.

"There's nothing more you can do to change my mind. In all the years I've been helping you, you've never been upfront about anything. You've even flat out lied to me. Jackson and I will be there tonight, end of discussion."

Freddy's expression looked about as close to annoyed as Allister guessed the older man was able to get. He stared at the ceiling as if carrying out complex maths problems. His brow furrowed slightly as he seemed to reach a decision he was not happy about.

"Fine," Freddy said eventually. For the first time since

entering the office, he looked directly at Allister, making eye contact for a long moment. "I need the memory stick back." He held out his hand expectantly.

Allister reached into his jacket pocket and retrieved the tiny device he had kept on his person for some time. He took a moment to examine the small, dark grey and nondescript item again. There were no outside clues to indicate its actual purpose or contents. Allister also knew he lacked the skill to attempt to crack it, something he did not admit to easily. After the briefest of pauses, he placed it into Freddy's waiting palm.

"Are you going to tell me what that does?" he asked, already anticipating the answer.

"No," Freddy replied before turning toward the door. Just as he was about to leave, he stopped and said over his shoulder, "Take some advice and leave the gun, Allister. She's far more likely to kill you with it." Then he was gone.

Chapter Sixteen

Jackson sat in the passenger seat of the car, watching through the windscreen. Allister had parked as close to the Gold Rush Casino as he had been able to, while still giving them the best view possible. The street was almost entirely empty, allowing him a clear look in every direction. Some of the street lamps were broken, which not only left several places in darkness but also attested to the kind of area it was.

Allister had filled him in about the visit from Freddy, and the advice he had offered. Jackson agreed with Allister that they were so close to helping Chloe that giving up now was not an option. Jackson also had a feeling about how Freddy fitted into all of this, and if he was right, he had an uncomfortable sensation in the pit of his stomach about who else might be playing a part behind the scenes. If he was right, then his whole life may be about to change.

After Freddy left, Allister had begun researching everything he had just learned about Alice. Most of the explanations about electromagnetic radiation, wavelengths and colour spectrums made little to no sense to Jackson when Allister tried to explain them to him. They were nothing more than scientific words from school he had long since forgotten. However, when Allister clarified that many old myths such as ghost and poltergeist encounters had been linked to electromagnetic energy, things began to fit into place. His conversation with George also began to make far more sense.

"Do you see anything?" Allister asked.

"Nothing," Jackson replied. "But honestly though, Al, it isn't the most illuminated street I've ever seen."

"It doesn't seem like the kind of place somebody like Chloe would hang out near. I know it's only a few miles from her house, but it definitely doesn't scream teenager friendly."

"I just cannot imagine why she would willingly come here. Especially tonight of all nights."

"I see somebody!" Allister announced, pointing down the street.

Jackson's gaze followed to where Allister indicated. Among the shadows, he caught sight of a girl walking quickly toward them. She had her arms wrapped around herself and her head was down. The nearer she got, the more familiar she became. It appeared that despite his recommendations, Chloe had found a reason to come anyway.

"That's definitely Chloe," Allister confirmed. "What the hell is she doing here?"

"I don't know and right now I don't care," Jackson replied. "Let's just get her out of here and then ask questions."

"How do you want to do this?"

"You're her friend and she trusts you. You're going to need to convince her to get in the car."

"Two grown men trying to talk a teenage girl into getting in the back of their car? I see no way this could possibly end badly," Allister said in a deadpan voice.

"Really not the time for jokes, Al. Let's just do this before Alice shows up, and it's too late."

They both opened their car doors and climbed out of the

vehicle together. Chloe still had her head down as she walked and did not appear to have noticed them.

"Hey, Chloe," Allister called, trying to look relaxed, but feeling far from it in this unusual situation.

Chloe looked up quickly with a small jump of surprise, then smiled when she saw them. "Hey guys," she replied. "What are you doing here?"

"Just driving," Jackson replied, immediately realising how unlikely it sounded. "Can we give you a lift anywhere?"

"No, I'm good, thanks. I'm supposed to be meeting somebody here."

"Trust me, Chloe," Allister began. "I don't think there's anybody around here that you want to be meeting." He reached out to place a reassuring hand on her arm, but she quickly took two steps backwards. He started to worry they had mishandled the situation as concern crossed her face.

"Honestly. I'll be ok," she assured them. "Stop acting weird," she added with a nervous laugh.

"Sorry, we are just looking out for you," Jackson explained. "We think Alice might be on her way here."

"Alice? You mean my..."

"Hi, man," a voice said from behind Jackson and Allister.

Chloe's face changed from a friendly smile to a look of total confusion as Jade stepped forward. Jackson could see by Allister's reaction that they were thinking the same thing about Jade's unexpected arrival. Was it really possible she could be Alice?

"You guys do know you look like you're in the middle of a drug deal, right?" Jade continued, seemingly oblivious to the change in atmosphere.

"What are you doing here?" Chloe asked, looking shaken by Jade's presence.

"Getting drugs from my dealer. He lives around here," Jade explained. She finally seemed to be seeing what was in front of her. As she looked between the three of them, she took a step forward, "I'll tell you what Chlo, let's get you out of here, man!"

Jackson and Allister stepped between the two girls, keeping Chloe safely behind them.

"That's close enough, Jade!" Jackson said, trying to think of ways he might be able to stop her if he needed to.

"What the fuck? Are you kidding me? I knew you two were some sort of grooming gang."

"Just go, Jade," Chloe said, her voice almost pleading. "I swear I'm ok. We'll chat later, yeah?"

"This just got beyond weird." Jade took another step towards them, "I ain't leaving without her."

"Listen to her, Jade," Allister insisted. "She said she would like you to leave!"

"It's honestly ok, Jade," Chloe said, trying to sound reassuring. "They're my friends. I'm safe with Jack and Al."

Allister's head whipped around to look at Chloe. "You never call me Al!" he said, suspicion clear in his voice.

Seeing the momentary distraction, Jade took the opportunity to push past Allister and Jackson. She reached out to grab hold of Chloe's hand. "I'm getting you out of here," she said firmly.

"DON'T TOUCH ME!" Chloe screamed, taking even more steps back.

Everybody seemed to freeze momentarily in place at Chloe's reaction. Jackson looked towards Jade and saw that her face did not wear a look of malice or hatred, but a look of pure fear. He turned to see Chloe. Except it did not appear to be Chloe anymore. Her eyes glowed bright red and a look of annoyance covered her face. It suddenly became clear to him; Alice had in fact been here all along.

"For God's sake, Jade," Alice raged. "Do you have any idea what you've just done?"

"You're Alice?" Jackson asked, trying to process what he was seeing. "You've been leading us on this entire time?"

"No," Allister said. "It's not Chloe. She... it may look like her, but it's not her. I'd bet my life on it!"

"How can you be sure?"

"Chloe would never call me Al. It's one thing she was always adamant about. Abbreviating names is lazy."

"Actually, I am Chloe," Alice interjected. "Just not exactly as you know her... well me. Not yet anyway." She looked at Allister, her eyes fading to their natural non-glowing blue. "It's actually really good to see you again. It's been so long. Over fifteen years to be exact."

"None of this is making any sense, Al!" Jackson said.

Alice looked at him and smiled, "However, Jackson and I have already caught up this week. Haven't we?"

For a moment the statement confused him, but then with a flash of realisation, the final missing piece of the puzzle clicked into place. "The coffee shop," he said.

"Top marks," Alice confirmed with a smile that made her look too much like Chloe. "Also at the bar on 80s night. Before poor Sean met a very fortunate end. Unfortunate for him anyway." She looked at Allister, "Don't hold it against Jackson. He never told you about meeting me as I gave him a mental nudge to keep it to himself. I couldn't have you talking and figuring things out too quickly. It was similar to the nudge I gave you, to look in her direction the day we met."

"I should have realised sooner. You said you had a germ phobia when I tried to shake your hand," Jackson said.

"You would probably be dead right now if I hadn't. Which means you should thank me." She shrugged and smiled.

"Who are you really?" Allister demanded. "Because there is no way you are Chloe. I do not believe for a moment she is capable of murder."

Alice tilted her head slightly, and her smile became a grin. She looked like an innocent girl who was incapable of harm. She fluttered her eyelashes, "Maybe not yet, but give her time. She really will surprise you. She even surprised herself."

"If you are, or were Chloe, then how have you been here since the 80s?" Jackson asked. "Chloe is fifteen. She was born in 2002."

"That is a very good question. Unfortunately, I don't know the answer. Which is why I need everything to go exactly as planned tonight. Otherwise, who knows what will happen to me."

"What the fuck is going on, man?" Jade asked, finding her voice but sounding terrified. "Who is she? Is it Chloe?"

"I don't think so," Allister replied. "At least, not exactly."

"Then where is Chloe?"

Jackson exchanged a concerned look with Allister. She had a good point, and he was surprised the two of them had not realised it yet. If Alice had brought them here by making them think she was Chloe, then that meant nobody was watching the real Chloe.

"It's a setup," Jackson said, mentally kicking himself for falling for another of Alice's distractions.

"Where is she?" Allister demanded, standing his ground against Alice, his concern for Chloe pushing down his fear.

Alice smiled, but this time there was no innocence, her malicious nature was shining through clearly. A wave of purple light slid down the length of her hair. She raised her hand toward him and wriggled her fingers, "You should know, Al. You just sent me... well her, there!" She nodded toward the pocket where Allister kept his phone.

A look of confusion covered his face as he reached into the pocket and took hold of his phone. He quickly tapped the screen several times. He read something, then looked at Jackson, blood visibly draining from his face.

"What is it?" Jackson asked.

Allister handed him the phone, and Jackson read a message that had been sent to Chloe's phone only moments before.

Chloe, go to your safe place. It's important. I will meet you there. Allister.

As soon as he finished reading the message, the screen cracked and went dark. Jackson checked his own phone to see that it too had been broken. He glanced at Jade who held up her own damaged device.

"Sorry guys," Alice said, sounding anything but apologetic. "I can't have you warning her."

"It doesn't matter," Allister replied confidently. "We told her to stay in her house. She won't fall for an obvious trick like this."

Alice shrugged, "I did."

Allister looked at Jackson, his eyes pleading. "She needs me," was all he said.

"Go!" Jackson replied. "I'll be ok."

Just as Allister turned to run toward the car, he seemed to freeze in place, only his head would move. Jackson tried to take a step toward him but found his own body seemed reluctant to move either. Every limb was locked solid, only his neck still seemed to follow instructions. Turning his head toward Alice, he saw she was holding one hand toward them, fingers spread out.

"You're both going to need to stay here, I'm afraid," she insisted. Her head turned to her left, so she could examine Jade. "I'm really sorry about what happened at school, mate. I hated doing that to you. But you've very nearly messed everything up for me."

"You can't hurt her. I won't let you!" Jade replied, trying to be defiant but visibly shaking. All signs of her tough girl persona were gone.

"Yes, I can. She's me. I can do whatever I choose with her!" She moved closer to Jade, "I really don't want to do this, you were a good friend to me. You made this week one of my best since moving to this damned city. But do you remember what I said would happen if you interfered again?" She began to raise her free hand toward a terrified Jade, her eyes turning red once more. She began to reach a hand out toward her friend.

"I can't let you do that, Chloe," a voice called from behind Alice.

As soon as she heard it, her eyes turned black and her face

became a mask of pure hatred. For a moment, Jackson was almost convinced he could hear her growling. Everything about her was becoming animalistic, as though instinct was taking over her actions.

"You!" she snarled, as she turned to face the newcomer.

As if from nowhere, the air was filled with what sounded like an incoherent stream of beeps and squeals, echoing off the surrounding buildings. As soon as Alice heard them, she grabbed her head and began screaming in agony. She seemed to flicker momentarily between visible, translucent and invisible, before finally remaining visible. She bent forward, as though barely able to keep her feet beneath her anymore.

Jackson and Allister found themselves able to move again. Allister looked at Jackson. "I need to get to her," he said.

"I understand," Jackson shouted, as Allister was already running toward the car. Turning to Jade he added, "You too. Get out of here."

"But..." Jade began to protest.

"I don't know how long we have, so go home. Now!"

Jade nodded in agreement, took one last look at Alice who was still clutching her head, then turned and began to run as fast as she was able to.

Jackson slowly approached Alice, who had stopped screaming, but still clutched her head as she quietly whimpered while rocking back and forth, now on her knees. She was clearly still in agony. He had no idea what the strange noises that continued their assault were, but they clearly appeared to be a form of torture for her. Part of him felt sorry for Alice, but he was more relieved that she had been incapacitated, even if only for now.

Looking past her, he saw a man walking toward them holding a megaphone. The sounds were clearly coming from the device, which were so loud, Jackson was surprised nobody else had come to investigate what was causing them.

The new arrival was a man who appeared to be in his fifties. Jackson was sure that he did not know him, but he looked familiar. Very familiar. He moved carefully forward toward them; the megaphone aimed unwaveringly at Alice, a determined look on his face. When he seemed satisfied she had been subdued, he switched off the noise and watched her carefully, ready to switch the megaphone back on again if needed.

"You should never have come back," Alice whispered, obviously still in pain, despite the silence.

"You need to be stopped. I'm sorry. I didn't want things to be like this. You left me no choice."

"Have you any idea how hard my life has been since you both abandoned me?" she demanded, her voice rising slightly.

"I can only imagine."

"I had to get through the 90s without you!"

"We both made sacrifices." At that moment he glanced at Jackson, who suddenly realised who he was. Jackson felt his knees wobble.

Alice got slowly to her feet, but it appeared she was still weak. She raised a hand toward the older man, but nothing happened. She sighed in frustration. "This isn't over, Martin!" she said, before turning and stumbling away, managing to remain invisible on her third attempt.

Martin lowered the megaphone and turned to Jackson. He tried a smile, but it did not seem to work. Finally, he gave up and just spoke. "Hello, Son," he said.

"Dad?" Jackson asked in disbelief.

***

Chloe sat swinging backwards and forwards on her favourite swing in the park she thought of as her safe place. The message from Allister had surprised her, not just in receiving it, but the urgency of it. Especially after Jackson had insisted that she remain home tonight. Fortunately, her parents had gone to a local shop to buy a bottle of wine, so she hadn't needed to make an excuse to leave the house so late.

Now she just needed to wait for Allister to arrive and tell her what was so important. She had tried dialling his number, but it went straight to voicemail. This really surprised her, as he did not seem like the kind of person who turned his phone off. Ever.

Feeling concerned, she tried both Jackson and Jade's numbers but was again met with the same response, an automated voicemail message. She knew for certain Jade would have her phone on, regardless of the time. Worried it might be her phone that was to blame, she called her mother's number instead. She relaxed slightly when she heard it connect.

"Hi, sweetheart," her mother said, answering after three rings. *"Is everything ok?"*

"Yeah," Chloe replied. "I was having some connection issues, so I was checking it wasn't my phone freaking out on me. It clearly isn't."

"That's good. I know you would be lost without it. Your father and I are about to pay, then we'll be on our way home."

"Ok. I'll see you then." Chloe was about to hang up when she stopped herself, "Mum?"

"Yes, sweetheart?" her mother sounded concerned.

"You know I love you right? You and Dad." Chloe was surprised by the words as soon as they were spoken. She was rarely so sentimental with her parents anymore. Especially in the last two years.

If her mum was surprised, she did not let it show. *"We know you do, Chloe. We love you too. We'll be home in about twenty minutes, ok?"*

"Yeah, I'll see you soon." She tapped the phone and ended the call.

She tried calling Allister again but once more received the same message. She sighed as she put her phone back into her bag, which she placed on the floor beside her. As Chloe continued to rock on the swing, she considered giving up and going home. Allister could find her there. It was cold, and she had a huge day tomorrow.

But instead, she stopped swinging as a strange smell reached her nose. Her brow furrowed in confusion as she tried to place it. It was bitter and sickly, but also familiar. She sniffed again, which was when fear and realisation hit her at the same time. Sour milk. Before she could react, a hand clamped over her mouth, preventing her from crying out, and she was pulled from the swing.

*** *

Jackson stood, staring at his father in utter disbelief. This man who had left him when he was too young to even remember. Abandoned with just photos, stories from his mother and an old car to prove he had ever existed at all. Two equally strong emotions fought for dominance within him, one wishing to hug his dad, the other wanting to punch him. If he had also abandoned Alice, then he guessed they had something in common.

"What are you doing here?" he finally asked, deciding to go with the safest response. "Where have you been?"

"I understand you have a lot of questions, Jackson," Martin replied, "and you deserve answers to all of them. But they will need to wait, I'm afraid. I may have hurt Chloe but be certain that she will be back, and she'll be angry." He held up the megaphone, "Sadly the same trick never works twice with her, so it's best we go."

Jackson considered what his father said and could not fault his logic. Chloe was still in danger, so everything else had to wait. "You're right. Our catch up can come later. So, what do you suggest for now?"

"Where did Allister go?"

"To meet Chloe. The real one, I mean."

"They are both equally real, Son," Martin replied. "Do you know where she is?"

Jackson nodded "At a park. The one near..."

"I know it," Martin replied, placing his finger against his ear. "Freddy, the girl is at the park. I'll meet you there."

Jackson guessed there must be some kind of two-way radio in his dad's ear. Martin had obviously come prepared for this evening, leading Jackson to believe that he had known what he was dealing with, and who she was.

"You knew what was going to happen tonight, didn't you? You knew Alice's real identity," Jackson said, the accusation clear in his voice.

"My car's just down here," Martin replied with a nod of his head. "We should go before Chloe recovers." They began walking in the direction indicated. "Yes. We did know. Freddy and I have known for some time. We also knew of her friendship with Allister. It was one of the reasons Freddy sought him out to work for us."

"Allister was working for you, and he didn't tell me?"

"He didn't know it was me, and Freddy operated under the name of Gates. But we always knew Chloe would eventually attempt to contact him, so we needed to be ready for when she did."

"Why didn't you tell us? We could have stopped all of this. We could have done things differently."

"The risk was too great. We knew when it happened. We didn't know how. Anything we did may have been the choice that makes Chloe who she becomes."

"So, you chose to do nothing?"

"We chose to follow fate as it happened. Hopefully to catch whatever takes Chloe down a certain path. To stop the cycle once and for all."

Again, Jackson figured it made a certain amount of logical sense not to intervene. He had chosen to change the future and save Lucy, and so far, nothing negative seemed to have happened as a result. But he could understand why his dad had chosen to take a different course of action. Especially as the stakes appeared to be that much higher.

He looked at the megaphone Martin still carried, "What did you do to hurt her like that?"

"It was a pilot signal," Martin replied. "I played her a corrupted data file."

"That makes no sense to me."

Martin chuckled at that, "I know exactly how you feel. Freddy could certainly explain it better. Chloe absorbs digital information from all around her: radio waves, television signals, Wi-Fi, anything that transmits information. Even the human mind to a lesser extent if she's close enough. It's essentially how she learns. But she has internal firewalls that prevent her from absorbing anything that could be harmful. Instead, a pilot signal sends information via an audio medium, just like an old dial-up modem or a cassette tape computer game would have. She has no defence against it. If she can hear it, she is affected by it."

"Can it kill her?"

"Sadly not. It is extremely painful, however, as you saw. She will eventually purge the bad data and be back to full strength. When she is, I'm going to be her first target." Martin shrugged, "Though to be honest, there is nothing new there. We have had a... rocky relationship to say the least."

"Can you stop Alice?" Jackson asked.

They reached Martin's car, which he unlocked with a key fob. His dad was clearly doing well for himself as it was an expensive looking sport coupe. A huge step up from the ancient car Jackson now owned. They got in as Martin considered his reply.

With a sigh, he said, "I honestly don't know. Freddy has something planned, but I don't understand a word of it." He paused for a moment before continuing, "Son, you have to stop calling her Alice. It's a name Freddy gave her, which she eventually adopted to distance herself from what she was doing. She may not be Chloe as you know her now, but she was, and she's who your Chloe will become one day if we don't stop this."

"I don't understand. George said that she died thirty-two years ago."

"George," Martin said with a smile as he began driving. "There's a name I haven't heard in some time. To answer your question; from Chloe's perspective, she was indeed murdered over thirty years ago. From mine too, I guess. But from yours, she dies tonight!"

***

Allister ran as fast as he was physically able towards the park, all the way cursing himself for falling for Alice's tricks. He had been the one to counsel Jackson on caution when it had been Lucy's life in danger. Yet, when he believed Chloe to be at risk, he refused to think rationally. Now Chloe could pay the price for that arrogance.

"Get off me!" he heard Chloe shout from the darkness ahead, spurring him to run faster than he could ever have believed himself capable. Adrenaline filled his body as he felt his feet power him forward.

He also cursed himself for listening to Freddy and leaving the gun behind in the office, even though deep down he knew it had been the wisest choice. He didn't know if he would even be capable of using it.

Barely slowing down to open the park gate, he immediately saw two figures struggling on the tarmac floor. He could make out Chloe attempting to shove her attacker from her, clearly not giving up without a fight. Her fist thrust upward to strike his face, sadly to little effect. As Allister drew closer, his eyes met with hers, and he saw relief flood into them. She knew she was saved.

"She said get off!" Allister yelled as he kicked the man hard in the side of his ribcage, knocking him away. The sound of a knife skidding across the floor briefly caught his attention. He immediately placed himself between Chloe and the attacker, intending to shield her from further harm. Relief flooded through him as he saw Chloe already getting back to her feet from the corner of his eye.

The other man growled at him in obvious irritation at being disturbed and looked at Allister with eyes that almost burned with hatred. He too began to get to his feet, picking up the knife he had dropped as he did. When the moonlight illuminated his face, Allister saw the dark birthmark across the left side of his face. He could barely believe it: Maxwell Solomon.

Allister was stunned as he faced the man who had escaped Jackson earlier in the week. Maxwell watched him, slowly turning the knife in his hand. His face held open hostility and no fear towards Allister.

"Allister?" Chloe said, her voice barely a whisper behind him.

Unable to look away from Maxwell, Allister did not reply as he considered his next move. He was beginning to realise that he was far out of his depth. Maybe he should have waited for Jackson, but then Chloe would still be alone with Solomon right now, possibly in a worse position.

"Allister!" she said again but with more urgency.

Before he could respond, a shadow seemed to breeze past him, attacking Maxwell with a flurry of punches so fast Allister could barely count them. Within seconds, Maxwell lay subdued and bleeding on the park floor. His knife could be heard skittering across the floor and out of harm's way. When

Allister looked around, instead of Jackson standing over Maxwell, he found Freddy, fists still clenched.

"Allister!" Chloe said in a voice so small and scared he knew he had to turn around. When he did, he felt his world begin to crumble.

She stood before him looking as white as snow. She held up a hand, and he saw the blood smeared across her fingers. Every fibre of his being screamed at him not to look, but his eyes dropped to her stomach and the growing red stain on her t-shirt. Seeing her legs were about to give way, Allister rushed forward and caught her. He gently held her against himself, as tears were already making damp tracks down her cheeks.

"No, no, no, no!" Allister repeated as he tried to think of what to do. All his knowledge about computers and technology, and he only now realised he knew nothing about how the human body worked. "Chloe, don't worry. You're going to be ok. Don't do this to me!"

"Please, I don't want to die, Allister," she begged, her body shaking against him. "Please don't let me die."

"You're not going to die, ok?" Allister replied firmly. "I won't allow it!" He looked up at Freddy to see if he could be of any help, but the older man just watched, almost as if he was having difficulty processing the scene he saw playing out before him. Allister could not help but wonder what his connection to Chloe and Alice actually was.

Jackson appeared beside Allister, took in what had happened and sprang into action. Without a word, he ripped a strip of fabric from his jacket, folded it into a tight wad, and gently taking her from him, laid her on the ground and pressed it firmly against Chloe's stomach.

"Dad," he said in a tone that expected to be obeyed, "call an ambulance. Tell them we have a fifteen-year-old girl with a stab wound to her abdomen losing blood fast. She will definitely need a transfusion." He looked at Allister, "Do you know her blood type?"

The question caught Allister by surprise. Of course he didn't know. Why would he know? He did not even know his own. "I-I've no idea..."

"A-negative," Freddy said from where he stood observing. Allister could not help but wonder how he could have known but knew now was not the time to ask.

If Jackson also thought it strange, he didn't say, instead simply passing the information onto Martin. "A-negative. Tell them she needs help now!" He looked at Allister. "Who did this?" he asked. Unable to answer, Allister pointed to Maxwell, who still lay on the ground. Despite the blood and swelling, it was clear Jackson had no difficulty remembering him, "Oh Christ, not him. Goddamn it. Why did I let him get away?"

"Now's not the time for blaming yourself," Martin said, reappearing behind him. "I imagine we will all have plenty of that to do tomorrow if tonight ends badly. Just focus on saving this girl. The ambulance is on its way!"

"Can you? Save her I mean?" Allister asked, his voice thick with emotion. He could feel his own warm tears stinging the corners of his eyes.

"I'm going to do everything I can to try," Jackson replied. Allister noted he gave him no guarantees.

"K-Ka..." Chloe gasped. Talking was clearly an effort.

"What was that, Chloe?" Allister asked, leaning down to hear her better.

"Kanga..." she tried again. "I want Kanga..." she pointed

over to the swings. "B-Bag..." Allister's gaze followed her finger, and he saw her bag lying next to the swings.

Jackson looked at Allister in confusion, "She wants what?"

"Kanga. It's her favourite stuffed animal from when she was little. She keeps it with her when she's scared," Allister explained. He looked back to Chloe, "I'll go get him."

As soon as he began to stand, he felt Chloe's hand grab his arm with a strength she no longer looked capable of. "No!" she said in a scared voice. "D-Don't leave me... Allister."

Allister looked at her, then at Jackson who was battling to stop the bleeding, the red liquid already covering his hands and wrists. The bag was so close, but he did not want to leave her, and Jackson could not.

"I'll get it," Freddy said. The look on his face suggested he was finding the unfolding events as hard to deal with as Allister was.

"Thank you," Allister replied gratefully. He looked at Chloe and stroked her hair gently, "Freddy has gone to get him." She gave his arm a squeeze, her grip beginning to feel weaker by the second. "How is she doing?" he asked Jackson.

It was clear from Jackson's expression what the answer was, but instead, he said, "I've managed to slow the bleeding. If an ambulance arrives soon, her chances will be a lot better." He looked over his shoulder at Martin, "Dad, did they say how long?"

"Less than ten minutes," Martin replied. "You're doing great, Son. You can do this."

Chloe coughed, blood appearing in the corner of her mouth. Her breathing seemed to become slower.

"That's not a good sign is it, Jackson?" Allister asked, panic rising in his voice again.

Jackson shook his head, "Internal bleeding. That ambulance needs to be here now!"

Freddy returned and held out the stuffed toy for Chloe. She took it with a thankful look and smiled weakly before clutching it tightly to her chest.

"It's close," Freddy said to Martin. "Where's George?"

Before Martin could reply, Maxwell suddenly pushed himself to his feet and began to stumble toward the park exit. Martin started to give chase when Maxwell just froze in place as he reached the exit. He let out a strangled scream of pain then his head twisted violently to the left accompanied by a loud snap that echoed through the air. As his body fell to the floor, Alice was revealed, standing casually on the opposite side of the gate. Her eyes glowed red, and she had a satisfied smile on her face.

"Oh my God, that felt good," she said in an almost musical voice. "I've waited over thirty-two years to do that!"

"Alice is here," Jackson said, briefly looking toward her, concern in his eyes.

"Don't worry," Allister replied. "She can't come in here. We're safe for now."

Alice looked at him and gave a sad smile that actually appeared genuine. With a wave of her hand, the gate opened, and she stepped forward into the park. "Sorry to disappoint you, Al. It's not that I couldn't enter; I've just never wanted to. I'm sure you can appreciate why." She turned her gaze on Freddy; her eyes seemed to soften slightly as they turned green at the sight of him, "As for your question, Freddy, unfortunately, Georgie couldn't make it. We talked, and he eventually got my point."

Martin held up the megaphone towards her, but before he could switch it on, Alice flicked her wrist and it was ripped from his grasp. Martin watched as it flew over the surrounding fence and disappeared into the darkness. She gave him an annoyed look, then began to approach Chloe. In the distance, the wail of an ambulance siren could be heard getting closer.

Chloe squeezed Allister's arm when she saw Alice. "Who's that?" she asked, her voice barely audible now.

"It's Alice," Allister replied, warily watching her approach.

"W-Why does she look like me?"

"Try not to worry about it. The ambulance will be here soon."

"Am... I going to be ok?" her voice was so small, so frightened, that it broke Allister's heart.

"Yes!" Allister said firmly. He glanced at Jackson, but his face told him everything. With the tiniest shake of his head, he confirmed Allister's fears. "Why did you do this, Alice?"

"I had to," she replied simply. "You see, if she doesn't die on this night, in this way, then there's a good chance I would never have existed. It's not personal, it's just about survival."

"That's why you saved her from Michael Johnson," Jackson said without looking at Alice. "It was the wrong time."

"That's right, Jackson. Also, he really did deserve it. If you had seen what he intended to do, you'd understand."

"What about her survival?" Allister demanded.

"She... I survive. It might not be what she wants right now, but in time she will," Alice explained, her eyes briefly flicking to Freddy.

"Allister," Chloe said, her voice coming out between breaths.

"What is it?" he asked gently, trying to keep the worry from his voice.

"It's... too late."

"No, don't give up. The ambulance will be here in just a minute. You've got to hang on! Don't you dare give up!"

"I-I..."

"Don't talk. Save your strength."

"I'll miss... you," she whispered. Allister watched as the life seemed to disappear from her eyes, and she took her last breath.

Chapter Seventeen

Jackson looked down at the lifeless body of the girl he had fought so hard to keep alive. But in the end, all the first aid knowledge he gained in the army had just not been enough to save her. Maybe if there had been a medical kit and plasma supplies to keep her going, he could have made more of a difference, but as it was, he had been able to do little more than try to stop the bleeding with compression alone. The knife wound was too deep, and she had lost too much blood for him to have stood any chance of saving her. Even if he had been able to get to her sooner. If she had been able to make it to the hospital, she could have had more of a chance, but out here, he had known the odds were slim from the moment he had laid eyes on her. Knowing that did not make any of this any easier to accept, however. He had seen death before, but not somebody so young; this was something he had never dreamt he would be forced to confront.

"No," Allister shouted. "Don't do this, Chloe. Please don't do this!" He squeezed her hand as he gently rocked her shoulder in a desperate attempt to wake her.

Jackson placed a hand on his best friend's back to comfort him, "I'm sorry, Al. There was nothing I could do. I'm afraid she's gone."

Allister looked for a moment as though he was going to argue with him, but in the end, he seemed to crumple as he accepted what was obviously the truth. He placed his hand against Chloe's cheek, then lifted her to him so he could hug her a final time.

"And I'm still here!" Alice said with relief, looking at her hands. "I wasn't sure if I would be."

Allister looked up at her, anger in his eyes, "You mean you had her killed and you were not even sure if it would even satisfy your sick idea of survival? It could have all been for nothing?"

Alice shrugged, "Not one hundred percent."

"But you killed her anyway?"

"You have to take risks, and it did work. That is what's important now." Alice attempted a smile, "Al, I know you're upset and angry, but I am still me. I am Chloe, and I was right, I have missed your friendship."

"Are you insane?" Allister asked, his voice rising. He gently laid Chloe back on the ground and got to his feet. He pointed to Chloe, "This girl here, the girl who just died in front of me, was my friend. Me and you? We are not friends. You're just the psychopath who killed her!"

Jackson was growing concerned that Allister was pushing Alice too far. Although her eyes remained their normal blue, they had both witnessed how quickly she could become angry.

"I would recommend you calm down," Freddy warned, seeming to read Jackson's mind.

"He has a point," Martin agreed. "I've seen her hurt people for far less."

Alice turned her eyes bright blue and she looked frustrated, "You've got it all wrong. I know what you think about me, Martin, but I don't want to hurt Allister!"

"No!" Allister snapped, seeming to throw her off balance. "You do not get to call me that."

"Please try to understand..."

"Freddy," Allister began, "whatever you've got planned, do it now!"

Alice looked from Allister to Freddy, her face showing fear for the first time. "Freddy? What is he talking about?" she asked.

"I'm sorry, Chloe," Freddy said as he tapped the screen on his phone. "I really am."

"Please don't..."

For a moment, Jackson thought he saw regret on Allister's face, maybe he thought he had acted too rashly. But when nothing happened, he began to wonder if whatever Freddy had attempted to do had failed. Seconds later, all of the lights he could see started to blink out. Street lamps, lights in nearby buildings, even the lights of passing cars. The ambulance, now so close its siren was almost deafening, fell silent. Within moments it looked as though every direction was now in total darkness, except for the pale light of the moon. Jackson searched for Alice, but she was gone, with nothing to show she had ever been there.

"What the hell was that?" he demanded, looking between his dad and Freddy.

"An EMP," Freddy replied. "A citywide detonation."

"Let me get this straight," Allister began. "You've just detonated an electromagnetic pulse, over the whole of Leeds?"

"We had to go for full saturation, make sure there was nowhere she could have escaped to," Martin explained. "If Freddy calculated correctly, and he always does, that blast should have covered the area almost all the way to the city's borders."

Jackson was pacing now, "This could be very bad."

"What could?" Allister asked.

"George. He said the night Alice, well Chloe, died, something happened that made her what she was. As I understand what Freddy told Allister, she was essentially made from electromagnetic radiation. Could that pulse in some way be responsible for everything that happens to her? Even displacing her in time?"

Freddy looked deep in thought, "It could make sense. Electromagnetism indeed has a history of being linked to time travel theories. Nikola Tesla certainly believed it possible. Among other scientists."

"What are you saying, Son?" Martin asked.

"I'm saying that I don't think you killed Alice," Jackson explained. "I think you may have just created her!"

"Did you know about any of this, Freddy?" Allister asked.

Freddy showed no emotion in his face, "I knew it could have been a possibility. But the odds were very slim."

Martin gave Freddy a suspicious look. "This conversation will have to wait," he said, indicating the paramedics who now made their way toward them on foot. "You three should go. I had a police team ready to move as soon as the city went dark. I will make sure Chloe receives everything she needs."

"Somebody will need to tell her parents," Allister said, his voice cracking slightly. "I could go..."

"It's good of you to offer, but I have officers trained to handle delicate situations like these. The best thing you can do for now is make yourself scarce. I will handle everything here."

"I agree," Jackson replied. He noticed Freddy was already walking away so he turned to Allister. "Let's go, Al," he said, gently placing his hand on Allister's shoulder.

"I need to be alone right now," Allister replied, shrugging the hand and the gesture away. Putting his head down, he began walking, leaving Jackson to wonder if their friendship would ever be the same again.

Chapter Eighteen

Early the following morning Jade sat with her back against the fence to the park that Chloe had loved so much, trying to figure out everything that had happened in the last twenty-four hours. It felt impossible to believe that just two days ago they had been sitting in Chloe's house, braiding each other's hair and laughing about things that no longer seemed important. Acting like the teenage girls they were. It was the best time she remembered having in so long.

They had only been friends for less than a week now but Jade already felt a hole inside herself she could not believe would ever be filled again. Some people really did come into your life and leave a huge impression. Chloe had, without a doubt, been one of those people.

Following Jackson's instructions, Jade had run towards her home. She hated leaving, but one meeting with Alice had given her nightmares, and she knew the smart thing to do was get as far away from her as fast as she was able to do. Growing up with the life she had, Jade did not scare easily, always choosing to fight over flight. Running was not in her nature, but it was clear Alice had been somebody she could not fight. So, she ran.

Once the power went out, she knew something bad had happened, and she sensed it was all connected. Jade knew she had to go to Chloe's home and make sure she was ok. She tried to ignore the growing feeling of dread that was already building in the pit of her stomach, trying to convince herself it was all in her head.

What she found as she approached the house, was Chloe's parents holding onto each other in the doorway and crying. They listened as two uniformed police officers told them Chloe's body had been found in the park nearby. Jade backed away before she could be seen. Her ears were filled with the desperate cries of Chloe's mother screaming her daughter's name, made all the more chilling in the silence of the night.

Jade ran straight to the park, her mind desperately clinging to the hope that it must be some kind of mistake. There was no way that Chloe could be gone. They had spoken on face time for over an hour the previous morning. Seeing the area lit up by portable lights running from a small generator dashed those hopes immediately. Black and yellow police crime tape surrounded the fence, while men and women in white boiler suits moved around gathering up items into plastic evidence bags.

The man who had saved Jackson, Allister and herself from Alice, looked to be in charge, directing the other officers and issuing orders. As she stood against the fence that ran around the edge of the park, she scanned the area and felt her heart miss a beat when she saw the black body bag laid out near the swings. She could see the outline of whoever was inside, and they looked so small. Far too small to be in such a big thing.

Jade's knees betrayed her then and she fell against the fence, sliding down against it until she was sitting on the floor. She cried. Tears for every missed opportunity over the years that she could have spent with Chloe, and for every moment they would now never have as friends. So much wasted time for nothing.

She remained sitting there, back resting against the metal bars for God only knew how long. Certainly the entire night, as the sky was by now beginning to lighten as the sun started to shine on a new day as if nothing had happened. She knew deep down it was time she should probably move but did not feel as though she could even if she wanted to, which she did not. She felt as though she would be abandoning Chloe if she left her here alone, surrounded by strangers.

"Hi," a voice from nearby said. "It's Jade, isn't it?"

She looked up to see the man from last night standing a short distance away. Not trusting her own voice to speak right now, she chose to nod.

"Have you been here all night?"

Another nod.

He squatted now so he was on her level, "I'm Superintendent Martin Clarke. Is there anything you need or anybody I can call for you?"

A shake of her head this time. Jade looked up at Martin, worried she might be asked to go. "Do I have to leave?" she managed to ask.

"Not at all. Stay as long as you want. If you need anything at all just ask one of my officers and they will help you out," Martin replied with a tight smile. He hesitated a moment then reached into an evidence bag he carried. "I really shouldn't do this, but on this occasion, I think I can bend the rules. Also, I think Chloe would have wanted you to have it." He held something out to her. "I think his name is Kanga. He looked after Chloe when she was scared or sad."

Jade reached out and took the small stuffed animal from him with a small smile of thanks. She examined it. Kanga was clearly quite old, with a chewed ear, scratched eyes and patches of fur worn away. Jade stroked her thumb along its body and noticed red flakes come away on her skin from a dark stain.

"Try not to worry about that," Martin said. "It should come out in the wash."

"No!" Jade said more quickly than she intended and felt awkward for wanting to keep it. "I mean, maybe, not yet..."

"I understand." Martin turned and began to walk away when he suddenly stopped. Without looking back, he added, "I don't know if this helps, but you were very important to her, and she talked about you often. Mostly about how much she missed you."

Jade's head snapped up, but Martin was already walking away. Unsure of what he meant, she lay on the cold, dew-covered grass with her back to the fence, clutched Kanga close to her, and cried until she fell asleep.

***

Jackson unlocked the door to his office and entered. He flicked the light switch on and, as expected, nothing happened. He sighed and crossed to his desk, placing a bag on its flat surface. He looked at the expensive electronic equipment that surrounded him, all of it now essentially worthless. He finally felt justified that he had kept paper files of their workload. Although the satisfaction felt hollower than he believed it would.

He opened the bag and removed the brand new boxed up smartphone he had purchased. He had walked the ten miles to the next town, Wakefield to purchase it as the town had been unaffected by the EMP Freddy detonated the previous evening. After a taxi ride back to his office, he sat at his desk feeling hollow inside.

Picking up a newspaper before returning to Leeds, he had been surprised by how quickly a cover story had been put into place to explain what happened. Calling the damage to electrical items in Leeds the result of a freak solar storm striking the city. Jackson could not help but shake his head at the absurdity of the claim, but also knew people would accept it and move on with their lives. Most of them anyway.

Taking the new phone from its box and turning it on, he saw there was a very weak signal. There must be a surviving phone tower outside the city limits. It was enough to begin the setup, and for the software to update so he could add his email account and activate its other features. A pop-up message advised him the setup could take several minutes to complete. Placing it down on the table, he sat back to wait.

Also in the news was the discovery of Detective Chief Inspector Nathan Cole's body. He had apparently met his end in the woods a few miles from his home. Jackson tried to feel pity for the man, but there had always been something suspicious about DCI Cole that made it difficult to feel sorry for him. Turning the newspaper's page, he began to read the next headline, about the murder of...

Jackson folded the paper and placed it into the wastepaper basket by his desk. He looked at his phone to check its progress, only to see it was still some way off completing the setup. He opened a drawer in his desk and took out the Winstable case file. He guessed he should use this quiet time to try to shift some of the work that had undoubtedly built up over the last week.

At the back of his mind, he was aware of what he was doing. He had followed the same routine when somebody was not here anymore. He kept himself busy to keep out the grief. It was all he could think to do right now. If he did not distract himself, then he knew that he would start to think. He would know what happened was partly his fault. That decisions he made, may have resulted in... in the night's events. He would eventually have to live with that knowledge, but not yet. He could not face it yet. So instead, he kept busy.

A beep from his phone indicated that the setup had been successfully completed. Another tone moments later alerted him that a new email had been received. Picking up the phone, he saw the email was from his bank, so he opened it:

Mr Clarke, a money transfer of £1,047 has been deposited into your account from a Miss C. Winchell.

Jackson felt as though he had been punched in the gut when he read the email. The feeling only grew worse when he realised Chloe had filled out an optional message to accompany the transfer:

Dear Jackson and Allister, I wanted to thank you for everything you have done for me this past week. I know you said you would waive my fee, but I wanted to show my appreciation. I'm sure that without the two of you, I would never have made it through the last seven days with my sanity still intact. I will let you know as soon as I land so you know that I am safe. Thank you again, lots of love, Chloe xx.

Jackson stared at the message, his hand already beginning to shake. Yelling in frustration, he threw his new phone across the office. When it hit the wall opposite him, it smashed into several pieces.

Reaching down, Jackson opened another drawer. He took hold of the half-full bottle of whiskey that still rested there, along with his mug. He placed them both on the desk and then removed the lid to begin pouring himself a large measure.

***

Freddy sat by himself in the departure lounge at Gatwick airport. After driving through the night in a car he had left some miles outside of Leeds, he reached the airport in the early hours of the morning. Once there, he had been able to purchase a ticket to Australia. He was informed there had been a last-minute cancellation on the next flight, and he tried not to think about whose seat he had now taken.

This had been his own plan from the moment Martin had set out to destroy Alice once and for all, forcing Freddy to question where his loyalty lay. For a long time now, he had hated calling her that name, but by her own admission, she stopped being Chloe some time ago. Alice stopped being a nickname and became an identity. Still, Freddy tried to stand by her in spite of what she did.

The last straw for him had come almost thirty years ago. He had only just managed to stop her from doing something so unspeakable, he still had trouble believing it had almost happened. Something that proved how far she had fallen and how lost she had become. How much George Senior's actions had damaged her. After that, nothing was ever the same between them again. He felt he had no choice but to leave with Martin.

Freddy had always believed that Chloe still existed somewhere inside Alice if he could just find her. The friendly but scared girl, who was still trying to figure out what she was when they met when he was only eighteen. The girl who first saw that he was not the slow kid everybody else believed he was, and who first suggested he might, in fact, be autistic. Something that later turned out to be true. But she saw beyond it. The funny, intelligent and loyal girl who had helped him realise he could achieve anything he wanted to. Who encouraged him outside of his comfort zone more than once.

The girl he had promised to return to her hometown one day.

There had been a glimpse of her last night before the EMP. When she had attempted to reconnect with Allister. Perhaps witnessing her own death had awoken something inside of her that could have been rescued. Unfortunately, Allister's reaction had left no time to see if there may have been more of her to emerge.

Watching the departure board as the time of his flight grew nearer, he held the memory stick that Allister had looked after carefully in one hand. The information stored upon it was invaluable to him. That was assuming his calculations were correct, of course.

New South Wales Airline flight AU375 to Sydney International Airport, Australia, is now ready for boarding! a female voice announced over the public address speaker.

Freddy looked down at the memory stick. "It's time to get you home," he whispered, before picking up his one piece of carry-on luggage.

Waiting once more in line to have his ticket and passport checked, he reached the front of the queue and the airline employee smiled at him politely, taking his documentation.

As she handed him his boarding pass she asked, "Is your trip to Australia business or pleasure?"

"I'm just keeping a promise," he replied.

***

After leaving Jackson in the park, Allister had found himself wandering the dark streets of Leeds. He had no real direction in mind, so just let his feet find their own way forward. It was peculiar how different the world was when the power was cut. The silence and darkness were strangely comforting in his current mood.

He was finding it impossible to come to terms with everything that happened last night. So much was his fault. He had underestimated Alice on so many levels. Not realising how dangerous she really was or what had driven her. It was not hatred for Chloe that had made her choices for her, but the need to survive. Allister could accept somebody wanting to live, but he could not accept her argument of survival at any cost. In trying to secure her own life, she had robbed Chloe of hers. Nobody would ever know the kind of future she could have had, what she may have achieved if she were given the chance. Alice's selfish needs had ruined a young girl's life.

Sometime early on Monday morning, he had found the way back to his apartment. He let himself in and headed straight to the shower so he could wash Chloe's blood off his skin. He stared at the plughole, visible in the gloom of the light filtering through the frosted glass window, until the water finally ran from red to pink, to clear, his head resting against the hard tiles as the cold, unheated water sprayed down on him.

Finally realising how tired he now was, Allister stumbled toward his bed. He climbed under the covers and closed his eyes. He had a restless sleep, filled with disturbing dreams of blood and glowing eyes. Each one always ending the same; in pain and death. In the end, he gave up on sleep and just lay in his bed staring at the ceiling and his mind in constant motion.

Every so often, it was as if he had forgotten what had happened and he would hope Chloe was safe in the power cut. But then, the memory would hit again full force and he would know with certainty that she was gone, and he was never going to see her again.

Briefly, Allister wondered if maybe he had acted too quickly in telling Freddy to do what he had planned. For a moment, when Alice had told him she had missed him, she looked so much like Chloe, vulnerable and scared. As though she needed him to be her friend again.

He guessed that it explained why she had befriended his sister Ruby, as a way of being close to him. Ruby was certain Alice had been a good person who had not harmed her on purpose. However, intentional or not, Alice had harmed Ruby, costing her years of her life. Both physically and the waste in a mental hospital. Not that she would be there for much longer. As soon as he was able to, he was going to get his sister out of that place.

Allister jumped slightly when there were four hard knocks on his front door. He chose to ignore it. When the knocks were repeated even harder and more insistently, he realised it would be easier to just answer.

With a heavy sigh, he sat up on his bed, stood and headed for the door, pausing only to pull on his bathrobe. He hoped it was not anybody he knew as he was in no mood to entertain.

Opening the door, he saw a deliveryman holding a medium-sized, very dusty looking, cardboard box.

"Allister Kelwick?" he asked expectantly.

"Yeah?" was all the reply Allister could manage.

"This is for you." He handed over the box and then thrust an electronic pad in front of Allister for a signature. *Must be from out of town if that thing works.*

After signing, Allister closed the door without a word and crossed to his sofa. He placed the box on the coffee table, then stared at it as if trying to decide if he was interested in its contents or not. The strange thing was, it was not just dusty like it had been in storage for some time, but it also looked old. The tape was beginning to peel and the address label fading.

Unable to contain his curiosity any longer, he tore open the box, coughing slightly as the dust flew up. He lifted the lid and found several audio cassette tapes. The type he had not seen since he was a child. Picking up the top cassette, he saw that it had 'Tape One' written on both sides in permanent marker. He picked up seven more tapes, each likewise numbered.

Also, inside the box was a rectangular shaped portable cassette player with a sticker that announced that batteries were not included. Which made sense. If the package was as old as he was starting to suspect it was, he doubted any batteries would have retained their charge for so long.

He stood and walked to a chest of drawers he kept against the far wall where he knew he kept batteries of all kinds in the top drawer. Taking out four of the size required, Allister inserted them into the tape player. He pushed in the first cassette ensuring side *A* was facing upwards then closed the brown translucent lid.

Pressing play, he waited while a small tinny speaker played a few seconds of static before a voice began talking, a voice he recognised instantly, but believed he would never hear again.

"Hi, Allister," Chloe began, her voice clear. *"I'm sorry it's taken me so long to get in touch, from my perspective anyway,"* she laughed then, and it was a happy laugh, *"but it's taken me a while to learn how to do this. To record my voice, I mean. I know what happened last night, for you anyway. God, this is all so confusing when I try to say it out loud. Anyway, I wanted to record these tapes for you. I wanted you to know what happened, you know, after..."*

As Chloe's voice continued to play, Allister listened intently, not wanting to miss a word of her story. He pulled his knees up to his chest and let the tears spill down his cheeks.

The End?

Epilogue

The first thing she became aware of, strangely, was the darkness. It seemed to surround her, hold her in place and be her entire existence. How long she was in this state she was not sure, as there was no way to follow time here. Wherever here was. Seconds, minutes, hours, days? Even years; she could not be certain. It felt like both an eternity and no time at all. She was just in the dark void. Aware. But also, not aware.

Soon, or maybe not so soon, the sounds began to filter through. They were indistinguishable from each other at first, but eventually, she was able to make out noises she recognised. The sound of cars, people, the occasional aeroplane, bird song. Oh, how much she had missed birdsong and never even realised it.

Finally, the blackness of the all-consuming void began to grow lighter. First to a dark grey, but soon brighter and following through a whole spectrum of colours until she was surrounded by the brightest white and the loudest symphony of sounds.

The white eventually dissipated, only to be replaced by blue. A beautiful sky blue in fact. It took several minutes of staring at the blue, with the passing of a cloud and two birds flying overhead that she finally realised she was indeed, looking at the sky.

Sitting up, Chloe immediately began to look herself over.

She appeared to be in the same clothes she had worn... She stopped and thought. She had difficulty remembering exactly what had happened. A vague memory of being stabbed began to return. Quickly checking her stomach, Chloe was relieved to find there did not appear to be any damage or blood.

She wondered where she was now. Getting slowly to her feet she looked around. She appeared to be in some kind of public garden judging by the grass surrounding her and the abundance of flowers. Not that she could smell them. In fact, she realised, she could not smell anything. Chloe breathed in deeply but there was nothing, as though her sense of smell was missing entirely.

Walking outside of the garden, she realised she was still in Leeds. At least she thought she was. It looked like Leeds city centre, but many of the buildings she knew so well were missing, replaced by ones Chloe did not recognise at all or were simply not there.

A car drove past. It was a make she did not know. It looked old but well maintained. It reminded her of the car she had seen Jackson driving. Similar cars were parked against the curb on both sides of the street. Everywhere she looked was confusing. Where was she?

Chloe spotted a woman standing by a bus stop a short distance away. Realising she needed answers, she decided to approach her. As she neared, she noticed that the woman was dressed strangely. Unlike anything she had seen before. And did she have a perm? She kind of looked how her own mother did in photos of her as a teenager. Chloe smiled, but the woman did not respond, she did not even look in her direction. Thinking of how rude the woman was, she decided to try to talk to her, regardless.

"Hi," she began. "I'm sorry to bother you but I'm a bit lost.

Can you help me, please?" There was no response, the woman just continued to stare up the road, looking for a bus.

Moving on, Chloe searched for somebody else to try to speak to. Noticing an elderly lady sitting on a bench a short walk away, she headed in her direction. In Chloe's experience, the elderly were always friendly to her. Especially when they heard her speak. They were always commenting on how exotic her accent was.

"Excuse me," she began. Chloe laid her accent on thick in the hopes it would help with a response. People usually wanted to talk to her about what Australia was like as soon as they realised where she was from.

Again, there was no response. The lady just sat and looked away from her. Figuring that maybe she was hard of hearing, Chloe moved to tap her gently on the arm. But instead of making contact, her hand seemed to bend around the lady's upper arm. It reminded her of watching light pass through a prism in a science lesson on one of the days she had actually turned up to school.

Jumping back, Chloe let out a yelp of fear. Looking at her hand, it had returned to normal, if more than a little shaky. Reaching forward again, she went to poke the lady's shoulder, but again she felt no contact and her finger seemed to bend again into shades of red, blue and green. The lady still did not respond.

What was going on? Was she invisible? Was she a ghost? Or had she finally been pushed over the edge? Walking to a nearby car, she looked into the door window, expecting to see herself looking back, but instead, she saw nothing, just the reflection of a tree behind her.

She started to walk quickly down the street, starting to

feel more than a little freaked out. She noticed that she did not feel the steps her feet took on the pavement. Admittedly, she had never really noticed if she could feel herself walking. But surely if you concentrated, you should be able to feel the impact in your foot when you took a step. Shouldn't you?

There was a newspaper stand a short distance away that advertised the Leeds Daily News, among others. She ran to it, realising there was no wind against her skin as she did so. In fact, she was starting to realise the only thing she did feel was her own touch. Reaching the stand, she was about to ask the man selling papers where she was when something caught her eye which made her stop. She bent down and read the date across the top of each newspaper.

21 March 1986.

"What the hell is going on?" Chloe whispered to herself, feeling more lost than she had ever felt before.

About the Author

Richard has been writing in one form or another since he was a child, but *Echo* is the first story he has self-published and is the first in a four-part story.

With a busy personal and work life, he wrote the book with a biro pen on a notepad before copying it on his phone, almost exclusively while travelling to work on the bus or during his lunch break, proving to himself that you can always find time to make a dream a reality.

Born in Birmingham, and having moved around England, Richard finally settled in Leeds, West Yorkshire, where he lives with his family and no pets, whatsoever.

You can follow Richard on:

Twitter: @EchoTheBook1

Instagram: @Echobook1

Website: www.rcglenn.co.uk

Printed in Great
Britain
by Amazon